# NEVER SAY DIE

# NEVER SAY DIE

## Tess Gerritsen

This first world hardcover edition published 2015
in Great Britain and in the USA by
SEVERN HOUSE PUBLISHERS LTD of
19 Cedar Road, Sutton, Surrey, England, SM2 5DA,
by arrangement with Harlequin Books S.A.
First published 1992 in the USA in mass market format only.

British Library Cataloguing in Publication Data

Gerritsen, Tess. author.
  Never say die.
  1. Fathers and daughters--Fiction. 2. Aircraft accidents--
  Investigation--Fiction. 3. Missing persons--Fiction.
  4. Suspense fiction.
  I. Title
  813.6-dc23

  ISBN-13: 978-0-7278-8483-1   (cased)

*All Severn House titles are printed on acid-free paper.*

Severn House Publishers support the Forest Stewardship Council™ [FSC™],
the leading international forest certification organisation.
All our titles that are printed on FSC certified paper carry the FSC logo.

Printed and bound in Great Britain by
TJ International, Padstow, Cornwall.

To Adam and Joshua, the little rascals

# Prologue

*1970*
*Laos–North Vietnam border*

Thirty miles out of Muong Sam, they saw the first tracers slash the sky.

Pilot William "Wild Bill" Maitland felt the DeHavilland Twin Otter buck like a filly as they took a hit somewhere back in the fuselage. He pulled into a climb, instinctively opting for the safety of altitude. As the misty mountains dropped away beneath them, a new round of tracers streaked past, splattering the cockpit with flak.

"Damn it, Kozy. You're bad luck," Maitland muttered to his copilot. "Seems like every time we go up together, I taste lead."

Kozlowski went right on chomping his wad of bubble gum. "What's to worry?" he drawled, nodding at the shattered windshield. "Missed ya by at least two inches."

"Try one inch."

"Big difference."

"One extra inch can make a *hell* of a lot of difference."

Kozy laughed and looked out the window. "Yeah, that's what my wife tells me."

The door to the cockpit swung open. Valdez, the cargo kicker, his shoulders bulky with a parachute pack, stuck his head in. "What the hell's goin' on any—" He froze as another tracer spiraled past.

"Got us some mighty big mosquitoes out there," Kozlowski said and blew a huge pink bubble.

"What was that?" asked Valdez. "AK-47?"

"Looks more like .57-millimeter," said Maitland.

"They didn't say nothin' about no .57s. What kind of briefing did we get, anyway?"

Kozlowski shrugged. "Only the best your tax dollars can buy."

"How's our 'cargo' holding up?" Maitland asked. "Pants still dry?"

Valdez leaned forward and confided, "Man, we got us one weird passenger back there."

"So what's new?" Kozlowski said.

"I mean, this one's *really* strange. Got flak flyin' all 'round and he doesn't bat an eye. Just sits there like he's floatin' on some lily pond. You should see the medallion he's got 'round his neck. Gotta weigh at least a kilo."

"Come on," said Kozlowski.

"I'm tellin' you, Kozy, he's got a kilo of gold hangin' around that fat little neck of his. Who is he?"

"Some Lao VIP," said Maitland.

"That all they told you?"

"I'm just the delivery boy. Don't need to know any more than that." Maitland leveled the DeHavilland off at eight thousand feet. Glancing back through the open cockpit doorway, he caught sight of their lone passenger sitting placidly among the jumble of supply crates. In the dim cabin, the Lao's face gleamed like burnished mahogany. His eyes were closed, and his lips were moving silently. In prayer? wondered Maitland. Yes, the man was definitely one of their more interesting cargoes.

Not that Maitland hadn't carried strange passengers before. In his ten years with Air America, he'd transported German shepherds and generals, gibbons and girlfriends. And he'd fly them anywhere they had to go. If hell had a landing strip, he liked to say, he'd take them there—as long as they had a ticket. Anything, anytime, anywhere, was the rule at Air America.

"Song Ma River," said Kozlowski, glancing down through the fingers of mist at the lush jungle floor. "Lot of cover. If they got any more .57s in place, we're gonna have us a hard landing."

"Gonna be a hard landing anyhow," said Maitland, taking stock of the velvety green ridges on either side of them. The valley was narrow; he'd have to swoop in fast and low. It was a hellishly short landing strip, nothing but a pin scratch in the jungle, and there was always the chance of an unreported gun emplacement. But the orders were to drop the Lao VIP, whoever he was, just inside North Vietnamese territory. No return pickup had been scheduled; it sounded to Maitland like a one-way trip to oblivion.

"Heading down in a minute," he called over his shoulder to Valdez. "Get the passenger ready. He's gonna have to hit the ground running."

"He says that crate goes with him."

"What? I didn't hear anything about a crate."

"They loaded it on at the last minute. Right after we took

on supplies for Nam Tha. Pretty heavy sucker. I might need some help.”

Kozlowski resignedly unbuckled his seatbelt. “Okay,” he said with a sigh. “But remember, I don’t get paid for kickin’ crates.”

Maitland laughed. “What the hell *do* you get paid for?”

“Oh, lots of things,” Kozlowski said lazily, ducking past Valdez and through the cockpit door. “Eatin’. Sleepin’. Tellin’ dirty jokes—”

His last words were cut off by a deafening blast that shattered Maitland’s eardrums. The explosion sent Kozlowski—or what was left of Kozlowski—flying backward into the cockpit. Blood spattered the control panel, obscuring the altimeter dial. But Maitland didn’t need the altimeter to tell him they were going down fast.

“Kozy!” screamed Valdez, staring down at the remains of the copilot. *“Kozy!”*

His words were almost lost in the howling maelstrom of wind. The DeHavilland shuddered, a wounded bird fighting to stay aloft. Maitland, wrestling with the controls, knew immediately that he’d lost hydraulics. The best he could hope for was a belly flop on the jungle canopy.

He glanced back to survey the damage and saw, through a swirling cloud of debris, the bloodied body of the Lao passenger, thrown against the crates. He also saw sunlight shining through oddly twisted steel, glimpsed blue sky and clouds where the cargo door should have been. What the hell? Had the blast come from *inside* the plane?

He screamed to Valdez, “Bail out!”

The cargo kicker didn’t respond; he was still staring in horror at Kozlowski.

Maitland gave him a shove. "Get the hell *out* of here!"

Valdez at last reacted. He stumbled out of the cockpit and into the morass of broken crates and rent metal. At the gaping cargo door he paused. "Maitland?" he yelled over the wind's shriek.

Their gazes met, and in that split second, they knew. They both knew. It was the last time they'd see each other alive.

"I'll be out!" Maitland shouted. *"Go!"*

Valdez backed up a few steps. Then he launched himself out the cargo door.

Maitland didn't glance back to see if Valdez's parachute had opened; he had other things to worry about.

The plane was sputtering into a dive.

Even as he reached for his harness release, he knew his luck had run out. He had neither the time nor the altitude to struggle into his parachute. He'd never believed in wearing one anyway. Strapping it on was like admitting you didn't trust your skill as a pilot, and Maitland knew—everyone knew—that he was the best.

Calmly he refastened his harness and grasped the controls. Through the shattered cockpit window he watched the jungle floor, lush and green and heartwrenchingly beautiful, swoop up to meet him. Somehow he'd always known it would end this way: the wind whistling through his crippled plane, the ground rushing toward him, his hands gripping the controls. This time he wouldn't be walking away....

It was startling, this sudden recognition of his own mortality. An astonishing thought. *I'm going to die.*

And astonishment was exactly what he felt as the DeHavilland sliced into the treetops.

*Vientiane, Laos*

At 1900 hours the report came in that Air America Flight 5078 had vanished.

In the Operations Room of the U.S. Army Liaison, Colonel Joseph Kistner and his colleagues from Central and Defense Intelligence greeted the news with shocked silence. Had their operation, so carefully conceived, so vital to U.S. interests, met with disaster?

Colonel Kistner immediately demanded confirmation.

The command at Air America provided the details. Flight 5078, due in Nam Tha at 1500 hours, had never arrived. A search of the presumed flight path—carried on until darkness intervened—had revealed no sign of wreckage. But flak had been reported heavy near the border, and .57-millimeter gun emplacements were noted just out of Muong Sam. To make things worse, the terrain was mountainous, the weather unpredictable and the number of alternative nonhostile landing strips limited.

It was a reasonable assumption that Flight 5078 had been shot down.

Grim acceptance settled on the faces of the men gathered around the table. Their brightest hope had just perished aboard a doomed plane. They looked at Kistner and awaited his decision.

"Resume the search at daybreak," he said.

"That'd be throwing away live men after dead," said the CIA officer. "Come on, gentlemen. We all know that crew's gone."

*Cold-blooded bastard,* thought Kistner. But as always, he was right. The colonel gathered together his papers and rose to his feet. "It's not the men we're searching for," he said. "It's the wreckage. I want it located."

"And then what?"

Kistner snapped his briefcase shut. "We melt it."

The CIA officer nodded in agreement. No one argued the point. The operation had met with disaster. There was nothing more to be done.

Except destroy the evidence.

# Chapter One

*Present*
*Bangkok, Thailand*

General Joe Kistner did not sweat, a fact that utterly amazed Willy Jane Maitland, since she herself seemed to be sweating through her sensible cotton underwear, through her sleeveless chambray blouse, all the way through her wrinkled twill skirt. Kistner looked like the sort of man who ought to be sweating rivers in this heat. He had a fiercely ruddy complexion, bulldog jowls, a nose marbled with spidery red veins, and a neck so thick, it strained to burst free of his crisp military collar. *Every inch the blunt, straight-talking, tough old soldier,* she thought. *Except for the eyes. They're uneasy. Evasive.*

Those eyes, a pale, chilling blue, were now gazing across the veranda. In the distance the lush Thai hills seemed to steam in the afternoon heat. "You're on a fool's errand, Miss Maitland," he said. "It's been twenty years. Surely you agree your father is dead."

"My mother's never accepted it. She needs a body to bury, General."

Kistner sighed. "Of course. The wives. It's always the wives. There were so many widows, one tends to forget—"

"*She* hasn't forgotten."

"I'm not sure what I can tell you. What I ought to tell you." He turned to her, his pale eyes targeting her face. "And really, Miss Maitland, what purpose does this serve? Except to satisfy your curiosity?"

That irritated her. It made her mission seem trivial, and there were few things Willy resented more than being made to feel insignificant. Especially by a puffed up, flat-topped warmonger. Rank didn't impress her, certainly not after all the military stuffed shirts she'd met in the past few months. They'd all expressed their sympathy, told her they couldn't help her and proceeded to brush off her questions. But Willy wasn't a woman to be stonewalled. She'd chip away at their silence until they'd either answer her or kick her out.

Lately, it seemed, she'd been kicked out of quite a few offices.

"This matter is for the Casualty Resolution Committee," said Kistner. "They're the proper channel to go—"

"They say they can't help me."

"Neither can I."

"We both know you can."

There was a pause. Softly, he asked, "Do we?"

She leaned forward, intent on claiming the advantage. "I've done my homework, General. I've written letters, talked to dozens of people—everyone who had anything to do with that last mission. And whenever I mention Laos or Air America or Flight 5078, your name keeps popping up."

He gave her a faint smile. "How nice to be remembered."

"I heard you were the military attaché in Vientiane. That

your office commissioned my father's last flight. And that you personally ordered that final mission."

"Where did you hear *that* rumor?"

"My contacts at Air America. Dad's old buddies. I'd call them a reliable source."

Kistner didn't respond at first. He was studying her as carefully as he would a battle plan. "I may have issued such an order," he conceded.

"Meaning you don't remember?"

"Meaning it's something I'm not at liberty to discuss. This is classified information. What happened in Laos is an extremely sensitive topic."

"We're not discussing military secrets here. The war's been over for fifteen years!"

Kistner fell silent, surprised by her vehemence. Given her unassuming size, it was especially startling. Obviously Willy Maitland, who stood five-two, tops, in her bare feet, could be as scrappy as any six-foot marine, and she wasn't afraid to fight. From the minute she'd walked onto his veranda, her shoulders squared, her jaw angled stubbornly, he'd known this was not a woman to be ignored. She reminded him of that old Eisenhower chestnut, "It's not the size of the dog in the fight but the size of the fight in the dog." Three wars, fought in Japan, Korea and Nam, had taught Kistner never to underestimate the enemy.

He wasn't about to underestimate Wild Bill Maitland's daughter, either.

He shifted his gaze across the wide veranda to the brilliant green mountains. In a wrought-iron birdcage, a macaw screeched out a defiant protest.

At last Kistner began to speak. "Flight 5078 took off

from Vientiane with a crew of three—your father, a cargo kicker and a copilot. Sometime during the flight, they diverted across North Vietnamese territory, where we assume they were shot down by enemy fire. Only the cargo kicker, Luis Valdez, managed to bail out. He was immediately captured by the North Vietnamese. Your father was never found."

"That doesn't mean he's dead. Valdez survived—"

"I'd hardly call the man's outcome 'survival.'"

They paused, a momentary silence for the man who'd endured five years as a POW, only to be shattered by his return to civilization. Luis Valdez had returned home on a Saturday and shot himself on Sunday.

"You left something out, General," said Willy. "I've heard there was a passenger...."

"Oh. Yes," said Kistner, not missing a beat. "I'd forgotten."

"Who was he?"

Kistner shrugged. "A Lao. His name's not important."

"Was he with Intelligence?"

"That information, Miss Maitland, is classified." He looked away, a gesture that told her the subject of the Lao was definitely off-limits. "After the plane went down," he continued, "we mounted a search. But the ground fire was hot. And it became clear that if anyone *had* survived, they'd be in enemy hands."

"So you left them there."

"We don't believe in throwing lives away, Miss Maitland. That's what a rescue operation would've been. Throwing live men after dead."

Yes, she could see his reasoning. He was a military tactician, not given to sentimentality. Even now, he sat ramrod straight in his chair, his eyes calmly surveying the verdant hills surrounding his villa, as though eternally in search of some enemy.

"We never found the crash site," he continued. "But that jungle could swallow up anything. All that mist and smoke hanging over the valleys. The trees so thick, the ground never sees the light of day. But you'll get a feeling for it yourself soon enough. When are you leaving for Saigon?"

"Tomorrow morning."

"And the Vietnamese have agreed to discuss this matter?"

"I didn't tell them my reason for coming. I was afraid I might not get the visa."

"A wise move. They aren't fond of controversy. What *did* you tell them?"

"That I'm a plain old tourist." She shook her head and laughed. "I'm on the deluxe private tour. Six cities in two weeks."

"That's what one has to do in Asia. You don't confront the issues. You dance around them." He looked at his watch, a clear signal that the interview had come to an end.

They rose to their feet. As they shook hands, she felt him give her one last, appraising look. His grip was brisk and matter-of-fact, exactly what she expected from an old war dog.

"Good luck, Miss Maitland," he said with a nod of dismissal. "I hope you find what you're looking for."

He turned to look off at the mountains. That's when she noticed for the first time that tiny beads of sweat were glistening like diamonds on his forehead.

* * *

General Kistner watched as the woman, escorted by a servant, walked back toward the house. He was uneasy. He remembered Wild Bill Maitland only too clearly, and the daughter was very much like him. There would be trouble.

He went to the tea table and rang a silver bell. The tinkling drifted across the expanse of veranda, and seconds later, Kistner's secretary appeared.

"Has Mr. Barnard arrived?" Kistner asked.

"He has been waiting for half an hour," the man replied.

"And Ms. Maitland's driver?"

"I sent him away, as you directed."

"Good." Kistner nodded. "Good."

"Shall I bring Mr. Barnard in to see you?"

"No. Tell him I'm canceling my appointments. Tomorrow's, as well."

The secretary frowned. "He will be quite annoyed."

"Yes, I imagine he will be," said Kistner as he turned and headed toward his office. "But that's his problem."

A Thai servant in a crisp white jacket escorted Willy through an echoing, cathedral-like hall to the reception room. There he stopped and gave her a politely questioning look. "You wish me to call a car?" he asked.

"No, thank you. My driver will take me back."

The servant looked puzzled. "But your driver left some time ago."

"He couldn't have!" She glanced out the window in annoyance. "He was supposed to wait for—"

"Perhaps he is parked in the shade beyond the trees. I will go and look."

Through the French windows, Willy watched as the servant skipped gracefully down the steps to the road. The estate was vast and lushly planted; a car could very well be hidden in that jungle. Just beyond the driveway, a gardener clipped a hedge of jasmine. A neatly graveled path traced a route across the lawn to a tree-shaded garden of flowers and stone benches. And in the far distance, a fairy blue haze seemed to hang over the city of Bangkok.

The sound of a masculine throat being cleared caught her attention. She turned and for the first time noticed the man standing in a far corner of the reception room. He cocked his head in a casual acknowledgment of her presence. She caught a glimpse of a crooked grin, a stray lock of brown hair drooping over a tanned forehead. Then he turned his attention back to the antique tapestry on the wall.

Strange. He didn't look like the sort of man who'd be interested in moth-eaten embroidery. A patch of sweat had soaked through the back of his khaki shirt, and his sleeves were shoved up carelessly to his elbows. His trousers looked as if they'd been slept in for a week. A briefcase, stamped U.S. Army ID Lab, sat on the floor beside him, but he didn't strike her as the military type. There was certainly nothing disciplined about his posture. He'd seem more at home slouching at a bar somewhere instead of cooling his heels in General Kistner's marble reception room.

"Miss Maitland?"

The servant was back, shaking his head apologetically. "There must have been a misunderstanding. The gardener says your driver returned to the city."

"Oh, no." She looked out the window in frustration. "How do I get back to Bangkok?"

"Perhaps General Kistner's driver can take you back? He has gone up the road to make a delivery, but he should return very soon. If you wish, you can see the garden in the meantime."

"Yes. Yes, I suppose that'd be nice."

The servant, smiling proudly, opened the door. "It is a very famous garden. General Kistner is known for his collection of dendrobiums. You will find them at the end of the path, near the carp pond."

She stepped out into the steam bath of late afternoon and started down the gravel path. Except for the *clack-clack* of the gardener's hedge clippers, the day was absolutely still. She headed toward a stand of trees. But halfway across the lawn she suddenly stopped and looked back at the house.

At first all she saw was sunlight glaring off the marble facade. Then she focused on the first floor and saw the figure of a man standing at one of the windows. The servant, perhaps?

Turning, she continued along the path. But every step of the way, she was acutely aware that someone was watching her.

Guy Barnard stood at the French windows and observed the woman cross the lawn to the garden. He liked the way the sunlight seemed to dance in her clipped, honey-colored hair. He also liked the way she moved, the coltish swing of her walk. Methodically, his gaze slid down, over the sleeveless blouse and the skirt with its regrettably sensible hemline, taking in the essentials. Trim waist. Sweet hips. Nice calves. Nice ankles. Nice...

He reluctantly cut off that disturbing train of thought.

This was not a good time to be distracted. Still, he couldn't help one last appreciative glance at the diminutive figure. Okay, so she was a touch on the scrawny side. But she had great legs. Definitely great legs.

Footsteps clipped across the marble floor. Guy turned and saw Kistner's secretary, an unsmiling Thai with a beardless face.

"Mr. Barnard?" said the secretary. "Our apologies for the delay. But an urgent matter has come up."

"Will he see me now?"

The secretary shifted uneasily. "I am afraid—"

"I've been waiting since three."

"Yes, I understand. But there is a problem. It seems General Kistner cannot meet with you as planned."

"May I remind you that I didn't request this meeting. General Kistner did."

"Yes, but—"

"I've taken time out of *my* busy schedule—" he took the liberty of exaggeration "—to drive all the way out here, and—"

"I understand, but—"

"At least tell me why he insisted on this appointment."

"You will have to ask him."

Guy, who up till now had kept his irritation in check, drew himself up straight. Though he wasn't a particularly tall man, he stood a full head taller than the secretary. "Is this how the general normally conducts business?"

The secretary merely shrugged. "I am sorry, Mr. Barnard. The change was entirely unexpected...." His gaze shifted momentarily and focused on something beyond the French windows.

Guy followed the man's gaze. Through the glass, he saw what the man was looking at: the woman with the honey-colored hair.

The secretary shuffled his feet, a signal that he had other duties to attend to. "I assure you, Mr. Barnard," he said, "if you call in a few days, we will arrange another appointment."

Guy snatched up his briefcase and headed for the door. "In a few days," he said, "I'll be in Saigon."

A whole afternoon wasted, he thought in disgust as he walked down the front steps. He swore again as he reached the empty driveway. His car was parked a good hundred yards away, in the shade of a poinciana tree. The driver was nowhere to be seen. Knowing Puapong, the man was probably off flirting with the gardener's daughter.

Resignedly Guy trudged toward the car. The sun was like a broiler, and waves of heat radiated from the gravel road. Halfway to the car, he happened to glance at the garden, and he spotted the honey-haired woman, sitting on a stone bench. She looked dejected. No wonder; it was a long drive back to town, and Lord only knew when her ride would turn up.

What the hell, he thought, starting toward her. He could use some company.

She seemed to be deep in thought; she didn't look up until he was standing right beside her

"Hi there," he said.

She squinted up at him. "Hello." Her greeting was neutral, neither friendly nor unfriendly.

"Did I hear you needed a lift back to town?"

"I have one, thank you."

"It could be a long wait. And I'm heading there anyway."
She didn't respond, so he added, "It's really no trouble."

She gave him a speculative look. She had silver-gray eyes,
direct, unflinching; they seemed to stare right through him.
No shrinking violet, this one. Glancing back at the house,
she said, "Kistner's driver was going to take me...."

"I'm here. He isn't."

Again she gave him that look, a silent third degree. She
must have decided he was okay, because she finally rose to
her feet. "Thanks. I'd appreciate it."

Together they walked the graveled road to his car. As they
approached, Guy noticed a back door was wide open and
a pair of dirty brown feet poked out. His driver was
sprawled across the seat like a corpse.

The woman halted, staring at the lifeless form. "Oh, my
God. He's not—"

A blissful snore rumbled from the car.

"He's not," said Guy. "Hey. Puapong!" He banged on
the car roof.

The man's answering rumble could have drowned out
thunder.

"Hello, Sleeping Beauty!" Guy banged the car again.
"You gonna wake up, or do I have to kiss you first?"

"What? What?" groaned a voice. Puapong stirred and
opened one bloodshot eye. "Hey, boss. You back so soon?"

"Have a nice nap?" Guy asked pleasantly.

"Not bad."

Guy graciously gestured for Puapong to vacate the back
seat. "Look, I hate to be a pest, but do you mind? I've
offered this lady a ride."

Puapong crawled out, stumbled around sleepily to the

driver's seat and sank behind the wheel. He shook his head a few times, then fished around on the floor for the car keys.

The woman was looking more and more dubious. "Are you sure he can drive?" she muttered under her breath.

"This man," said Guy, "has the reflexes of a cat. When he's sober."

"*Is* he sober?"

"Puapong! Are you sober?"

With injured pride, the driver asked, "Don't I look sober?"

"There's your answer," said Guy.

The woman sighed. "That makes me feel *so* much better." She glanced back longingly at the house. The Thai servant had appeared on the steps and was waving goodbye.

Guy motioned for the woman to climb in. "It's a long drive back to town."

She was silent as they drove down the winding mountain road. Though they both sat in the back seat, two feet apart at the most, she seemed a million miles away. She kept her gaze focused on the scenery.

"You were in with the general quite a while," he noted.

She nodded. "I had a lot of questions."

"You a reporter?"

"What?" She looked at him. "Oh, no. It was just...some old family business."

He waited for her to elaborate, but she turned back to the window.

"Must've been some pretty important family business," he said.

"Why do you say that?"

"Right after you left, he canceled all his appointments. Mine included."

"You didn't get in to see him?"

"Never got past the secretary. And Kistner's the one who asked to see *me*."

She frowned for a moment, obviously puzzled. Then she shrugged. "I'm sure I had nothing to do with it."

*And I'm just as sure you did,* he thought in sudden irritation. Lord, why was the woman making him so antsy? She was sitting perfectly still, but he got the distinct feeling a hurricane was churning in that pretty head. He'd decided that she *was* pretty after all, in a no-nonsense sort of way. She was smart not to use any makeup; it would only cheapen that girl-next-door face. He'd never before had any interest in the girl-next-door type. Maybe the girl down the street or across the tracks. But this one was different. She had eyes the color of smoke, a square jaw and a little boxer's nose, lightly dusted with freckles. She also had a mouth that, given the right situation, could be quite kissable.

Automatically he asked, "So how long will you be in Bangkok?"

"I've been here two days already. I'm leaving tomorrow."

*Damn,* he thought.

"For Saigon."

His chin snapped up in surprise. "Saigon?"

"Or Ho Chi Minh City. Whatever they call it these days."

"Now that's a coincidence," he said softly.

"What is?"

"In two days, *I'm* leaving for Saigon."

"Are you?" She glanced at the briefcase, stenciled with U.S. Army ID Lab, lying on the seat. "Government affairs?"

He nodded. "What about you?"

She looked straight ahead. "Family business."

"Right," he said, wondering what the hell business her family was in. "You ever been to Saigon?"

"Once. But I was only ten years old."

"Dad in the service?"

"Sort of." Her gaze stayed fixed on some faraway point ahead. "I don't remember too much of the city. Lot of dust and heat and cars. One big traffic jam. And the beautiful women..."

"It's changed a lot since then. Most of the cars are gone."

"And the beautiful women?"

He laughed. "Oh, they're still around. Along with the heat and dust. But everything else has changed." He was silent a moment. Then, almost as an afterthought, he added, "If you get stuck, I might be able to show you around."

She hesitated, obviously tempted by his invitation. *Come on, come on, take me up on it,* he thought. Then he caught a glimpse of Puapong, grinning and winking wickedly at him in the rearview mirror.

He only hoped the woman hadn't noticed.

But Willy most certainly *had* seen Puapong's winks and grins and had instantly comprehended the meaning. *Here we go again,* she thought wearily. *Now he'll ask me if I want to have dinner and I'll say no I can't, and then he'll say, what about a drink? and I'll break down and say yes because he's such a damnably good-looking man....*

"Look, I happen to be free tonight," he said. "Would you like to have dinner?"

"I can't," she said, wondering who had written this tired script and how one ever broke out of it.

"Then how about a drink?" He shot her a half smile and she felt herself teetering at the edge of a very high cliff. The crazy part was, he really *wasn't* a handsome man at all. His nose was crooked, as if, after managing to get it broken, he hadn't bothered to set it back in place. His hair was in need of a barber or at least a comb. She guessed he was somewhere in his late thirties, though the years scarcely showed except around his eyes, where deep laugh lines creased the corners. No, she'd seen far better-looking men. Men who offered more than a sweaty one-night grope in a foreign hotel.

*So why is this guy getting to me?*

"Just a drink?" he offered again.

"Thanks," she said. "But no thanks."

To her relief, he didn't press the issue. He nodded, sat back and looked out the window. His fingers drummed the briefcase. The mindless rhythm drove her crazy. She tried to ignore him, just as he was trying to ignore her, but it was hopeless. He was too imposing a presence.

By the time they pulled up at the Oriental Hotel, she was ready to leap out of the car. She practically did.

"Thanks for the ride," she said, and slammed the door shut.

"Hey, wait!" called the man through the open window. "I never caught your name!"

"Willy."

"You have a last name?"

She turned and started up the hotel steps. "Maitland," she said over her shoulder.

"See you around, Willy Maitland!" the man yelled.

*Not likely,* she thought. But as she reached the lobby doors, she couldn't help glancing back and watching the car disappear around the corner. That's when she realized she didn't even know the man's name.

* * *

Guy sat on his bed in the Liberty Hotel and wondered what had compelled him to check into this dump. Nostalgia, maybe. Plus cheap government rates. He'd always stayed here on his trips to Bangkok, ever since the war, and he'd never seen the need for a change until now. Certainly the place held a lot of memories. He'd never forget those hot, lusty nights of 1973. He'd been a twenty-year-old private on R and R; she'd been a thirty-year-old army nurse. Darlene. Yeah, that was her name. The last he'd seen of her, she was a chain-smoking mother of three and about fifty pounds overweight. What a shame. The woman, like the hotel, had definitely gone downhill.

*Maybe I have, too,* he thought wearily as he stared out the dirty window at the streets of Bangkok. How he used to love this city, loved the days of wandering through the markets, where the colors were so bright they hurt the eyes; loved the nights of prowling the back streets of Pat Pong, where the music and the girls never quit. Nothing bothered him in those days—not the noise or the heat or the smells.

Not even the bullets. He'd felt immune, immortal. It was always the *other* guy who caught the bullet, the other guy who got shipped home in a box. And if you thought otherwise, if you worried too long and hard about your own mortality, you made a lousy soldier.

Eventually, he'd become a lousy soldier.

He was still astonished that he'd survived. It was something he'd never fully understand: the simple fact that he'd made it back alive.

Especially when he thought of all the other men on that transport plane out of Da Nang. Their ticket home, the magic bird that was supposed to deliver them from all the madness.

He still had the scars from the crash. He still harbored a mortal dread of flying.

He refused to think about that upcoming flight to Saigon. Air travel, unfortunately, was part of his job, and this was just one more plane he couldn't avoid.

He opened his briefcase, took out a stack of folders and lay down on the bed to read. The file he opened first was one of dozens he'd brought with him from Honolulu. Each contained a name, rank, serial number, photograph and a detailed history—as detailed as possible—of the circumstances of disappearance. This one was a naval airman, Lieutenant Commander Eugene Stoddard, last seen ejecting from his disabled bomber forty miles west of Hanoi. Included was a dental chart and an old X-ray report of an arm fracture sustained as a teenager. What the file left out were the nonessentials: the wife he'd left behind, the children, the questions.

There were always questions when a soldier was missing in action.

Guy skimmed the pages, made a few mental notes and reached for another file. These were the most likely cases, the men whose stories best matched the newest collection of remains. The Vietnamese government was turning over three sets, and Guy's job was to confirm the skeletons were non-Vietnamese and to give each one a name, rank and serial number. It wasn't a particularly pleasant job, but one that had to be done.

He set aside the second file and reached for the next.

This one didn't contain a photograph; it was a supplementary file, one he'd reluctantly added to his briefcase at the last minute. The cover was stamped Confidential, then, a year ago, restamped Declassified. He opened the file and frowned at the first page.

Code Name: Friar Tuck
Status: Open (Current as of 10/85)
File Contains:
1. Summary of Witness Reports
2. Possible Identities
3. Search Status

*Friar Tuck.* A legend known to every soldier who'd fought in Nam. During the war, Guy had assumed those tales of a rogue American pilot flying for the enemy were mere fantasy.

Then, a few weeks ago, he'd learned otherwise.

He'd been at his desk at the Army Lab when two men, representatives of an organization called the Ariel Group, had appeared in his office. "We have a proposition," they'd said. "We know you're visiting Nam soon, and we want you to look for a war criminal." The man they were seeking was Friar Tuck.

"You've got to be kidding." Guy had laughed. "I'm not a military cop. And there's no such man. He's a fairy tale."

In answer, they'd handed him a twenty-thousand-dollar check—"for expenses," they'd said. There'd be more to come if he brought the traitor back to justice.

"And if I don't want the job?" he'd asked.

"You can hardly refuse," was their answer. Then they'd told Guy exactly what they knew about him, about his past, the thing he'd done in the war. A brutal secret that could destroy him, a secret he'd kept hidden away behind a wall of fear and self-loathing. They told him exactly what he could expect if it came to light. The hard glare of publicity. The trial. The jail cell.

They had him cornered. He took the check and awaited the next contact.

The day before he left Honolulu, this file had arrived special delivery from Washington. Without looking at it, he'd slipped it into his briefcase.

Now he read it for the first time, pausing at the page listing possible identities. Several names he recognized from his stack of MIA files, and it struck him as unfair, this list. These men were missing in action and probably dead; to brand them as possible traitors was an insult to their memories.

One by one, he went over the names of those voiceless pilots suspected of treason. Halfway down the list, he stopped, focusing on the entry "William T. Maitland, pilot, Air America." Beside it was an asterisk and, below, the footnote: "Refer to File #M-70-4163, Defense Intelligence. (Classified.)"

*William T. Maitland,* he thought, trying to remember where he'd heard the name. Maitland, Maitland.

Then he thought of the woman at Kistner's villa, the little blonde with the magnificent legs. I'm here on family business, she'd said. For that she'd consulted General Joe Kistner, a man whose connections to Defense Intelligence were indisputable.

*See you around, Willy Maitland.*

It was too much of a coincidence. And yet...

He went back to the first page and reread the file on Friar

Tuck, beginning to end. The section on Search Status he read twice. Then he rose from the bed and began to pace the room, considering his options. Not liking any of them.

He didn't believe in using people. But the stakes were sky-high, and they were deeply, intensely personal. *How many men have their own little secrets from the war?* he wondered. *Secrets we can't talk about? Secrets that could destroy us?*

He closed the file. The information in this folder wasn't enough; he needed the woman's help.

*But am I cold-blooded enough to use her?*

*Can I afford not to?* whispered the voice of necessity.

It was an awful decision to make. But he had no choice.

It was 5:00 P.M., and the Bong Bong Club was not yet in full swing. Up onstage, three women, bodies oiled and gleaming, writhed together like a trio of snakes. Music blared from an old stereo speaker, a relentlessly primitive beat that made the very darkness shudder.

From his favorite corner table, Siang watched the action, the men sipping drinks, the waitresses dangling after tips. Then he focused on the stage, on the girl in the middle. She was special. Lush hips, meaty thighs, a pink, carnivorous tongue. He couldn't define what it was about her eyes, but she had *that look*. The numeral 7 was pinned on her G-string. He would have to inquire later about number seven.

"Good afternoon, Mr. Siang."

Siang looked up to see the man standing in the shadows. It never failed to impress him, the size of that man. Even now, twenty years after their first meeting, Siang could not help feeling he was a child in the presence of this giant.

The man ordered a beer and sat down at the table. He watched the stage for a moment. "A new act?" he asked.

"The one in the middle is new."

"Ah, yes, very nice. Your type, is she?"

"I will have to find out." Siang took a sip of whiskey, his gaze never leaving the stage. "You said you had a job for me."

"A small matter."

"I hope that does not mean a small reward."

The man laughed softly. "No, no. Have I ever been less than generous?"

"What is the name?"

"A woman." The man slid a photograph onto the table. "Her name is Willy Maitland. Thirty-two years old. Five foot two, dark blond hair cut short, gray eyes. Staying at the Oriental Hotel."

"American?"

"Yes."

Siang paused. "An unusual request."

"There is some...urgency."

*Ah. The price goes up,* thought Siang. "Why?" he asked.

"She departs for Saigon tomorrow morning. That leaves you only tonight."

Siang nodded and looked back at the stage. He was pleased to see that the girl in the middle, number seven, was looking straight at him. "That should be time enough," he said.

Willy Maitland was standing at the river's edge, staring down at the swirling water.

From across the dining terrace, Guy spotted her, a tiny figure leaning at the railing, her short hair fluffing in the wind. From the hunch of her shoulders, the determined focus of her gaze, he got the impression she wanted to be left alone. Stopping at the bar, he picked up a beer—Oranjeboom, a good Dutch brand he hadn't tasted in years. He stood there a moment, watching her, savoring the touch of the frosty bottle against his cheek.

She still hadn't moved. She just kept gazing down at the river, as though hypnotized by something she saw in the muddy depths. He moved across the terrace toward her, weaving past empty tables and chairs, and eased up beside her at the railing. He marveled at the way her hair seemed to reflect the red and gold sparks of sunset.

"Nice view," he said.

She glanced at him. One look, utterly uninterested, was all she gave him. Then she turned away.

He set his beer on the railing. "Thought I'd check back with you. See if you'd changed your mind about that drink."

She stared stubbornly at the water.

"I know how it is in a foreign city. No one to share your frustrations. I thought you might be feeling a little—"

"Give me a break," she said, and walked away.

He must be losing his touch, he thought. He snatched up his beer and followed her. Pointedly ignoring him, she strolled along the edge of the terrace, every so often flicking her hair off her face. She had a cute swing to her walk, just a little too frisky to be considered graceful.

"I think we should have dinner," he said, keeping pace. "And maybe a little conversation."

"About what?"

"Oh, we could start off with the weather. Move on to politics. Religion. My family, your family."

"I assume this is all leading up to something?"

"Well, yeah."

"Let me guess. An invitation to your room?"

"Is that what you think I'm trying to do?" he asked in a hurt voice. "Pick you up?"

"Aren't you?" she said. Then she turned and once again walked away.

This time he didn't follow her. He didn't see the point. Leaning back against the rail, he sipped his beer and watched her climb the steps to the dining terrace. There, she sat down at a table and retreated behind a menu. It was too late for tea and too early for supper. Except for a dozen boisterous Italians sitting at a nearby table, the terrace was empty. He lingered there a while, finishing off the beer, wondering what his next approach should be. Wondering if anything would work. She was a tough nut to crack, surprisingly fierce for a dame who barely came up to his shoulder. A mouse with teeth.

He needed another beer. And a new strategy. He'd think of it in a minute.

He headed up the steps, back to the bar. As he crossed the dining terrace, he couldn't help a backward glance at the woman. Those few seconds of inattention almost caused him to collide with a well-dressed Thai man moving in the opposite direction. Guy murmured an automatic apology. The other man didn't answer; he walked right on past, his gaze fixed on something ahead.

Guy took about two steps before some inner alarm went off in his head. It was pure instinct, the soldier's premonition of disaster. It had to do with the eyes of the man who'd just passed by.

He'd seen that look of deadly calm once before, in the eyes of a Vietnamese. They had brushed shoulders as Guy was leaving a popular Da Nang nightclub. For a split second their gazes had locked. Even now, years later, Guy still remembered the chill he'd felt looking into that man's eyes. Two minutes later, as Guy had stood waiting in the street for his buddies, a bomb ripped apart the building. Seventeen Americans had been killed.

Now, with a growing sense of alarm, he watched the Thai stop and survey his surroundings. The man seemed to spot what he was looking for and headed toward the dining terrace. Only two of the tables were occupied. The Italians sat at one, Willy Maitland at the other. At the edge of the terrace, the Thai paused and reached into his jacket.

Reflexively, Guy took a few steps forward. Even before his eyes registered the danger, his body was already reacting. Something glittered in the man's hand, an object that caught the bloodred glare of sunset. Only then could Guy rationally acknowledge what his instincts had warned him was about to happen.

He screamed, "Willy! Watch out!"

Then he launched himself at the assassin.

# Chapter Two

At the sound of the man's shout, Willy lowered her menu and turned. To her amazement, she saw it was the crazy American, toppling chairs as he barreled across the cocktail lounge. What was that lunatic up to now?

In disbelief, she watched him shove past a waiter and fling himself at another man, a well-dressed Thai. The two bodies collided. At the same instant, she heard something hiss through the air, felt an unexpected flick of pain in her arm. She leapt up from her chair as the two men slammed to the ground near her feet.

At the next table, the Italians were also out of their chairs, pointing and shouting. The bodies on the ground rolled over and over, toppling tables, sending sugar bowls crashing to the stone terrace. Willy was lost in utter confusion. What was happening? Why was that idiot fighting with a Thai businessman?

Both men staggered to their feet. The Thai kicked high, his heel thudding squarely into the other man's belly. The American doubled over, groaned and landed with his back propped up against the terrace wall.

The Thai vanished.

By now the Italians were hysterical.

Willy scrambled through the fallen chairs and shattered crockery and crouched at the man's side. Already a bruise the size of a golf ball had swollen his cheek. Blood trickled alarmingly from his torn lip. "Are you all right?" she cried.

He touched his cheek and winced. "I've probably looked worse."

She glanced around at the toppled furniture. "Look at this mess! I hope you have a good explanation for— What are you doing?" she demanded as he suddenly gripped her arm. "Get your hands off me!"

"You're bleeding!"

"What?" She followed the direction of his gaze and saw that a shocking blotch of red soaked her sleeve. Droplets splattered to the flagstones.

Her reaction was immediate and visceral. She swayed dizzily and sat down smack on the ground, right beside him. Through a cottony haze, she felt her head being shoved down to her knees, heard her sleeve being ripped open. Hands probed gently at her arm.

"Easy," he murmured. "It's not bad. You'll need a few stitches, that's all. Just breathe slowly."

"Get your hands off me," she mumbled. But the instant she raised her head, the whole terrace seemed to swim. She caught a watery view of mass confusion. The Italians chattering and shaking their heads. The waiters staring open-mouthed in horror. And the American watching her with a look of worry. She focused on his eyes. Dazed as she was, she registered the fact that those eyes were warm and steady.

By now the hotel manager, an effete Englishman wearing an immaculate suit and an appalled expression, had appeared. The waiters pointed accusingly at Guy. The manager kept clucking and shaking his head as he surveyed the damage.

"This is dreadful," he murmured. "This sort of behavior is simply not tolerated. Not on *my* terrace. Are you a guest? You're not?" He turned to one of the waiters. "Call the police. I want this man arrested."

"Are you all blind?" yelled Guy. "Didn't any of you see he was trying to kill her?"

"What? What? Who?"

Guy poked around in the broken crockery and fished out the knife. "Not your usual cutlery," he said, holding up the deadly looking weapon. The handle was ebony, inlaid with mother of pearl. The blade was razor sharp. "This one's designed to be thrown."

"Oh, rubbish," sputtered the Englishman.

"Take a look at her arm!"

The manager turned his gaze to Willy's blood-soaked sleeve. Horrified, he took a stumbling step back. "Good God. I'll—I'll call a doctor."

"Never mind," said Guy, sweeping Willy off the ground. "It'll be faster if I take her straight to the hospital."

Willy let herself be gathered into Guy's arms. She found his scent strangely reassuring, a distinctly male mingling of sweat and aftershave. As he carried her across the terrace, she caught a swirling view of shocked waiters and curious hotel guests.

"This is embarrassing," she complained. "I'm all right. Put me down."

"You'll faint."

"I've never fainted in my life!"

"It's not a good time to start." He got her into a waiting taxi, where she curled up in the backseat like a wounded animal.

The emergency-room doctor didn't believe in anesthesia. Willy didn't believe in screaming. As the curved suture needle stabbed again and again into her arm, she clenched her teeth and longed to have the lunatic American hold her hand. If only she hadn't played tough and sent him out to the waiting area. Even now, as she fought back tears of pain, she refused to admit, even to herself, that she needed any man to hold her hand. Still, it would have been nice. It would have been wonderful.

*And I still don't know his name.*

The doctor, whom she suspected of harboring sadistic tendencies, took the final stitch, tied it off and snipped the silk thread. "You see?" he said cheerfully. "That wasn't so bad."

She felt like slugging him in the mouth and saying, *You see? That wasn't so bad, either.*

He dressed the wound with gauze and tape, then gave her a cheerful slap—on her wounded arm, of course—and sent her out into the waiting room.

*He* was still there, loitering by the reception desk. With all his bruises and cuts, he looked like a bum who'd wandered in off the street. But the look he gave her was warm and concerned. "How's the arm?" he asked.

Gingerly she touched her shoulder. "Doesn't this country believe in Novocaine?"

"Only for wimps," he observed. "Which you obviously aren't."

Outside, the night was steaming. There were no taxis available, so they hired a *tuk-tuk,* a motorcycle-powered rickshaw, driven by a toothless Thai.

"You never told me your name," she said over the roar of the engine.

"I didn't think you were interested."

"Is that my cue to get down on my knees and beg for an introduction?"

Grinning, he held out his hand. "Guy Barnard. Now do I get to hear what the Willy's short for?"

She shook his hand. "Wilone."

"Unusual. Nice."

"Short of Wilhelmina, it's as close as a daughter can get to being William Maitland, Jr."

He didn't comment, but she saw an odd flicker in his eyes, a look of sudden interest. She wondered why. The *tuk-tuk* puttered past a *klong,* its stagnant waters shimmering under the streetlights.

"Maitland," he said casually. "Now that's a name I seem to remember from the war. There was a pilot, a guy named Wild Bill Maitland. Flew for Air America. Any relation?"

She looked away. "Just my father."

"No kidding! You're Wild Bill Maitland's kid?"

"You've heard the stories about him, have you?"

"Who hasn't? He was a living legend. Right up there with Earthquake Magoon."

"That's about what he was to me, too," she muttered. "Nothing but a legend."

There was a pause in their exchange, and she wondered if Guy Barnard was shocked by the bitterness in her last statement. If so, he didn't show it.

"I never actually met your old man," he said. "But I saw him once, on the Da Nang airstrip. I was working ground crew."

"With Air America?"

"No. Army Air Cav." He sketched a careless salute.

"Private First Class Barnard. You know, the real scum of the earth."

"I see you've come up in the world."

"Yeah." He laughed. "Anyway, your old man brought in a C-46, engine smoking, fuel zilch, fuselage so shot up you could almost see right through her. He sets her down on the tarmac, pretty as you please. Then he climbs out and checks out all the bullet holes. Any other pilot would've been down on his knees kissing the ground. But your dad, he just shrugs, goes over to a tree and takes a nap." Guy shook his head. "Your old man was something else."

"So everyone tells me." Willy shoved a hank of wind-blown hair off her face and wished he'd stop talking about her father. That's how it'd been, as far back as she could remember. When she was a child in Vientiane, at every dinner party, every cocktail gathering, the pilots would invariably trot out another Wild Bill story. They'd raise toasts to his nerves, his daring, his crazy humor, until she was ready to scream. All those stories only emphasized how unimportant she and her mother were in the scheme of her father's life.

Maybe that's why Guy Barnard was starting to annoy her.

But it was more than just his talk about Bill Maitland. In some odd, indefinable way, Guy reminded her too much of her father.

The *tuk tuk* suddenly hit a bump in the road, throwing her against Guy's shoulder. Pain sliced through her arm and her whole body seemed to clench in a spasm.

He glanced at her, alarmed. "Are you all right?"

"I'm—" She bit her lip, fighting back tears. "It's really starting to hurt."

He yelled at the driver to slow down. Then he took Willy's hand and held it tightly. "Just a little while longer. We're almost there...."

It was a long ride to the hotel.

Up in her room, Guy sat her down on the bed and gently stroked the hair off her face. "Do you have any pain killers?"

"There's—there's some aspirin in the bathroom." She started to rise to her feet. "I can get it."

"No. You stay right where you are." He went into the bathroom, came back out with a glass of water and the bottle of aspirin. Even through her cloud of pain, she was intensely aware of him watching her, studying her as she swallowed the tablets. Yet she found his nearness strangely reassuring. When he turned and crossed the room, the sudden distance between them left her feeling abandoned.

She watched him rummage around in the tiny refrigerator. "What are you looking for?"

"Found it." He came back with a cocktail bottle of whiskey, which he uncapped and handed to her. "Liquid anesthesia. It's an old-fashioned remedy, but it works."

"I don't like whiskey."

"You don't have to like it. By definition, medicine's not supposed to taste good."

She managed a gulp. It burned all the way down her throat. "Thanks," she muttered. "I think."

He began to walk a slow circle, surveying the plush furnishings, the expansive view. Sliding glass doors opened onto a balcony. From the Chaophya River flowing just below came the growl of motorboats plying the waters. He wandered over to the nightstand, picked up a rambutan from the complimentary fruit basket and peeled off the prickly shell. "Nice room," he said, thoughtfully chewing the fruit. "Sure beats my dive—the Liberty Hotel. What do you do for a living, anyway?"

She took another sip of whiskey and coughed. "I'm a pilot."

"Just like your old man?"

"Not exactly. I fly for the paycheck, not the excitement. Not that the pay's great. No money in flying cargo."

"Can't be too bad if you're staying here."

"I'm not paying for this."

His eyebrows shot up. "Who is?"

"My mother."

"Generous of her."

His note of cynicism irritated her. What right did he have to insult her? Here he was, this battered vagabond, eating *her* fruit, enjoying *her* view. The *tuk-tuk* ride had tossed his hair in all directions, and his bruised eye was swollen practically shut. Why was she even putting up with this jerk?

He was watching her with curiosity. "So what else is Mama paying for?" he asked.

She looked him hard in the eye. "Her own funeral arrangements," she said, and was satisfied to see his smirk instantly vanish.

"What do you mean? Is your mother dead?"

"No, but she's dying." Willy gazed out the window at the lantern lights along the river's edge. For a moment they seemed to dance like fireflies in a watery haze. She swallowed; the lights came back into focus. "God," she sighed, wearily running her fingers through her hair. "What the hell am I doing here?"

"I take it this isn't a vacation."

"You got that right."

"What is it, then?"

"A wild-goose chase." She swallowed the rest of the whiskey and set the tiny bottle down on the nightstand. "But it's Mom's last wish. And you're always supposed to grant people their dying wish." She looked at Guy. "Aren't you?"

He sank into a chair, his gaze locked on her face. "You told me before that you were here on family business. Does it have to do with your father?"

She nodded.

"And that's why you saw Kistner today?"

"We were hoping—I was hoping—that he'd be able to fill us in about what happened to Dad."

"Why go to Kistner? Casualty resolution isn't his job."

"But Military Intelligence is. In 1970, Kistner was stationed in Laos. He was the one who commissioned my father's last flight. And after the plane went down, he directed the search. What there was of a search."

"And did Kistner tell you anything new?"

"Only what I expected to hear. That after twenty years, there's no point pursuing the matter. That my father's dead. And there's no way to recover his remains."

"It must've been tough hearing that. Knowing you've come all this way for nothing."

"It'll be hard on my mother."

"And not on you?"

"Not really." She rose from the bed and wandered out onto the balcony, where she stared down at the water. "You see, I don't give a damn about my father."

The night was heavy with the smells of the river. She

knew Guy was watching her; she could feel his gaze on her back, could imagine the shocked expression on his face. Of course, he would be shocked; it was appalling, what she'd just said. But it was also the truth.

She sensed, more than heard, his approach. He came up beside her and leaned against the railing. The glow of the river lanterns threw his face into shadow.

She stared down at the shimmering water. "You don't know what it's like to be the daughter of a legend. All my life, people have told me how brave he was, what a hero he was. God, he must have loved the glory."

"A lot of men do."

"And a lot of women suffer for it."

"Did your mother suffer?"

She looked up at the sky. "My mother..." She shook her head and laughed. "Let me tell you about my mother. She was a nightclub singer. All the best New York clubs. I went through her scrapbook, and I remember some reviewer wrote, 'Her voice spins a web that will trap any audience in its magic.' She was headed for the moon. Then she got married. She went from star billing to a—a footnote in some man's life. We lived in Vientiane for a few years. I remember what a trouper she was. She wanted so badly to go home, but there she was, scraping the store shelves for decent groceries. Laughing off the hand grenades. Dad got the glory. But she's the one who raised me." Willy looked at Guy. "That's how the world works. Isn't it?"

He didn't answer.

She turned her gaze back to the river. "After Dad's contract ended with Air America, we tried it for a while in San Francisco. He worked for a commuter airline. And

Mom and I, well, we just enjoyed living in a town without mortars and grenades going off. But..." She sighed. "It didn't last. Dad got bored. I guess he missed the old adrenaline high. And the glory. So he went back."

"They got divorced?"

"He never asked for one. And Mom wouldn't hear of it anyway. She loved him." Willy's voice dropped. "She still loves him."

"He went back to Laos alone, huh?"

"Signed up for another two years. Guess he preferred the company of danger junkies. They were all like that, those A.A. pilots—all volunteers, not draftees—all of 'em laughing death in the face. I think flying was the only thing that gave them a rush, made them feel alive. Must've been the ultimate high for Dad. Dying."

"And here you are, over twenty years later."

"That's right. Here I am."

"Looking for a man you don't give a damn about. Why?"

"It's not me asking the questions. It's my mother. She's never wanted much. Not from me, not from anyone. But this was something she had to know."

"A dying wish."

Willy nodded. "That's the one nice thing about cancer. You get some time to tie up the loose ends. And my father is one hell of a big loose end."

"Kistner gave you the official verdict—your father's dead. Doesn't that tie things up?"

"Not after all the lies we've been told."

"Who's lied to you?"

She laughed. "Who hasn't? Believe me, we've made the rounds. We've talked to the Joint Casualty Resolution Committee. Defense Intelligence. The CIA. They all had the same advice—drop it."

"Maybe they have a point."

"Maybe they're hiding the truth."

"Which is?"

"That Dad survived the crash."

"What's your evidence?"

She studied Guy for a moment, wondering how much to tell him. Wondering why she'd already told him as much as she had. She knew nothing about him except that he had fast reflexes and a sense of humor. That his eyes were brown, and his grin distinctly crooked. And that, in his own rumpled way, he was the most attractive man she'd ever met.

That last thought was as jolting as a bolt of lightning on a clear summer's day. But he *was* attractive. There was nothing she could specifically point to that made him that way. Maybe it was his self-assurance, the confident way he carried himself. *Or maybe it's the damn whiskey,* she thought. That's why she was feeling so warm inside, why her knees felt as if they were about to buckle.

She gripped the steel railing. "My mother and I, we've had, well, *hints* that secrets have been kept from us."

"Anything concrete?"

"Would you call an eyewitness concrete?"

"Depends on the eyewitness."

"A Lao villager."

"He saw your father?"

"No, that's the whole point—he didn't."

"I'm confused."

"Right after the plane went down," she explained, "Dad's buddies printed up leaflets advertising a reward of two kilos of gold to anyone who brought in proof of the crash. The leaflets were dropped along the border and all over Pathet Lao territory. A few weeks later a villager came out of the jungle to claim the reward. He said he'd found the wreckage of a plane, that it had crashed just inside the Vietnam border. He described it right down to the number on the tail. And he swore there were only two bodies on board, one in the cargo hold, another in the cockpit. The plane had a crew of *three*."

"What did the investigators say about that?"

"We didn't hear this from them. We learned about it only after the classified report got stuffed into our mailbox, with a note scribbled 'From a friend.' I think one of Dad's old Air America buddies got wind of a cover-up and decided to let the family know about it."

Guy was standing absolutely still, like a cat in the shadows. When he spoke, she could tell by his voice that he was very, very interested.

"What did your mother do then?" he asked.

"She pursued it, of course. She wouldn't give up. She hounded the CIA. Air America. She got nothing out of them. But she did get a few anonymous phone calls telling her to shut up."

"Or?"

"Or she'd learn things about Dad she didn't want to know. Embarrassing things."

"Other women? What?"

This was the part that made Willy angry. She could barely bring herself to talk about it. "They implied—" She let out a breath. "They implied he was working for the other side. That he was a traitor."

There was a pause. "And you don't believe it," he said softly.

Her chin shot up. "Hell, no, I don't believe it! Not a word. It was just their way to scare us off. To keep us from digging up the truth. It wasn't the only stunt they pulled. When we kept asking questions, they stopped release of Dad's back pay, which by then was somewhere in the tens of thousands. Anyway, we floundered around for a while, trying to get information. Then the war ended, and we thought we'd finally hear the answers. We watched the POWs come back. It was tough on Mom, seeing all those reunions on TV. Hearing Nixon talk about our brave men finally coming home. Because hers didn't. But we were surprised to hear of one man who did make it home—one of the crew members on Dad's plane."

Guy straightened in surprise. "Then there *was* a survivor?"

"Luis Valdez, the cargo kicker. He bailed out as the plane was going down. He was captured almost as soon as he hit the ground. Spent the next five years in a North Vietnamese prison camp."

"Doesn't that explain the missing body? If Valdez bailed out—"

"There's more. The very day Valdez flew back to the States, he called us. I answered the phone. I could hear he was scared. He'd been warned by Intelligence not to talk to anyone. But he thought he owed it to Dad to let us know what had happened. He told us there was a passenger on that flight, a Lao who was already dead when the plane went down. And that the body in the cockpit was probably Kozlowski, the copilot. That still leaves a missing body."

"Your father."

She nodded. "We went back to the CIA with this information. And you know what? They denied there was any passenger on that plane, Lao or otherwise. They said it carried only a shipment of aircraft parts."

"What did Air America say?"

"They claim there's no record of any passenger."

"But you had Valdez's testimony."

She shook her head. "The day after he called, the day he was supposed to come see us, he shot himself in the head. Suicide. Or so the police report said."

She could tell by his long silence that Guy was shocked. "How convenient," he murmured.

"For the first time in my life, I saw my mother scared. Not for herself, but for me. She was afraid of what might happen, what they might do. So she let the matter drop. Until..." Willy paused.

"There was something else?"

She nodded. "About a year after Valdez died—I guess it was around '76—a funny thing happened to my mother's bank account. It picked up an extra fifteen thousand dollars. All the bank could tell her was that the deposit had been made in Bangkok. A year later, it happened again, this time, around ten thousand."

"All that money, and she never found out where it came from?"

"No. All these years she's been trying to figure it out. Wondering if one of Dad's buddies, or maybe Dad himself—" Willy shook her head and sighed. "Anyway, a few months ago, she found out she had cancer. And suddenly it seemed very important to learn the truth. She's too sick to make this trip herself, so she asked me to come. And I'm hitting the same brick wall she hit twenty years ago."

"Maybe you haven't gone to the right people."

"Who *are* the right people?"

Quietly, Guy shifted toward her. "I have connections," he said softly. "I could find out for you."

Their hands brushed on the railing; Willy felt a delicious shock race through her whole arm. She pulled her hand away.

"What sort of connections?"

"Friends in the business."

"Exactly what *is* your business?"

"Body counts. Dog tags. I'm with the Army ID Lab."

"I see. You're in the military."

He laughed and leaned sideways against the railing. "No way. I bailed out after Nam. Went back to college, got a master's in stones and bones. That's physical anthropology, emphasis on Southeast Asia. Anyway, I worked a while in a museum, then found out the army paid better. So I hired on as a civilian contractor. I'm still sorting bones, only these have names, ranks and serial numbers."

"And that's why you're going to Vietnam?"

He nodded. "There are new sets of remains to pick up in Saigon and Hanoi."

*Remains.* Such a clinical word for what was once a human being.

"I know a few people," he said. "I might be able to help you."

"Why?"

"You've made me curious."

"Is that all it is? Curiosity?"

His next move startled her. He reached out and brushed

back her short, tumbled hair. The brief contact of his fingers seemed to leave her whole neck sizzling. She froze, unable to react to this unexpectedly intimate contact.

"Maybe I'm just a nice guy," he whispered.

*Oh, hell, he's going to kiss me,* she thought. *He's going to kiss me and I'm going to let him, and what happens next is anyone's guess....*

She batted his hand away and took a panicked step back. "I don't believe in nice guys."

"Afraid of men?"

"I'm not afraid of men. But I don't trust them, either."

"Still," he said with an obvious note of laughter in his voice, "you let me into your room."

"Maybe it's time to let you out." She stalked across the room and yanked open the door. "Or are you going to be difficult?"

"Me?" To her surprise, he followed her to the door. "I'm never difficult."

"I'll bet."

"Besides, I can't hang around tonight. I've got more important business."

"Really."

"Really." He glanced at the lock on her door. "I see you've got a heavy-duty dead bolt. Use it. And take my advice—don't go out on the town tonight."

"Darn! That was next on my agenda."

"Oh, and in case you need me—" he turned and grinned at her from the doorway "—I'm staying at the Liberty Hotel. Call anytime."

She started to snap, *Don't hold your breath.* But before she could get out the words, he'd left.

She was staring at a closed door.

# Chapter Three

Tobias Wolff swiveled his wheelchair around from the liquor cabinet and faced his old friend. "If I were you, Guy, I'd stay the hell out of it."

It had been five years since they'd last seen each other. Toby still looked as muscular as ever—at least from the waist up. Fifteen years' confinement to a wheelchair had bulked out those shoulders and arms. Still, the years had taken their inevitable toll. Toby was close to fifty now, and he looked it. His bushy hair, cut Beethoven style, was almost entirely gray. His face was puffy and sweating in the tropical heat. But the dark eyes were as sharp as ever.

"Take some advice from an old Company man," he said, handing Guy a glass of Scotch. "There's no such thing as a coincidental meeting. There are only planned encounters."

"Coincidence or not," said Guy, "Willy Maitland could be the break I've been waiting for."

"Or she could be nothing but trouble."

"What've I got to lose?"

"Your life?"

"Come on, Toby! You're the only one I can trust to give me a straight answer."

"It was a long time ago. I wasn't directly connected to the case."

"But you were in Vientiane when it happened. You must remember something about the Maitland file."

"Only what I heard in passing, none of it confirmed. Hell, it was like the Wild West out there. Rumors flying thicker'n the mosquitoes."

"But not as thick as you covert-action boys."

Toby shrugged. "We had a job to do. We did it."

"You remember who handled the Maitland case?"

"Had to be Mike Micklewait. I know he was the case officer who debriefed that villager—the one who came in for the reward."

"Did Micklewait think the man was on the level?"

"Probably not. I know the villager never got the reward."

"Why wasn't Maitland's family told about all this?"

"Hey, Maitland wasn't some poor dumb draftee. He was working for Air America. In other words, CIA. That's a job you don't talk about. Maitland knew the risks."

"The family deserved to hear about any new evidence." Guy thought about the surreptitious way Willy and her mother *had* learned of it.

Toby laughed. "There was a secret war going on, remember? We weren't even supposed to be in Laos. Keeping families informed was at the bottom of anyone's priority list."

"Was there some other reason it was hushed up? Something to do with the passenger?"

Toby's eyebrows shot up. "Where did you hear that rumor?"

"Willy Maitland. She heard there was a Lao on board.

Everyone's denying his existence, so my guess is he was a very important person. Who was he?"

"I don't know." Toby wheeled around and looked out the open window of his apartment. From the darkness came the sounds and smells of the Bangkok streets. Meat sizzling on an open-air grill. Women laughing. The rumble of a *tuk-tuk*. "There was a hell of a lot going on back then. Things we never talked about. Things we were even ashamed to talk about. What with all the agents and counteragents and generals and soldiers of fortune, you could never really be sure who was running the place. Everyone was pulling strings, trying to get rich quick. I couldn't wait to get the hell out." He slapped the wheel-chair in anger. "And this is where I end up. Great retirement." Sighing, he leaned back and stared out at the night. "Let it be, Guy," he said softly. "If you're right—if someone's out to hit Maitland's kid—then this is too hot to handle."

"Toby, that's the point! *Why* is the case so hot? Why, after all these years, would Maitland's brat be making them nervous? What do they think she'll find out?"

"Does she know what she's getting into?"

"I doubt it. Anyway, nothing'll stop this dame. She's a chip off the old block."

"Meaning she's trouble. How're you going to get her to work with you?"

"That's the part I haven't figured out yet."

"There's always the Romeo approach."

Guy grinned. "I'll keep it in mind."

In fact, that was precisely the tactic he'd been considering all evening. Not because he was so sure it would work, but because she was an attractive woman and he couldn't help wondering what she was really like under that tough-gal facade.

"Alternatively," Toby said, "you could try telling her the truth. That you're not after her. You're after the three million bounty."

"Two million."

"Two million, three million, what's the difference? It's a lot of dough."

"And I could use a lot of help," Guy said with quiet significance.

Toby sighed. "Okay," he said, at last wheeling around to look at him. "You want a name, I'll give you one. May or may not help you. Try Alain Gerard, a Frenchman, living these days in Saigon. He used to have close ties with the Company, knew all the crap going on in Vientiane."

"Ex-Company and living in Saigon? Why haven't the Vietnamese kicked him out?"

"He's useful to them. During the war he made his money exporting, shall we say, raw pharmaceuticals. Now he's turned humanitarian in his old age. U.S. trade embargoes cut the Viets off from Western markets. Gerard brings in medical supplies from France, antibiotics, X-ray film. In return, they let him stay in the country."

"Can I trust him?"

"He's ex-Company."

"Then I can't trust him."

Toby grunted. "You seem to trust me."

"You're different."

"That's only because I owe you, Barnard. Though I often think you should've left me to burn in that plane."

Toby kneaded his senseless thighs. "No one has much use for half a man."

"Doesn't take legs to make a man, Toby."

"Ha. Tell that to Uncle Sam." Using his powerful arms, Toby shifted his weight in the chair. "When're you leaving for Saigon?"

"Tomorrow morning. I moved my flight up a few days." Guy's palms were already sweating at the thought of boarding that Air France plane. He tossed back a mind-numbing gulp of Scotch. "Wish I could take a boat instead."

Toby laughed. "You'd be the first boat person going *back* to Vietnam. Still scared to fly, huh?"

"White knuckles and all." He set his glass down and headed for the door. "Thanks for the drink. And the tip."

"I'll see what else I can do for you," Toby called after him. "I still might have a few contacts in-country. Maybe I can get 'em to watch over you. And the woman. By the way, is anyone keeping an eye on her tonight?"

"Some buddies of Puapong's. They won't let anyone near her. She should get to the airport in one piece."

"And what happens then?"

Guy paused in the doorway. "We'll be in Saigon. Things'll be safer there."

"In Saigon?" Toby shook his head. "Don't count on it."

The crowd at the Bong Bong Club had turned wild, the men drunkenly shouting and groping at the stage as the girls, dead-eyed, danced on. No one took notice of the two men huddled at a dark corner table.

"I am disappointed, Mr. Siang. You're a professional, or

so I thought. I fully expected you to deliver. Yet the woman is still alive."

Stung by the insult, Siang felt his face tighten. He was not accustomed to failure—or to criticism. He was glad the darkness hid his burning cheeks as he set his glass of vodka down on the table. "I tell you, this could not be predicted. There was interference—a man—"

"Yes, an American, so I've been told. A Mr. Barnard."

Siang was startled. "You've learned his name?"

"I make it a point to know everything."

Siang touched his bruised face and winced. This Mr. Barnard certainly had a savage punch. If they ever crossed paths again, Siang would make him pay for this humiliation.

"The woman leaves for Saigon tomorrow," said the man.

"Tomorrow?" Siang shook his head. "That does not leave me enough time."

"You have tonight."

"Tonight? Impossible." Siang had, in fact, already spent the past four hours trying to get near the woman. But the desk clerk at the Oriental had stood watch like a guard dog over the passkeys, the hotel security officer refused to leave his post near the elevators, and a bellboy kept strolling up and down the hall. The woman had been untouchable. Siang had briefly considered climbing up the balcony, but his approach was hampered by two vagrants camped on the riverbank beneath her window. Though hostile-looking, the tramps had posed no real threat to a man like Siang, but he hadn't wanted to risk a foolish, potentially messy scene.

And now his professional reputation was at stake.

"The matter grows more urgent," said the man. "This must be done soon."

"But she leaves Bangkok tomorrow. I can make no guarantees."

"Then do it in Saigon. Whether you finish it here or there, *it has to be done.*"

Siang was stunned. "Saigon? I cannot return—"

"We'll send you under Thai diplomatic cover. A cultural attaché, perhaps. I'll decide and arrange the entry papers accordingly."

"Vietnamese security is tight. I will not be able to bring in any—"

"The diplomatic pouch goes out twice a week. Next drop is in three days. I'll see what weapons I can slip through. Until then, you'll have to improvise."

Siang fell silent, wondering how it would feel to once again walk the streets of Saigon. And he wondered about Chantal. How many years had it been since he'd seen her? Did she still hate him for leaving her behind? Of course, she would; she never forgot a grudge. Somehow, he'd have to work his way back into her affections. He didn't think that would be too difficult. Life in the new Vietnam must be hard these days, especially for a woman. Chantal liked her comforts; for a few precious luxuries, she might do anything. Even sell her soul.

She was a woman he could understand.

He looked across the table. "There will be expenses."

The man nodded. "I can be generous. As you well know."

Already Siang was making a mental list of what he'd need. Old clothes—frayed shirts and faded trousers—so he wouldn't stand out in a crowd. Cigarettes, soap and razor blades for bartering favours on the streets. And then he'd need a few special gifts for Chantal....

He nodded. The bargain was struck.

"One more thing," said the man as he rose to leave.

"Yes?"

"Other...parties seem to be involved. The Company, for instance. I wouldn't want to pull that particular tiger's tail. So keep bloodshed to a minimum. Only the woman dies. No one else."

"I understand."

After the man had left, Siang sat alone at the corner table, thinking. Remembering Saigon. Had it really been fifteen years? His last memories of the city were of panicked faces, of hands clawing frantically at a helicopter door, of the roar of chopper blades and the swirl of dust as the rooftops fell away.

Siang took a deep swallow of vodka and stood to leave. Just then, whistles and applause rose from the crowd gathered around the dance stage. A lone girl stood brown and naked in the spotlight. Around her waist was wrapped an eight-foot boa constrictor. The girl seemed to shudder as the snake slithered down between her thighs. The men shouted their approval.

Siang grinned. Ah, the Bong Bong Club. Always something new.

*Saigon*

FROM THE ROOFTOP GARDEN of the Rex Hotel, Willy watched the bicycles thronging the intersection of Le Loi and Nguyen Hue. A collision seemed inevitable, only a matter of time. Riders whisked through at breakneck speed, blithely ignoring the single foolhardy pedestrian inching fearfully across the street. Willy was so intent on silently cheering the man on that she scarcely registered the monotonous voice of her government escort.

"And tomorrow, we will take you by car to see the National Palace, where the puppet government ruled in luxury, then on to the Museum of History, where you will learn about our struggles against the Chinese and the French imperialists. The next day, you will see our lacquer factory, where you can buy many beautiful gifts to bring home. And then—"

"Mr. Ainh," Willy said with a sigh, turning at last to her guide. "It all sounds very fascinating, this tour you've planned. But have you looked into my other business?"

Ainh blinked. Though his frame was chopstick thin, he had a cherubic face made owlish by his thick glasses. "Miss Maitland," he said in a hurt voice, "I have arranged a private car! And many wonderful meals."

"Yes, I appreciate that, but—"

"You are unhappy with your itinerary?"

"To be perfectly honest, I don't really care about a tour. I want to find out about my father."

"But you have paid for a tour! We must provide one."

"I paid for the tour to get a visa. Now that I'm here, I need to talk to the right people. You can arrange that for me, can't you?"

Ainh shifted nervously. "This is a...a complication. I do not know if I can...that is, it is not what I..." He drifted into helpless silence.

"Some months ago, I wrote to your foreign ministry about my father. They never wrote back. If you could arrange an appointment..."

"How many months ago did you write?"

"Six, at least."

"You are impatient. You cannot expect instant results."

She sighed. "Obviously not."

"Besides, you wrote the Foreign Ministry. I have nothing to do with them. I am with the Ministry of Tourism."

"And you folks don't communicate with each other, is that it?"

"They are in a different building."

"Then maybe—if it's not too much trouble—you could take me to their building?"

He looked at her bleakly. "But then who will take the tour?"

"Mr. Ainh," she said with gritted teeth, "*cancel* the tour."

Ainh looked like a man with a terrible headache. Willy almost felt sorry for him as she watched him retreat across the rooftop garden. She could imagine the bureaucratic quicksand he would have to wade through to honor her request. She'd already seen how the system operated—or, rather, how it didn't operate. That afternoon, at Ton Son Nhut Airport, it had taken three hours in the suffocating heat just to run the gauntlet of immigration officials.

A breeze swept the terrace, the first she'd felt all afternoon. Though she'd showered only an hour ago, her clothes were already soaked with sweat. Sinking into a chair, she gazed off at the skyline of Saigon, now painted a dusty gold in the sunset. Once, this must have been a glorious town of tree-lined boulevards and outdoor cafés where one could while away the afternoons sipping coffee.

But after its fall to the North, Saigon slid from the dizzy impudence of wealth to the resignation of poverty. The signs of decay were everywhere, from the chipped paint on the old French colonials to the skeletons of buildings left permanently unfinished. Even the Rex Hotel, luxurious by local standards, seemed to be fraying at the edges. The terrace stones were cracked. In the fish pond, three listless carp drifted like dead leaves. The rooftop swimming pool had bloomed an unhealthy shade of green. A lone Russian tourist sat on the side and dangled his legs in the murky water, as though weighing the risks of a swim.

It occurred to Willy that her immediate situation was every bit as murky as that water. The Vietnamese obviously believed in a proper channel for everything, and without Ainh's help, there was no way she could navigate *any* channel, proper or otherwise.

*What then?* she thought wearily. *I can't do this alone. I need help. I need a guide. I need—*

"Now *there's* a lady who looks down on her luck," said a voice.

She looked up to see Guy Barnard's tanned face framed against the sunset. Her instant delight at seeing someone familiar—even *him*—only confirmed the utter depths of despair to which she'd sunk.

He flashed her a smile that could have charmed the habit off a nun. "Welcome to Saigon, capital of fallen dreams. How's it goin', kid?"

She sighed. "You need to ask?"

"Nope. I've been through it before, running around like a headless chicken, scrounging up seals of approval for every piddly scrap of paper. This country has got bureaucracy down to an art."

"I could live without the pep talk, thank you."

"Can I buy you a beer?"

She studied that smile of his, wondering what lay behind it. Suspecting the worst.

Seeing her weaken, he called for two beers, then dropped into a chair and regarded her with rumpled cheerfulness.

"I thought you weren't due in Saigon till Wednesday," she said.

"Change of plans."

"Pretty sudden, wasn't it?"

"Flexibility happens to be one of my virtues." He added, ruefully, "Maybe my only virtue."

The bartender brought over two frosty Heinekens. Guy waited until the man left before he spoke again.

"They brought in some new remains from Dak To," he said.

"MIAs?"

"That's what I have to find out. I knew I'd need a few extra days to examine the bones. Besides—" he took a gulp of beer "—I was getting bored in Bangkok."

"Sure."

"No, I mean it. I was ready for a change of scenery."

"You left the fleshpot of the East to come here and check out a few dead soldiers?"

"Believe it or not, I take my job seriously." He set the bottle down on the table. "Anyway, since I happen to be in town, maybe I could help you out. Since you probably need it."

Something about the way he looked at her, head cocked, teeth agleam in utter self-assurance, irritated her. "I'm doing okay," she said.

"Are you, now? So when's your first official meeting?"

"Things are being arranged."

"What sorts of things?"

"I don't know. Mr. Ainh's handling the details, and—"

"Mr. Ainh? You don't mean your *tour guide?*" He burst out laughing.

"Just why is that so funny?" she demanded.

"You're right," Guy said, swallowing his laughter. "It's not funny. It's pathetic. Do you want an advance look in my crystal ball? Because I can tell you exactly what's going to happen. First thing in the morning, your guide will show up with an apologetic look on his face."

"Why apologetic?"

"Because he'll tell you the ministry is closed for the day. After all, it's the grand and glorious holiday of July 18."

"Holiday? What holiday?"

"Never mind. He'll make something up. Then he'll ask if you wouldn't rather see the lacquer factory, where you can buy many beautiful gifts to bring home...."

Now she was laughing. Those were, in fact, Mr. Ainh's exact words.

"Then, the following day, he'll come up with some other reason you can't visit the ministry. Say, they're all sick with the swine flu or there's a critical shortage of pencil erasers. *But*—you can visit the National Palace!"

She stopped laughing. "I think I'm beginning to get your point."

"It's not that the man's deliberately sabotaging your plans. He simply knows how hopeless it is to untangle this bureaucracy. All he wants is to do his own little job, which is to be a tour guide and file innocuous reports about the nice lady tourist. Don't expect more from him. The poor guy isn't paid enough for what he already does."

"I'm not helpless. I can always start knocking on a few doors myself."

"Yeah, but *which* doors? And where are they hidden? And do you know the secret password?"

"Guy, you're making this country sound like a carnival funhouse."

"*Fun* is not the operative word here."

"What *is* the operative word?"

"*Chaos.*" He pointed down at the street, where pedestrians and bicycles swarmed in mass anarchy. "See that? That's how this government works. It's every man for himself. Ministries competing with ministries, provinces with provinces. Every minor official protecting his own turf. Everyone scared to move an inch without a nod from the powers that be." He shook his head. "Not a system for the faint of heart."

"That's one thing I've never been."

"Wait till you've been sitting in some sweatbox of a 'reception' area for five hours. And your belly hurts from the bad water. And the closest bathroom is a hole in the—"

"I get the picture."

"Do you?"

"What are you suggesting I do?"

Smiling, he sat back. "Hang around with me. I have a contact here and there. Not in the Foreign Ministry, I admit, but they might be able to help you."

*He wants something,* she thought. *What is it?* Though his gaze was unflinching, she sensed a new tension in his posture, saw in his eyes the anticipation rippling beneath the surface.

"You're being awfully helpful. Why?"

He shrugged. "Why not?"

"That's hardly an answer."

"Maybe at heart I'm still the Boy Scout helping old ladies cross the street. Maybe I'm a nice guy."

"Maybe you could tell me the truth."

"Have you always had this problem trusting men?"

"Yes, and don't change the subject."

For a moment, he didn't speak. He sat drumming his fingers against the beer bottle. "Okay," he admitted. "So I fibbed a little. I was never a Boy Scout. But I meant it about helping you out. The offer stands."

She didn't say a thing. For Guy, that silence, that look of skepticism, said it all. The woman didn't trust him. But why not, when he'd sounded his most sincere? He wondered what had made her so mistrustful. Too many hard knocks in life? Too many men who'd lied to her?

*Well, watch out, baby, 'cause this one's no different,* he thought with a twinge of self-disgust.

He just as quickly shook off the feeling. The stakes were too high to be developing a conscience. Especially at his age.

Now he'd have to tell another lie. He'd been lying a lot lately. It didn't get any easier.

"You're right," he said. "I'm not doing this out of the kindness of my heart."

She didn't look surprised. That annoyed him. "What do you expect in return?" she asked, her eyes hard on his. "Money?" She paused. "Sex?"

That last word, flung out so matter-of-factly, made his belly do a tiny loop-the-loop. Not that he hadn't already thought about that particular subject. He'd thought about it a lot ever since he'd met her. And now that she was sitting only a few feet away, watching him with those unyielding eyes, he was having trouble keeping certain images out of his head. Briefly he considered the possibility of throwing a little sex into the deal, but he just as quickly discarded the idea. He felt low enough as it was.

He calmly reached for the Heineken. The frostiness had gone out of the bottle. "No," he said. "Sex isn't part of the bargain."

"I see." She bit her lip. "Then it's money."

He gave a nod.

"I think you should know that I don't have any. Not for you, anyway."

"It's not *your* money I'm after."

"Then whose?"

He paused, willing his expression to remain bland. His voice dropped to a murmur. "Have you ever heard of the Ariel Group?"

"Never."

"Neither had I. Until two weeks ago, when I was contacted by two of their representatives. They're a veterans' organization, dedicated to bringing our MIAs home—alive. Even if it means launching a Rambo operation."

"I see," she said, her lips tightening. "We're talking about paramilitary kooks."

"That's what I thought—at first. I was about to kick 'em out of my office when they pulled out a check—a very generous one, I might add. Twenty thousand. For expenses, they said."

"Expenses? What are they asking you to do?"

"A little moonlighting. They knew I was scheduled to fly in-country. They wanted me to conduct a small, private search for MIAs. But they aren't interested in skeletons and dog tags. They're after flesh and blood."

"Live ones? You don't really think there are any, do you?"

"They do. And they only have to produce one. A single living MIA to back up their claims. With the publicity that'd generate, Washington would be forced to take action."

He fell silent as the waiter came by to collect the empty beer bottles. Only when the man had left did Willy ask softly, "And where do I come in?"

"It's not you. It's your father. From what you've told me, there's a chance—a small one, to be sure—that he's still alive. If he is, I can help you find him. I can help you bring him home."

His words, uttered so quietly, so confidently, made Willy fall still. Guy could tell she was trying to read his face, trying to figure out what he wasn't telling her. And he wasn't telling her a lot.

"What do you get out of this?" she asked.

"You mean besides the pleasure of your company?"

"You said there was money involved. Since I'm not paying you, I assume someone else is. The Ariel Group? Are they offering you more than just expenses?"

"Move to the head of the class."

"How much?"

"For an honest to God live one? Two million."

"Two million *dollars?*"

He squeezed her hand, hard. "Keep it down, will you? This isn't exactly public information."

She dropped her voice to a whisper. "You're serious? Two million?"

"That's their offer. Now you think about *my* offer. Work with me, and we could both come out ahead. You'd get your father back. I'd pick up a nice little retirement fund. A win-

win situation." He grinned, knowing he had her now. She'd be stupid to refuse. And Willy Maitland was definitely not stupid. "I think you'll agree," he said. "It's a match made in heaven."

"Or hell," she muttered darkly. She sat back and gave him a look of pure cast iron. "You're nothing but a bounty hunter."

"If that's what you want to call me."

"I could call you quite a few things. None of them flattering."

"Before you start calling me names, maybe you should think about your options. Which happen to be pretty limited. The way I see it, you can go it alone, which so far hasn't gotten you a helluva lot of mileage. Or—" he leaned forward and beamed her his most convincing smile "—you could work with me."

Her mouth tightened. "I don't work with mercenaries."

"What've you got against mercenaries?"

"Just a minor matter—principle."

"It's the money that bothers you, isn't it? The fact that I'm doing it for cash and not out of the goodness of my heart."

"This isn't some big-game hunt! We're talking about *men*. Men whose families have wiped out their savings to pay worthless little Rambos like you! I know those families. Some of them are still hanging in, twisting around on that one shred of hope. And you know as well as I do that those soldiers aren't sitting around in some POW camp, waiting to be rescued. They're *dead*."

"You think *your* old man's alive."

"He's a different story."

"Right. And every one of those five hundred other MIAs could be another 'different story.'"

"*I* happen to have evidence!"

"But you don't have the smarts it takes to find him." Guy leaned forward, his gaze hard on hers. In the last light of sunset, her face seemed alight with fire, her cheeks glowing a beautiful dusky red. "If he's alive, you can't afford to screw up this chance. And you may get only one chance to find him. Because I'll tell you now, the Vietnamese won't let you back in the country for another deluxe tour. Admit it, Willy. You need me."

"No," she shot back. "You need *me*. Without my help, how are you going to cash in on your 'live one'?"

"How're *you* going to find him?"

She was the one leaning forward now, so close, he almost pulled back in surprise. "Don't underestimate me, sleazeball," she muttered.

"And don't overestimate yourself, Junior. It's not easy finding answers in this country. No one, nothing's ever what it seems here. A flicker in the eye, a break in the voice can mean all the difference in the world. You *need* a partner. And, hey, I'm not unreasonable. I'll even think about splitting the reward with you. Say, ten percent. That's money you never expected, just to let me—"

"I don't give a damn about the money!" She rose sharply to her feet. "Go get rich off someone else's old man." She spun around and walked away.

"Won't you even think about it?" he yelled.

She just kept marching away across the rooftop garden, oblivious to the curious glances aimed her way.

"Take it from me, Willy! You need me!"

A trio of Russian tourists, their faces ruddy from a few rounds of vodka, glanced up as she passed. One of the men raised his glass in a drunken salute. "Maybe you like Russian man better?" he shouted.

She didn't even break her stride. But as she walked away, every guest on that rooftop heard her answer, which came floating back with disarming sweetness over her shoulder. "Go to hellski."

# Chapter Four

Guy watched her storm away, her chambray skirt snapping smartly about those fabulous legs. Annoyed as he was, he couldn't help laughing when he heard that comeback to the Russian.

*Go to hellski.* He laughed harder. He was still laughing as he wandered over to the bar and called for another Heineken. The beer was so cold, it made his teeth ache.

"For a fellow who's just gotten the royal heave-ho," said a voice, obviously British, "you seem to be in high spirits."

Guy glanced at the portly gentleman hunched next to him at the bar. With those two tufts of hair on his bald head, he looked like a horned owl. China blue eyes twinkled beneath shaggy eyebrows.

Guy shrugged. "Win some, lose some."

"Sensible attitude. Considering the state of womanhood these days." The man hoisted a glass of Scotch to his lips. "But then, I could have predicted she'd be a no go."

"Sounds like an expert talking."

"No, I sat behind her on the plane. Listened to some oily Frenchman ooze his entire repertoire all over her. Smashing lines, I have to say, but she didn't fall for it." He squinted at Guy. "Weren't *you* on that flight out of Bangkok?"

Guy nodded. He didn't remember the man, but then, he'd spent the entire flight white-knuckling his armrest and gulping down whiskey. Airplanes did that to him. Even nice big 747s with nice French stewardesses. It never failed to astonish him that the wings didn't fall off.

At the other end of the garden, the trio of Russians had started to sing. Not, unfortunately, in the same key. Maybe not even the same song. It was hard to tell.

"Never would've guessed it," the Englishman said, glancing over at the Russians. "I still remember the Yanks drinking at that very table. Never would've guessed there'd be Russians sitting there one day."

"When were you here?"

"Sixty-eight to '75." He held out a pudgy hand in greeting. "Dodge Hamilton, *London Post*."

"Guy Barnard. Ex-draftee." He shook the man's hand. "Reporter, huh? You here on a story?"

"I was." Hamilton looked mournfully at his Scotch. "But it's fallen through."

"What has? Your interviews?"

"No, the concept. I called it a sentimental journey. Visit to old friends in Saigon. Or, rather, to one friend in particular." He took a swallow of Scotch. "But she's gone."

"Oh. A woman."

"That's right, a woman. Half the human race, but they might as well be from Mars for all I understand the sex." He slapped down the glass and motioned for another refill. The bartender resignedly shoved the whole bottle of Scotch over to Hamilton. "See, the story I had in mind was the search for a lost love. You know, the sort of copy that sells papers. My editor went wild about it." He poured the Scotch, recklessly filling the glass to the brim. "Ha! Lost love! I stopped by her old house today, over on Rue Catinat. Or what used to be Rue Catinat. Found her brother still living there. But it seems my old love ran away with some new love. A sergeant. From Memphis, no less."

Guy shook his head in sympathy. "A woman has a right to change her mind."

"One day after I left the country?"

There wasn't much a man could say to that. But Guy couldn't blame the woman. He knew how it was in Saigon—the fear, the uncertainty. No one knowing if there'd be a slaughter and everyone expecting the worst. He'd seen the news photos of the city's fall, recognized the look of desperation on the faces of the Vietnamese scrambling aboard the last choppers out. No, he couldn't blame a woman for wanting to get out of the country, any way she could.

"You could still write about it," Guy pointed out. "Try a different angle. How one woman escaped the madness. The price of survival."

"My heart's not in it any longer." Hamilton gazed sadly around the rooftop. "Or in this town. I used to love it here! The noise, the smells. Even the whomp of the mortar rounds. But Saigon's changed. The spirit's flown out of it. The funny part is, this hotel looks exactly the same. I used to stand at this very bar and hear your generals whisper to each other, 'What the hell are we doing here?' I don't think they ever quite figured it out." He laughed and took another gulp of Scotch. "Memphis. Why would she want to go to Memphis?"

He was muttering to himself now, some private monologue about women causing all the world's miseries. An opinion with which Guy could almost agree. All he had to do was think about his own miserable love life and he, too, would get the sudden, blinding urge to get thoroughly soused.

Women. All the same. Yet, somehow, all different.

He thought about Willy Maitland. She talked tough, but he could tell it was an act, that there was something soft, something vulnerable beneath that hard-as-nails surface. Hell, she was just a kid trying to live up to her old man's name, pretending she didn't need a man when she did. He had to admire her for that: her pride.

She was smart to turn down his offer. He wasn't sure he had the stomach to go through with it anyway. Let the Ariel Group tighten his noose. He'd lived with his skeletons long enough; maybe it was time to let them out of the closet.

*I should just do my job,* he thought. *Go to Hanoi, pick up a few dead soldiers, fly them home.*

And forget about Willy Maitland.

Then again...

He ordered another beer. Drank it while the debate raged on in his head. Thought about all the ways he could help her, about how much she needed *someone's* help. Considered doing it not because he was being forced into it, but because he wanted to. *Out of the goodness of my heart?* Now that was a new concept. No, he'd never been a Boy Scout. Something about those uniforms, about all that earnest goodliness and godliness, had struck him as faintly ridiculous. But here he was, Boy Scout Barnard, ready to offer his services, no strings attached.

Well, maybe a few strings. He couldn't help fantasizing about the possibilities. He thought of how it would be, taking her up to his room. Undressing her. Feeling her yield beneath him. He swallowed hard and reached automatically for the Heineken.

"No doubt about it," Hamilton muttered. "I tell you, it's all their fault."

"Hmm?" Guy turned. "Whose fault?"

"Women, of course. They cause more trouble than they're worth."

"You said it, pal." Guy sighed and lifted the beer to his lips. "You said it."

Men. They cause more trouble than they're worth, Willy thought as she viciously wound her alarm clock.

A bounty hunter. She should have guessed. Warning bells should have gone off in her head the minute he so generously offered his help. *Help.* What a laugh. She thought of all the solicitation letters she and her mother had received, all the mercenary groups who'd offered, for a few thousand dollars, to provide just such worthless help. There'd been the MIA Search Fund, the Men Alive Committee, Operation Chestnut—Let's Pull 'em Out Of The Fire! had been *their* revolting slogan. How many grieving families had invested their hopes and savings on such futile dreams?

She stripped down to a tank top and flopped onto the bed. A decent night's sleep, she could tell, was another futile dream. The mattress was lumpy, and the pillow seemed to be stuffed with concrete. Not that it mattered. How could she get any rest with that damned disco music vibrating through the walls? At 8:00 the first driving drumbeats had announced the opening of Dance Night at the Rex Hotel.

*Lord,* she thought, *what good is communism if it can't even stamp out disco?*

It occurred to her that, at that very minute, Guy Barnard was probably loitering downstairs in that dance hall, checking out the action. Sometimes she thought that was the real reason men started wars—it was an excuse to run away from home and check out the action.

*What do I care if he's down there eyeing the ladies? The man's scum. He's not worth a second thought.*

Still, she had to admit he had a certain tattered charm. Nice straight teeth and a dazzling smile and eyes that were brown as a wolf's. A woman could get in trouble for the sake of those eyes. *And heaven knows, I don't need that kind of trouble.*

Someone knocked on the door. She sat up straight and called out, "Who is it?"

"Room service."

"There must be a mistake. I didn't order anything."

There was no response. Sighing, she pulled on a robe and padded over to open the door.

Guy grinned at her from the darkness. "Well?" he inquired. "Have you thought about it?"

"Thought about what?" she snapped back.

"You and me. Working together."

She laughed in disbelief. "Either you're hard of hearing or I didn't make myself clear."

"That was two hours ago. I figured you might have changed your mind."

"I will *never* change my mind. Good *night.*" She slammed the door, shoved the bolt home and stepped back, seething.

There was a tapping on her window. She yanked the curtain aside and saw Guy smiling through the glass.

"Just one more question," he called.

"*What?*"

"Is that answer final?"

She jerked the curtain closed and stood there, waiting to see where he'd turn up next. Would he drop down from the ceiling? Pop up like a jack-in-the-box through the floor?

What was that rustling sound?

Glancing down sharply, she saw a piece of paper slide under the door. She snatched it up and read the scrawled message. "Call me if you need me."

*Ha!* she thought, ripping the note to pieces. "The day I need you is the day hell freezes over!" she yelled.

There was no answer. And she knew, without even looking, that he had already walked away.

Chantel gazed at the bottle of champagne, the tins of caviar and foie gras, and the box of chocolates, and she licked her lips. Then she said, "How dare you show up after all these years."

Siang merely smiled. "You have lost your taste for champagne? What a pity. It seems I shall have to drink it all myself." He reached for the bottle. Slowly, he untwisted the wire. The flight from Bangkok had jostled the contents; the cork shot out, spilling pale gold bubbles all over the earthen floor. Chantal gave a little sob. She appeared ready to drop to her knees and lap up the precious liquid. He poured champagne into one of two fluted glasses he'd brought all the way from Bangkok. One could not, after all, drink champagne from a teacup. He took a sip and sighed happily. "Taittinger. Delightful."

"Taittinger?" she whispered.

He filled the second glass and set it on the rickety table in front of her. She kept staring at it, watching the bubbles spiral to the surface.

"I need help," he said.

She reached for the glass, put it to her trembling lips, tasted the rim, then the contents. He could almost see the bubbles sliding over her tongue, slipping down that fine, long throat. Even if the rest of her was sagging, she still had that beautiful throat, slender as a stalk of grass. A legacy from her Vietnamese mother. Her Asian half had held up over the years; the French half hadn't done so well. He could see the freckles, the fine lines tracing the corners of her greenish eyes.

She was no longer merely tasting the champagne; she was guzzling. Greedily, she drained the last drop from her glass and reached for the bottle.

He slid it out of her reach. "I said I need your help."

She wiped her chin with the back of her hand. "What kind of help?"

"Not much."

"Ha. That's what you always say."

"A pistol. Automatic. Plus several clips of ammunition."

"What if I don't have a pistol?"

"Then you will find me one."

She shook her head. "This is not the old days. You don't know what it's like here. Things are difficult." She paused, looking down at her slightly crepey hands. "Saigon is a hell."

"Even hell can be made comfortable. I can see to that."

She was silent. He could read her mind almost as easily as if her eyes were transparent. She gazed down at the treasures he'd brought from Bangkok. She swallowed, her mouth still tingling with the taste of champagne. At last she said, "The gun. What do you want it for?"

"A job."

"Vietnamese?"

"American. A woman."

A spark flickered in Chantal's eyes. Curiosity. Maybe jealousy. Her chin came up. "Your lover?"

He shook his head.

"Then why do you want her dead?"

He shrugged. "Business. My client has offered generous compensation. I will split it with you."

"The way you did before?" she shot back.

He shook his head apologetically. "Chantal, Chantal." He sighed. "You know I had no choice. It was the last flight out of Saigon." He touched her face; it had lost its former silkiness. That French blood again: it didn't hold up well under years of harsh sunlight. "This time, I promise. You'll be paid."

She sat there looking at him, looking at the champagne. "What if it takes me time to find a gun?"

"Then I'll improvise. And I will need an assistant. Someone I can trust, someone discreet." He paused. "Your cousin, is he still in need of money?"

Their gazes met. He gave her a slow, significant smile. Then he filled her glass with champagne.

"Open the caviar," she said.


"I need your help," said Willy.

Guy, dazed and still half-asleep, stood in his doorway, blinking at the morning sunlight. He was uncombed, unshaven and wearing only a towel—a skimpy one at that. She tried to stay focused on his face, but her gaze kept dropping to his chest, to that mat of curly brown hair, to the scar knotting the upper abdomen.

He shook his head in disbelief. "You couldn't have told me this last night? You had to wait till the crack of dawn?"

"Guy, it's eight o'clock."

He yawned. "No kidding."

"Maybe you should try going to bed at a decent hour."

"Who says I didn't?" He leaned carelessly in the doorway and grinned. "Maybe sleep didn't happen to be on my agenda."

Dear God. Did he have a woman in his room? Automatically, Willy glanced past him into the darkened room. The bed was rumpled but unoccupied.

"Gotcha," he said, and laughed.

"I can see you're not going to be any help at all." She turned and walked away.

"Willy! Hey, come on." He caught her by the arm and pulled her around. "Did you mean it? About wanting my help?"

"Forget it. It was a lapse in judgment."

"Last night, hell had to freeze over before you'd come to me for help. But here you are. What made you change your mind?"

She didn't answer right off. She was too busy trying not to notice that his towel was slipping. To her relief, he snatched it together just in time and fastened it more securely around his hips.

At last she shook her head and sighed. "You were right. It's all going exactly as you said it would. No official will talk to me. No one'll answer my calls. They hear I'm coming and they all dive under their desks!"

"You could try a little patience. Wait another week."

"Next week's no good, either."

"Why?"

"Haven't you heard? It's Ho Chi Minh's birthday."

Guy looked heavenward. "How could I forget?"

"So what should I do?"

For a moment, he stood there thoughtfully rubbing his unshaven chin. Then he nodded. "Let's talk about it."

Back in his room, she sat uneasily on the edge of the bed while he dressed in the bathroom. The man was a restless sleeper, judging by the rumpled sheets. The blanket had been kicked off the bed entirely, the pillows punched into formless lumps by the headboard. Her gaze settled on the nightstand, where a stack of files lay. The top one was labeled Operation Friar Tuck. Declassified. Curious, she flipped open the cover.

"It's the way things work in this country," she heard him say through the bathroom door. "If you want to get from point A to point B, you don't go in a straight line. You walk two steps to the left, two to the right, turn and walk backward."

"So what should I do now?"

"The two-step. Sideways." He came out, dressed and freshly shaved. Spotting the open file on the nightstand, he calmly closed the cover. "Sorry. Not for public view," he said, sliding the stack of folders into his briefcase. Then he turned to her. "Now. Tell me what else is going on."

"What do you mean?"

"I get the feeling there's something more. It's eight o'clock in the morning. You can't have battled the bureaucracy this early. What really made you change your mind about me?"

"Oh, I haven't changed my mind about *you*. You're still a mercenary." Her disgust seemed to hang in the air like a bad odor.

"But now you're willing to work with me. Why?"

She looked down at her lap and sighed. Reluctantly she opened her purse and pulled out a slip of paper. "I found this under my door this morning."

He unfolded the paper. In a spidery hand was written "Die Yankee." Just seeing those two words again made her angry. A few minutes ago, when she'd shown the message to Mr. Ainh, his only reaction was to shake his head in regret. At least Guy was an American; surely *he'd* share her sense of outrage.

He handed the note back to her. "So?"

"'*So?*'" She stared at him. "I get a death threat slipped under my door. The entire Vietnamese government hides at the mention of my name. Ainh practically *commands* me to tour his stupid lacquer factory. And that's all you can say? 'So?'"

Clucking sympathetically, he sat down beside her. *Why does he have to sit so close?* she thought. She tried to ignore the tingling in her leg as it brushed against his, struggled to sit perfectly straight though his weight on the mattress was making her sag toward him.

"First of all," he explained, "this isn't necessarily a personal death threat. It could be merely a political statement."

"Oh, is *that* all," she said blandly.

"And think of the lacquer factory as a visit to the dentist. You don't want to go, but everyone thinks you should. And as for the elusive Foreign Ministry, you wouldn't learn a thing from those bureaucrats anyway. Speaking of bureaucrats, where's your babysitter?"

"You mean Mr. Ainh?" She sighed. "Waiting for me in the lobby."

"You have to get rid of him."

"I wish."

"We can't have him around." Rising, Guy took her hand and pulled her to her feet. "Not where we're going."

"Where *are* we going?" she demanded, following him out the door.

"To see a friend. I think."

"Meaning he might not see us?"

"Meaning I can't be sure he's a friend."

She groaned as they stepped into the elevator. "Terrific."

Down in the lobby, they found Ainh by the desk, waiting to ambush her. "Miss Maitland!" he called. "Please, you must hurry. We have a very busy schedule today."

Willy glanced at Guy, who simply shrugged and looked off in another direction. Drat the man, he was leaving it up to her. "Mr. Ainh," she said, "about this little tour of the lacquer factory—"

"It will be quite fascinating! But they do not take dollars, so if you wish to exchange for dong, I can—"

"I'm afraid I don't feel up to it," she said flatly.

Ainh blinked in surprise. "You are ill?"

"Yes, I…" She suddenly noticed that Guy was shaking his head. "Uh, no, I'm not. I mean—"

"What she means," said Guy, "is that I offered to show her around. You know—" he winked at Ainh "—a little *personal* tour."

"P-personal?" Flushing, Ainh glanced at Willy. "But what about *my* tour? It is all arranged! The car, the sightseeing, a special lunch—"

"I tell you what, pal," said Guy, bending toward him conspiratorially. "Why don't *you* take the tour?"

"I have been on the tour," Ainh said glumly.

"Ah, but that was work, right? This time, why don't you take the day off, both you and the driver. Go see the sights of Saigon. And enjoy Ms. Maitland's lunch. After all, it's been paid for."

Ainh suddenly looked interested. "A free lunch?"

"And a beer." Guy slipped a few dollars into the man's breast pocket and patted the flap. "On me." He took Willy's arm and directed her across the lobby.

"But, Miss Maitland!" Ainh called out bleakly.

"Boy, what a blast you two guys're gonna have!" Guy sounded almost envious. "Air-conditioned car. Free lunch. No schedule to tie you down."

Ainh followed them outside, into a wall of morning heat so thick, it made Willy draw a breath of surprise. "Miss Maitland!" he said in desperation. "This is *not* the way it is supposed to be done!"

Guy turned and gave the man a solemn pat on the shoulder. "That, Mr. Ainh, is the whole idea."

They left the poor man standing alone on the steps, staring after them.

"What do you think he'll do?" whispered Willy.

"I think," said Guy, moving her along the crowded sidewalk, "he's going to enjoy a free lunch."

She glanced back and saw that Mr. Ainh had, indeed, disappeared into the hotel. She also noticed they were being followed. A street urchin, no more than twelve years old, caught up and danced around on the hot pavement.

"*Lien-xo?*" he chirped, dark eyes shining in a dirty face. They tried to ignore him, but the boy skipped along beside them, chattering all the way. His shirt hung in tatters; his feet were stained an apparently permanent brown. He pointed at Guy. "*Lien-xo?*"

"No, not Russian," said Guy. "Americanski."

The boy grinned. "Americanski? Yes?" He stuck out a smudgy hand and whooped. "Hello, Daddy!"

Resigned, Guy shook the boy's hand. "Yeah, it's nice to meet you too."

"Daddy rich?"

"Sorry. Daddy poor."

The boy laughed, obviously thinking that a grand joke. As Guy and Willy continued down the street, the boy hopped along at their side, shooing all the other urchins who had joined the procession. It was a tattered little parade marching through a sea of confusion. Bicycles whisked by, a multitude of wheels. And on the sidewalks, merchants squatted beside their meager collections of wares.

The boy tugged on Guy's arm. "Hey, Daddy. You got cigarette?"

"No," said Guy.

"Come on, Daddy. I do you favor, keep the beggars away."

"Oh, all right." Guy fished a pack of Marlboro cigarettes from his shirt pocket and handed the boy a cigarette.

"Guy, how could you?" Willy protested. "He's just a kid!"

"Oh, he's not going to smoke it," said Guy. "He'll trade it for something else. Like food. See?" He nodded at the boy, who was busy wrapping his treasure in a grimy piece of cloth. "That's why I always pack a few cartons when I come. They're handy when you need a favor." He turned and frowned up at one of the street signs. "Which, come to think of it, we do." He beckoned to the boy. "Hey, kid, what's your name?"

The boy shrugged.

"They must call you something."

"Other Americanski, he say I look like Oliver."

Guy laughed. "Probably meant Oliver Twist. Okay, Oliver. I got a deal for you. You do us a favor."

"Sure thing, Daddy."

"I'm looking for a street called Rue des Voiles. That's the old name, and it's not on the map. You know where it is?"

"Rue des Voiles? Rue des Voiles..." The boy scrunched up his face. "I think that one they call Binh Tan now. Why you want to go there? No stores, nothing to see."

Guy took out a thousand-dong note. "Just get us there."

The boy snapped up the money. "Okay, Daddy. You wait. Promise, you wait!" The boy trotted off down the street. At the corner, he glanced back and yelled again for good measure, "You wait!"

A minute later, he reappeared, trailed by a pair of bicycle-driven cyclos. "I find you the best. Very fast," said Oliver.

Guy and Willy stared in dismay at the two drivers. One smiled back toothlessly; the other was wheezing like a freight train.

Guy shook his head. "Where on earth did he dig up these fossils?" he muttered.

Oliver pointed proudly to the two old men and grinned. "My uncles!"

* * *

A voice behind the door said, "Go away."

"Mr. Gerard?" Guy called. There was no answer, but the man was surely lurking near the door; Willy could almost feel him crouched silently on the other side. Guy reached for the knocker fashioned after some grotesque face—either a horned lion or a goat with teeth—that hung on the door like a brass wart. He banged it a few times. "Mr. Gerard!"

Still no answer.

"It's important! We have to talk to you!"

"I said, go away!"

Willy muttered, "Do you suppose it's just possible he doesn't want to talk to us?"

"Oh, he'll talk to us." Guy banged on the door again. "The name's Guy Barnard!" he yelled. "I'm a friend of Toby Wolff."

The latch slid open. One pale eye peeped out through a crack in the door. The eye flicked back and forth, squinting first at Guy, then at Willy. The voice attached to the eye hissed, "Toby Wolff is an idiot."

"Toby Wolff is also calling in his chips."

The eye blinked. The door opened a fraction of an inch wider, the slit revealing a bald, crablike little man. "Well?" he snapped. "Are you just going to stand there?"

Inside, the house was dark as a cave, all the curtains drawn tightly over the windows. Guy and Willy followed the crustacean of a Frenchman down a narrow hallway. In the shadows, Gerard's outline was barely visible, but Willy could hear him just ahead of her, scuttling across the wood floor.

They emerged into what appeared to be a large sitting

room. Slivers of light shimmered through worn curtains. In the suffocating darkness hulked vaguely discernible furniture.

"Sit, sit," ordered Gerard. Guy and Willy moved toward a couch, but Gerard snapped, "Not *there!* Can't you see that's a genuine Queen Anne?" He pointed at a pair of massive rosewood chairs. "Sit there." He settled into a brocade armchair by the window. With his arms crossed and his knobby knees jutting out at them, he looked like a disagreeable pile of bones. "So what does Toby want from me now?" he demanded.

"He said you could pass us some information."

Gerard snorted. "I am not in the business."

"You used to be."

"No longer. The stakes are too high."

Willy glanced thoughtfully around the room, noting in the shadows the soft gleam of ivory, the luster of fine old china. She suddenly realized they were surrounded by a treasure trove of antiques. Even the house was an antique, one of Saigon's lovely old French colonials, laced with climbing vines. By law it belonged to the state. She wondered what the Frenchman had done to keep such a home.

"It has been years since I had any business with the Company," said Gerard. "I know nothing that could possibly help you now."

"Maybe you do," said Guy. "We're here about an old matter. From the war."

Gerard laughed. "These people are perpetually at war! Which enemy? The Chinese? The French? The Khmer Rouge?"

"You know which war," Guy said.

Gerard sat back. "*That* war is over."

"Not for some of us," said Willy.

The Frenchman turned to her. She felt him studying her, measuring her significance. She resented being appraised this way. Deliberately she returned his stare.

"What's the girl got to do with it?" Gerard demanded.

"She's here about her father. Missing in action since 1970."

Gerard shrugged. "My business is imports. I know nothing about missing soldiers."

"My father wasn't a soldier," said Willy. "He was a pilot for Air America."

"Wild Bill Maitland," Guy added.

The sudden silence in the room was thick enough to slice. After a long pause, Gerard said softly, "Air America."

Willy nodded. "You remember him?"

The Frenchman's knobby fingers began to tap the armrest. "I knew of them, the pilots. They carried goods for me on occasion. At a price."

"Goods?"

"Pharmaceuticals," said Guy.

Gerard slapped the armrest in irritation. "Come, Mr. Barnard, we both know what we're talking about! Opium. I don't deny it. There was a war going on, and there was money to be made. So I made it. Air America happened to provide the most reliable delivery service. The pilots never asked questions. They were good that way. I paid them what they were worth. In gold."

Again there was a silence. It took all Willy's courage to ask the next question. "And my father? Was he one of the pilots you paid in gold?"

Alain Gerard shrugged. "Would it surprise you?"

Somehow, it wouldn't, but she tried to imagine what all those old family friends would say, the ones who'd thought her father a hero.

"He was one of the best," said Gerard.

She looked up. "The best?" She felt like laughing. "At what? Running drugs?"

"Flying. It was his calling."

"My father's calling," she said bitterly, "was to do whatever he wanted. With no thought for anyone else."

"Still," insisted Gerard, "he was one of the best."

"The day his plane went down..." said Guy. "Was he carrying something of yours?"

The Frenchman didn't answer. He fidgeted in his chair, then rose and went to the window, where he fussed prissily with the curtains.

"Gerard?" Guy prodded.

Gerard turned and looked at them. "Why are you here? What purpose do these questions serve?"

"I have to know what happened to him," said Willy.

Gerard turned to the window and peered out through a slit in the curtains. "Go home, Miss Maitland. Before you learn things you don't want to know."

"What things?"

"Unpleasant things."

"He was my father! I have a right—"

"A right?" Gerard laughed. "He was in a war zone! He knew the risks. He was just another man who did not come back alive."

"I want to know why. I want to know what he was doing in Laos."

"Since when does *anyone* know what they were really doing in Laos?" He moved around the room, covetously touching his precious treasures. "You cannot imagine the things that went on in those days. Our secret war. Laos was the country we didn't talk about. But we were all there. Russians, Chinese, Americans, French. Friends and enemies, packed into the same filthy bars of Vientiane. Good soldiers, all of us, out to make a living." He stopped and looked at Willy. "I still do not understand that war."

"But you knew more than most," said Guy. "You were working with Intelligence."

"I saw only part of the picture."

"Toby Wolff suggested you took part in the crash investigation."

"I had little to do with it."

"Then who was in charge?"

"An American colonel by the name of Kistner."

Willy looked up in surprise. "*Joseph* Kistner?"

"Since promoted to general," Guy noted softly.

Gerard nodded. "He called himself a military attaché."

"Meaning he was really CIA."

"Meaning any number of things. I was liaison for French Intelligence, and I was told only the minimum. That was the way the colonel worked, you see. For him, information was power. He shared very little of it."

"What do you know about the crash?"

Gerard shrugged. "They called it 'a routine loss.' Hostile fire. A search was called at the insistence of the other pilots, but no survivors were found. After a day, Colonel Kistner put out the order to melt any wreckage. I don't know if the order was ever executed."

Willy shook her head. "Melt?"

"That's jargon for destroy," explained Guy. "They do it whenever a plane goes down during a classified mission. To get rid of the evidence."

"But my father wasn't flying a classified mission. It was a routine supply flight."

"They were *all* listed as routine supply flights," said Gerard.

"The cargo manifest listed aircraft parts," said Guy. "Not a reason to melt the plane. What was really on that flight?"

Gerard didn't answer.

"There was a passenger," Willy said. "They were carrying a passenger."

Gerard's gaze snapped toward her. "Who told you this?"

"Luis Valdez, Dad's cargo kicker. He bailed out as the plane went down."

"You spoke to this man Valdez?"

"It was only a short phone call, right after he was released from the POW camp."

"Then...he is still alive?"

She shook her head. "He shot himself the day after he got back to the States."

Gerard began to pace around the room again, touching each piece of furniture. He reminded her of a greedy gnome fingering his treasures.

"Who was the passenger, Gerard?" asked Guy.

Gerard picked up a lacquer box, set it back down again.

"Military? Intelligence? What?"

Gerard stopped pacing. "He was a phantom, Mr. Barnard."

"Meaning you don't know his name?"

"Oh, he had many names, many faces. A rumor always

does. Some said he was a general. Or a prince. Or a drug lord." Turning, he stared out the curtain slit, a shriveled silhouette against the glow of light. "Whoever he was, he represented a threat to someone in a high place."

*Someone in a high place.* Willy thought of the intrigue that must have swirled in Vientiane, 1970. She thought of Air America and Defense Intelligence and the CIA. Who among all those players would have felt threatened by this one unnamed Lao?

"Who do *you* think he was, Mr. Gerard?" she asked.

The silhouette at the window shrugged. "It makes no difference now. He's dead. Everyone on that plane is dead."

"Maybe not all of them. My father—"

"Your father has not been seen in twenty years. And if I were you, I would leave well enough alone."

"But if he's alive—"

"If he's alive, he may not wish to be found." Gerard turned and looked at her, his expression hidden against the backglow of the window. "A man with a price on his head has good reason to stay dead."

# Chapter Five

She stared at him. "A price? I don't understand."

"You mean no one has told you about the bounty?"

"Bounty for what?"

"For the arrest of Friar Tuck."

She fell instantly still. An image took shape in her mind: words typed on a file folder. *Operation Friar Tuck. Declassified.* She turned to Guy. "You know what he's talking about, don't you. Who's Friar Tuck?"

Guy's expression was unreadable, as if a mask had fallen over his face. "It's nothing but a story."

"But you had his file in your room."

"It's just a nickname for a renegade pilot. A legend—"

"Not just a legend," insisted Gerard. "He was a real man, a traitor. Intelligence does not offer two-million-dollar bounties for mere legends."

Willy's gaze shot back to Guy. She wondered how he had the nerve—the gall—to meet her eyes. *You knew,* she thought. *You bastard. All the time, you knew.* Rage had tightened her throat almost beyond speech.

She barely managed to force out her next question, which

she directed at Alain Gerard. "You think this—this renegade pilot is my father?"

"Intelligence thought so."

"Based on what evidence? That he could fly planes? The fact that he's not here to defend himself?"

"Based on the timing, the circumstances. In July 1970, William Maitland vanished from the face of the earth. In August of the same year, we heard the first reports of a foreign pilot flying for the enemy. Running weapons and gold."

"But there were hundreds of foreign pilots in Laos! Friar Tuck could have been a Frenchman, a Russian, a—"

"This much we did know—he was American."

She raised her chin. "You're saying my father was a traitor."

"I am telling you this only because it's something you should know. If he's alive, this is the reason he may not want to be found. You think you are on some sort of rescue mission, Miss Maitland, but you may be sadly mistaken. Your father could go home to a jail cell."

In the silence that followed, she turned her gaze to Guy. He still hadn't said a word; that alone proved his guilt. *Who do you work for?* she wondered. *The CIA? The Ariel Group? Or your lying, miserable self?*

She couldn't stand the sight of him. Even being in the same room with him made her recoil in disgust.

She rose. "Thank you, Mr. Gerard. You've told me things I needed to hear. Things I didn't expect."

"Then you agree it's best you drop the matter?"

"I don't agree. You think my father's a traitor. Obviously you're not the only one who thinks so. But you're all wrong."

"And how will you prove it?" Gerard snorted. "Tell me, Miss Maitland, how will you perform this grand miracle after twenty years?"

She didn't have an answer. The truth was, she didn't know what her next move would be. All she knew was that she would have to do it alone.

Her spine was ramrod straight as she followed Gerard back down the hall. The whole time, she was intensely aware of Guy moving right behind her. *I knew I couldn't trust him,* she thought. *From the very beginning I knew it.*

No one said a word until they reached the front door. There Gerard paused. Quietly he said, "Mr. Barnard? You will relay a message to Toby Wolff?"

Guy nodded. "Certainly. What's the message?"

"Tell him he has just called in his last chip." Gerard opened the front door. Outside, the sunshine was blinding. "There will be no more from me."

She made it scarcely five steps before her rage burst through.

"You lied to me. You scum, you were *using* me!"

The look on his face was the only answer Willy needed. It was written there clearly; the acknowledgment, the guilt.

"You knew about Friar Tuck. About the bounty. You weren't after just any 'live one,' were you? You were after a particular man—my father!"

Guy gave a shrug as though, now that the truth was out, it hardly mattered.

"How was this 'deal' with me supposed to work?" she pressed on. "Tell me, I'm curious. Were you going to turn him in the instant we found him—and my part of the deal be damned? Or were you going to humor me awhile, give me a chance to get my father home, let him step off the plane and onto American soil before you had him arrested? What was the plan, Guy? What *was* it?"

"There was no plan."

"Come on. A man like you always has a plan."

He looked tired. Defeated. "There was no plan."

She stared straight up at him, her fists clenching, un-clenching. "I bet you had plans for that two million dollars. I bet you knew exactly how you were going to spend it. Every penny. And all you had to do was put my father away. You bastard." She should have slugged him right then and there. Instead, she walked away.

"Sure, I could use two million bucks!" he yelled. "I could use a lot of things! But I didn't want to use *you!*"

She kept walking. It took him only a few quick strides to catch up to her.

"Willy. Dammit, will you listen?"

"To what? More of your lies?"

"No. The truth."

"The truth?" She laughed. "Since when have you bothered with the truth?"

He grabbed her arm and pulled her around to face him. "Since right now."

"Let me go."

"Not until you hear me out."

"Why should I believe anything you say?"

"Look, I admit it. I knew about Friar Tuck. About the reward. And—"

"And you knew my father was on their list."

"Yes."

"Then why didn't you tell me?"

"I would have. I was going to."

"It was all worked out from the beginning, wasn't it? Use me to track down my father."

"I thought about it. At first."

"Oh, you're low, Guy. You're really scraping bottom. Does money mean so much to you?"

"I wasn't doing it for the money. I didn't have a choice. They backed me into it."

"Who?"

"The Ariel Group. I told you—two weeks ago they showed up in my office. They knew I was headed back to Nam. What I didn't tell you was the real reason they wanted me to work for them. They weren't tracking MIAs. They were tracking an old war criminal."

"Friar Tuck."

He nodded. "I told them I wasn't interested. They offered me money. A lot of it. I got a little interested. Then they made me an offer I couldn't refuse."

"Ah," she said with disdain.

"Not money…" he protested.

"Then what's the payoff?"

He ran his hand through his hair and let out a tired breath. "Silence."

She frowned, not understanding. He didn't say a thing, but she could see in his eyes some deep, dark agony. "Then that's it," she finally whispered. "Blackmail. What do they have on you, Guy? What are you hiding?"

"It's not—" he swallowed "—something I can talk about."

"I see. It must be pretty damn shocking. Which is no big

surprise, I guess. But it still doesn't justify what you tried to do to me." She turned and walked away in disgust.

The road shimmered in the midmorning heat. Guy was right on her heels, like a stray dog that refused to be left behind. And he wasn't the only stray following her. The slap of bare feet announced the reappearance of Oliver, who skipped along beside her, chirping, "You want cyclo ride? It is very hot day! A thousand dong—I get you ride!"

She heard the squeak of wheels, the wheeze of an out-of-breath driver. Now Oliver's uncles had joined the procession.

"Go away," she said. "I don't want a ride."

"Sun very hot, very strong today. Maybe you faint. Once I see Russian lady faint." Oliver shook his head at the memory. "It was very bad sight."

"Go *away!*"

Undaunted, Oliver turned to Guy. "How about you, Daddy?"

Guy slapped a few bills into Oliver's grubby hand. "There's a thousand. Now scram."

Oliver vanished. Unfortunately, Guy wasn't so easily brushed off. He followed Willy into the town marketplace, past stands piled high with melons and mangoes, past counters where freshly butchered meat gathered flies.

"I was going to tell you about your father," Guy said. "I just wasn't sure how you'd take it."

"I'm not afraid of the truth."

"Sure you are! You're trying to protect him. That's why you keep ignoring the evidence."

"He wasn't a traitor!"

"You still love him, don't you?"

She turned sharply and walked away. Guy was right beside her. "What's wrong?" he said. "Did I hit a nerve?"

"Why should I care about him? He walked out on us."

"And you still feel guilty about it."

"Guilty?" She stopped. "Me?"

"That's right. Somewhere in that little-girl head of yours, you still blame yourself for his leaving. Maybe you had a fight, the way kids and dads always do, and you said something you shouldn't have. But before you had the chance to make up, he took off. And his plane went down. And here you are, twenty years later, still trying to make it up to him."

"Practicing psychiatry without a license now?"

"It doesn't take a shrink to know what goes on in a kid's head. I was fourteen when *my* old man walked out. I never got over being abandoned, either. Now I worry about my own kid. And it hurts."

She stared at him, astonished. "You have a child?"

"In a manner of speaking." He looked down. "The boy's mother and I, we weren't married. It's not something I'm particularly proud of."

"Oh."

"Yeah."

*You walked out on them,* she thought. *Your father left you. You left your son. The world never changes.*

"He wasn't a traitor," she insisted, returning to the matter at hand. "He was a lot of things—irresponsible, careless, insensitive. But he wouldn't turn against his own country."

"But he's on that list of suspects. If he's not Friar Tuck himself, he's probably connected somehow. And it's got to be a dangerous link. That's why someone's trying to stop you. That's why you're hitting brick walls wherever you turn. That's why, with every step you take, you're being followed."

"What!" In reflex, she turned to scan the crowd.

"Don't be so obvious." Guy grabbed her arm and dragged her to a pharmacy window. "Man at two o'clock," he murmured, nodding at a reflection in the glass. "Blue shirt, black trousers."

"Are you sure?"

"Absolutely. I just don't know who he's working for."

"He looks Vietnamese."

"But he could be working for the Russians. Or the Chinese. They both have a stake in this country."

Even as she stared at the reflection, the man in the blue shirt melted into the crowd. She knew he was still lingering nearby; she could feel his gaze on her back.

"What do I do, Guy?" she whispered. "How do I get rid of him?"

"You can't. Just keep in mind he's there. That you're probably under constant surveillance. In fact, we seem to be under the surveillance of a whole damn army." At least a dozen faces were now reflected there, all of them crowded close and peering curiously at the two foreigners. In the back, a familiar figure kept bouncing up and down, waving at them in the glass.

"Hello, Daddy!" came a yell.

Guy sighed. "We can't even get rid of *him*."

Willy stared hard at Guy's reflection. And she thought, *But I can get rid of you.*

Major Nathan Donnell of the Casualty Resolution team had shocking red hair, a booming voice and a cigar that stank to high heaven. Guy didn't know which was worse—the stench of that cigar or the odor of decay emanating from the four skeletons on the table. Maybe that's why Nate smoked those rotten cigars; they masked the smell of death.

The skeletons, each labeled with an ID number, were laid out on separate tarps. Also on the table were four plastic bags containing the personal effects and various other items found with the skeletons. After twenty or more years in this climate, not much remained of these bodies except dirt-encrusted bones and teeth. At least that much was left; sometimes fragments were all they had to work with.

Nate was reading aloud from the accompanying reports. In that grim setting, his resonant voice sounded somehow obscene, echoing off the walls of the Quonset hut. "Number 784-A, found in jungle, twelve klicks west of Camp Hawthorne. Army dog tag nearby—name, Elmore Stukey, Pfc."

"The tag was lying nearby?" Guy asked. "Not around the neck?"

Nate glanced at the Vietnamese liaison officer, who was standing off to the side. "Is that correct? It wasn't around the neck?"

The Vietnamese man nodded. "That is what the report said."

"Elmore Stukey," muttered Guy, opening the man's military medical record. "Six foot two, Caucasian, perfect teeth." He looked at the skeleton. Just a glance at the femur told him the man on the table couldn't have stood much taller than five-six. He shook his head. "Wrong guy."

"Cross off Stukey?"

"Cross off Stukey. But note that someone made off with his dog tag."

Nate let out a morbid laugh. "Not a good sign."

"What about these other three?"

"Oh, those." Nate flipped to another report. "Those three were found together eight klicks north of LZ Bird. Had that U.S. Army helmet lying close by. Not much else around."

Guy focused automatically on the relevant details: pelvic shape, configuration of incisors. "Those two are females, probably Asian," he noted. "But that one..." He took out a tape measure, ran it along the dirt-stained femur. "Male, five foot nine or thereabouts. Hmm. Silver fillings on numbers one and two." He nodded. "Possible."

Nate glanced at the Vietnamese liaison officer. "Number 786-A. I'll be flying him back for further examination."

"And the others?"

"What do you think, Guy?"

Guy shrugged. "We'll take 784-A, as well. Just to be safe. But the two females are yours."

The Vietnamese nodded. "We will make the arrangements," he said, and quietly withdrew.

There was a silence as Nate lit up another cigar, shook out the match. "Well, you sure made quick work of it. I wasn't expecting you here till tomorrow."

"Something came up."

"Yeah?" Nate's expression was thoughtful through the stinking cloud of smoke. "Anything I can help you with?"

"Maybe."

Nate nodded toward the door. "Come on. Let's get out of here. This place gives me the creeps."

They walked outside and stood in the dusty courtyard of the old military compound. Barbed wire curled on the wall above them. A rattling air conditioner dripped water from a window of the Quonset hut.

"So," said Nate, contentedly puffing on his cigar. "Is this business or personal?"

"Both. I need some information."

"Not classified, I hope."

"You tell me."

Nate laughed and squinted up at the barbed wire. "I may not tell you anything. But ask anyway."

"You were on the repatriation team back in '73, right?"

"Seventy-three through '75. But my job didn't amount to much. Just smiled a lot and passed out razors and tooth-brushes. You know, a welcome-home handshake for return-ing POWs."

"Did you happen to shake hands with any POWs from Tuyen Quan?"

"Not many. Half a dozen. That was a pretty miserable camp. Had an outbreak of typhoid near the end. A lot of 'em died in captivity."

"But not all of them. One of the POWs was a guy named Luis Valdez. Remember him?"

"Just the name. And only because I heard he shot himself the day after he got home. I thought it was a crying shame."

"Then you never met him?"

"No, he went through closed debriefing. Totally separate channel. No outside contact."

Guy frowned, wondering about that closed debriefing. Why had Intelligence shut Valdez off from the others?

"What about the other POWs from Tuyen Quan?" asked Guy. "Did anyone talk about Valdez? Mention why he was kept apart?"

"Not really. Hey, they were a pretty delirious bunch. All they could talk about was going home. Seeing their families. Anyway, I don't think any of them knew Valdez. The camp held its prisoners two to a cell, and Valdez's cellmate wasn't in the group."

"Dead?"

"No. Refused to get on the plane. If you can believe it."

"Didn't want to fly?"

"Didn't want to go home, period."

"You remember his name?"

"Hell, yes. I had to file a ten-page report on the guy. Lassiter. Sam Lassiter. Incident got me a reprimand."

"What happened?"

"We tried to drag him aboard. He kept yelling that he wanted to stay in Nam. And he was this big blond Viking, you know? Six foot four, kicking and screaming like a two-year-old. Should've seen the Vietnamese, laughing at it all. Anyway, the guy got loose and tore off into the crowd. At that point, we figured, what the hell. Let the jerk stay if he wants to."

"Then he never went home?"

Nate blew out a cloud of cigar smoke. "Never did. For a while, we tried to keep tabs on him. Last we heard, he was sighted over in Cantho, but that was a few years ago. Since then he could've moved on. Or died." Nate glanced around at the barren compound. "Nuts—that's my diagnosis. Gotta be nuts to stay in this godforsaken country."

*Maybe not,* thought Guy. *Maybe he didn't have a choice.*

"What happened to the other guys from Tuyen?" Guy asked. "After they got home?"

"They had the usual problems. Post-traumatic-stress reaction, you know. But they adjusted okay. Or as well as could be expected."

"All except Valdez."

"Yeah. All except Valdez." Nate flicked off a cigar ash. "Couldn't do a thing for him, or for wackos like Lassiter. When they're gone, they're gone. All those kids—they were too young for that war. Didn't have their heads together to begin with. Whenever I think of Lassiter and Valdez, it makes me feel pretty damn useless."

"You did what you could."

Nate nodded. "Well, I guess we're good for something." Nate sighed and looked over at the Quonset hut. "At least 786-A's finally going home."

The Russians were singing again. Otherwise it was a pleasant enough evening. The beer was cold, the bartender discreetly attentive. From his perch at the rooftop bar, Guy watched the Russkies slosh another round of Stolichnaya into their glasses. They, at least, seemed to be having a good time; it was more than he could say for himself.

He had to come up with a plan, and fast. Everything he'd learned, from Alain Gerard that morning and from Nate Donnell that afternoon, had backed up what he'd already suspected: that Willy Maitland was in over her pretty head. He was convinced that the attack in Bangkok hadn't been a robbery attempt. Someone was out to stop her. Someone who didn't want her rooting around in Bill Maitland's past. The CIA? The Vietnamese? Wild Bill himself?

That last thought he discarded as impossible. No man, no matter how desperate, would send someone to attack his own daughter.

But what if it had been meant only as a warning? A scare tactic?

All the possibilities, all the permutations, were giving Guy a headache. Was Maitland alive? What was his connection to Friar Tuck? Were they one and the same man?

Why was the Ariel Group involved?

That was the other part of the puzzle—the Ariel Group. Guy mentally replayed that visit they'd paid him two weeks ago. The two men who'd appeared in his office had been unremarkable: clean shaven, dark suits, nondescript ties, the sort of faces you'd forget the instant they walked out your door. Only when they'd presented the check for twenty thousand dollars did he sit up and take notice. Whoever they were, they had cash to burn. And there was more money waiting—a lot more—if only he'd do them one small favor: locate a certain pilot known as Friar Tuck. "Your patriotic duty," they'd called it. The man was a traitor, a red-blooded American who'd gone over to the other side. Still, Guy had hesitated. It wasn't his kind of job. He wasn't a bounty hunter.

That's when they'd played their trump card.

Ariel, Ariel. He kept mulling over the name. Something Biblical. Lionlike men. Odd name for a vets organization. If that's what they were.

Ariel wasn't the only group hunting the elusive Friar Tuck. The CIA had a bounty on the man. For all Guy knew, the Vietnamese, the French and the men from Mars were after the pilot, as well.

And at the very eye of the hurricane was naive, stubborn, impossible Willy Maitland.

That she was so damnably attractive only made things worse. She was a maddening combination of toughness and vulnerability, and he'd been torn between using her and protecting her. Did any of that make sense?

The rhythmic thud of disco music drifted up from a lower floor. He considered heading downstairs to find some willing dance partner and trample a few toes. As he took another swallow of beer, a familiar figure passed through his peripheral vision. Turning, he saw Willy head for a table near the railing. He wondered if she'd consider joining him for a drink.

Obviously not, he decided, seeing how determinedly she was ignoring him. She stared off at the night, her back rigid, her gaze fixed somewhere in the distance. A strand of tawny hair slid over her cheek, and she tucked it behind her ear, a tight little gesture that made him think of a schoolmarm.

He decided to ignore her, too. But the more fiercely he tried to shove all thought of her from his mind, the more her image seemed to burn into his brain. Even as he focused his gaze on the bartender's dwindling bottle of Stolichnaya, he felt her presence, like a crackling fire radiating somewhere behind him.

What the hell. He'd give it one more try.

He shoved to his feet and strode across the rooftop.

Willy sensed his approach but didn't bother to look up, even when he grabbed a chair, sat down and leaned across the table.

"I still think we can work together," he said.

She sniffed. "I doubt it."

"Can't we at least talk about it?"

"I don't have a thing to say to you, Mr. Barnard."

"So it's back to Mr. Barnard."

Her frigid gaze met his across the table. "I could call you something else. I could call you a—"

"Can we skip the sweet talk? Look, I've been to see a friend of mine—"

"You have friends? Amazing."

"Nate was part of the welcome-home team back in '75. Met a lot of returning POWs. Including the men from Tuyen Quan."

Suddenly she looked interested. "He knew Luis Valdez?"

"No. Valdez was routed through classified debriefing. No one got near him. But Valdez had a cellmate in Tuyen Quan, a man named Sam Lassiter. Nate says Lassiter didn't go home."

"He died?"

"He never left the country."

She leaned forward, her whole body suddenly rigid with excitement. "He's still here in Nam?"

"Was a few years ago anyway. In Cantho. It's a river town in the Delta, about a hundred and fifty kilometers southwest of here."

"Not very far," she said, her mind obviously racing. "I could leave tomorrow morning...get there by afternoon..."

"And just how are you going to get there?"

"What do you mean, how? By car, of course."

"You think Mr. Ainh's going to let you waltz off on your own?"

"That's what bribes are for. Some people will do anything for a buck. Won't they?"

He met her hard gaze with one equally unflinching. "Forget the damn money. Don't you see someone's trying to use *both* of us? I want to know why." He leaned forward, his voice soft, coaxing. "I've made arrangements for a driver to Cantho first thing in the morning. We can tell Ainh I've invited you along for the ride. You know, just another tourist visiting the—"

She laughed. "You must think I have the IQ of a turnip. Why should I trust you? Bounty hunter. Opportunist. *Jerk.*"

"Lovely evening, isn't it?" cut in a cheery voice.

Dodge Hamilton, drink in hand, beamed down at them. He was greeted with dead silence.

"Oh, dear. Am I intruding?"

"Not at all," Willy said with a sigh, pulling a chair out for the ubiquitous Englishman. No doubt he wanted company for his misery, and she would do fine. They could commiserate a little more about his lost story and her lost father.

"No, really, I wouldn't dream of—"

"I insist." Willy tossed a lethal glance at Guy. "Mr. Barnard was just leaving."

Hamilton's gaze shifted from Guy to the offered chair. "Well, if you insist." He settled uneasily into the chair, set his glass down on the table and looked at Willy. "What I wanted to ask you, Miss Maitland, is whether you'd consent to an interview."

"Me? Why on earth?"

"I decided on a new focus for my Saigon story—a daughter's search for her father. Such a touching angle. A sentimental journey into—"

"Bad idea," Guy said, cutting in.

"Why?" asked Hamilton.

"It...has no passion," he improvised. "No romance. No excitement."

"Of course, there's excitement. A missing father—"

"Hamilton." Guy leaned forward. "No."

"He's asking *me*," Willy said. "After all, it's about my father."

Guy's gaze swung around to her. "Willy," he said quietly, "think."

"I'm thinking a little publicity might open a few doors."

"More likely it'd close doors. The Vietnamese hate to hang out their dirty laundry. What if they know what happened to your father, and it wasn't a nice ending? They're not going to want the details all over the London papers. It'd be much easier to throw you out of the country."

"Believe me," said Hamilton, "I can be discreet."

"A discreet reporter. Right," Guy muttered.

"Not a word would be printed till she's left the country."

"The Vietnamese aren't dumb. They'd find out what you were working on."

"Then I'll give them a cover story. Something to throw them off the track."

"Excuse me..." Willy said politely.

"The matter's touchier than you realize, Hamilton," Guy said.

"I've covered delicate matters before. When I say something's off the record, I keep it off the record."

Willy rose to her feet. "I give up. I'm going to bed."

Guy looked up. "You can't go to bed. We haven't finished talking."

"You and I have definitely finished talking."

"What about tomorrow?"

"What about my story?"

"Hamilton," she said, "if it's dirty laundry you're looking

for, why don't you interview *him?*" She pointed to Guy.
Then she turned and walked away.

Hamilton looked at Guy. "What dirty laundry do you
have?"

Guy merely smiled.

He was still smiling as he crumpled his beer can in his
bare hands.

Lord, deliver me from the jerks of the world, Willy
thought wearily as she stepped into the elevator. The doors
slid closed. *Above all, deliver me from Guy Barnard.*

Leaning back, she closed her eyes and waited for the
elevator to creep down to the fourth floor. It moved at a
snail's pace, like everything else in this country. The stale air
was rank with the smell of liquor and sweat. Through the
creak of the cables she could hear a faint squeaking, high
in the elevator shaft. Bats. She'd seen them the night before,
flapping over the courtyard. Wonderful. Bats and Guy
Barnard. Could a girl ask for anything more?

If only there was some way she could have the benefit of
his insider's knowledge without having to put up with *him.*
The man was clever and streetwise, and he had those shadowy
but all-important connections. Too bad he couldn't be trusted.
Still, she couldn't help wondering what it would be like to take
him up on his offer. Just the thought of working cheek to cheek
with the man made her stomach dance a little pirouette of excitement. An ominous sign. The man was getting to her.

Oh, she'd been in love before; she knew how unreasonable hormones could be, how much havoc they could wreak,
cavorting in a deprived female body.

*I just won't think about him. It's the wrong time, the wrong place, the wrong situation.*

*And definitely the wrong man.*

The elevator groaned to a halt, and the doors slid open to the deserted outdoor walkway. The night trembled to the distant beat of disco music as she headed through the shadows to her room. The entire fourth floor seemed abandoned this evening, all the windows unlit, the curtains drawn. She whirled around in fright as a chorus of shrieks echoed off the building and spiraled up into the darkness. Beyond the walkway railing, the shadows of bats rose and fluttered like phantoms over the courtyard.

Her hands were still shaking when she reached her door, and it took a moment to find the key. As she rummaged in her purse, a figure glided into her peripheral vision. Some sixth sense—a premonition of danger—made her turn.

At the end of the walkway, a man emerged from the shadows. As he passed beneath the glow of an outdoor lamp, she saw slick black hair and a face so immobile it seemed cast in wax. Then something else drew her gaze. Something in his hand. He was holding a knife.

She dropped her purse and ran.

Just ahead, the walkway turned a corner, past a huge air-conditioning vent. If she kept moving, she would reach the safety of the stairwell.

The man was yards behind. Surely the purse was what he wanted. But as she tore around the corner, she heard his footsteps thudding in pursuit. Oh, God, he wasn't after her money.

He was after her.

The stairwell lay ahead at the far end of the walkway.

Just one flight down was the dance hall. She'd find people there. Safety...

With a desperate burst of speed, she sprinted forward. Then, through a fog of panic, she saw that her escape route was cut off.

Another man had appeared. He stood in the shadows at the far end of the walkway. She couldn't see his expression; all she saw was the faint gleam of his face.

She halted, spun around. As she did, something whistled past her cheek and clattered onto the walkway. A knife. Automatically, she snatched it up and wielded it in front of her.

Her gaze shifted first to one man, then the other. They were closing in.

She screamed. Her cry mingled with the dance music, echoed off the buildings and funneled up into the night. A wave of startled bats fluttered up through the darkness. *Can't anyone hear me?* she thought in desperation.

She cast another frantic look around, searching for a way out. In front of her, beyond the railing, lay a four-story drop to the courtyard. Just behind her, sunk into a square expanse of graveled roof, was the enormous air-conditioning vent. Through the rusted grating she saw its giant fan blades spinning like a plane's propeller. The blast of warm air was so powerful it made her skirt billow.

The men moved in for the kill.

# Chapter Six

She had no choice. She scrambled over the railing and dropped onto the grating. It sagged under her weight, lowering her heart-stoppingly close to the deadly blades. A rusted fragment crumbled off into the fan; the clatter of metal was deafening.

She inched her way over the grate, heading for a safe island of rooftop. It was only a few steps across, but it felt like miles of tightrope suspended over oblivion. Her legs were trembling as she finally stepped off the grate. It was a dead end; beyond lay a sheer drop. And a crumbling expanse of grating was all that separated her from the killers.

The two men glanced around in frustration, searching for a safe way to reach her. There was no other route; they would have to cross the vent. But the grating had barely supported her weight; these men were far heavier. She looked at the deadly whirl of the blades. They wouldn't risk it, she thought.

But to her disbelief, one of the men climbed over the railing and eased himself onto the vent. The mesh sagged but held. He stared at her over the spinning blades, and she saw in his eyes the impassive gaze of a man who'd simply come to do his job.

*Trapped,* she thought. *Dear God, I'm trapped!*

She screamed again, but her cry of terror was lost in the fan's roar.

He was halfway across, his knife poised. She clutched her knife and backed away to the very edge of the roof. She had two choices: a four-story drop to the pavement below, or hand-to-hand combat with an experienced assassin. Both prospects seemed equally hopeless.

She crouched, knife in trembling hand, to slash, to claw— anything to stay alive. The man took another step. The blade moved closer.

Then gunfire ripped the night.

Willy stared in bewilderment as the killer clutched his belly and looked down at his bloody hand, his face a mask of astonishment. Then, like a puppet whose strings have been cut, he crumpled. As dead weight hit the weakened grating, Willy closed her eyes and cringed.

She never saw his body fall through. But she heard the squeal of metal, felt the wild shuddering of the fan blades. She collapsed to her knees, retching into the darkness below.

When the heaving finally stopped, she forced her head up.

Her other attacker had vanished.

Across the courtyard, on the opposite walkway, some-thing gleamed. The barrel of a gun being lowered. A small face peering at her over the railing. She struggled to make sense of why the boy was there, why he had just saved her life. Stumbling to her feet, she whispered, "Oliver?"

The boy merely put a finger to his lips. Then, like a ghost, he slipped away into the darkness.

Dazed, she heard shouts and the thud of approaching footsteps.

"Willy! Are you all right?"

She turned and saw Guy. And she heard the panic in his voice.

"Don't move! I'll come get you."

"No!" she cried. "The grate—it's broken—"

For a moment, he studied the spinning blades. Then, glancing around, he spotted a workman's ladder propped beneath a broken window. He dragged it to the railing, hoisted it over and slid it horizontally across the broken grate. Then he eased himself over the railing, carefully stepped onto a rung and extended his arm to Willy. "I'm right here," he said. "Put your left foot on the ladder and grab my hand. I won't let you fall, I swear it. Come on, sweetheart. Just reach for my hand."

She couldn't look down at the fan blades. She looked across them at Guy's face, tense and gleaming with sweat. At his hand, reaching for her. And in that instant she knew, without a shred of doubt, that he would catch her. That she could trust him with her life.

She took a breath for courage, then took the step forward, over the whirling blades.

Instantly his hand locked over hers. For a split second she teetered. Guy's rigid grasp steadied her. Slowly, jerkily, she lunged forward onto the rung where he balanced.

"I've got you!" he yelled as he swept her into his arms, away from the yawning vent. He swung her easily over the railing onto the walkway, then dropped down beside her. He pulled her into the safety of his arms.

"It's all right," he murmured over and over into her hair. "Everything's all right...."

Only then, as she felt his heart pounding against hers, did she realize how terrified he'd been for her.

She was shaking so hard she could barely stand on her own two legs. It didn't matter. She knew the arms now wrapped around her would never let her fall.

They both stiffened as a harsh command was issued in Vietnamese. The people gathered about them quickly stepped aside to let a policeman through. Willy squinted as a blinding light shone in her eyes. The flashlight's beam shifted and froze on the air-conditioning vent. From the spectators came a collective gasp of horror.

"Dear God," she heard Dodge Hamilton whisper. "What a bloody mess."

Mr. Ainh was sweating. He was also hungry and tired, and he needed badly to use the toilet. But all these concerns would have to wait. He had learned that much from the war: patience. *Victory comes to those who endure.* This was what he kept saying to himself as he sat in his hard chair and stared down at the wooden table.

"We have been careless, Comrade." The minister's voice was soft, no more than a whisper; but then, the voice of power had no need to shout.

Slowly Ainh raised his head. The man sitting across from him had eyes like smooth, sparkling river stones. Though the face was wrinkled and the hair hung in silver wisps as delicate as cobwebs, the eyes were those of a young man— bold and black and brilliant. Ainh felt their gaze slice through him.

"The death of an American tourist would be most embarrassing," said the minister.

Ainh could only nod in meek agreement.

"You are certain Miss Maitland is uninjured?"

Ainh cleared his throat. Nodded again.

The minister's voice, so soft just a moment before, took on a razor's edge. "This Barnard fellow—he prevented an international incident, something our own people seem incapable of."

"But we had no warning, no reason to think this would happen."

"The attack in Bangkok—was that not a warning?"

"A robbery attempt! That's what the report—"

"And reports are never wrong, are they?" The minister's smile was disconcertingly bland. "First Bangkok. Then tonight. I wonder what our little American tourist has gotten herself into."

"The two attacks may not be connected."

"Everything, Comrade, is connected." The minister sat very still, thinking. "And what about Mr. Barnard? Are he and Miss Maitland—" the minister paused delicately "—involved?"

"I think not. She called him a…what is that American expression? A *jerk*."

The minister laughed. "Ah. Mr. Barnard has trouble with the ladies!"

There was a knock on the door. An official entered, handed a report to the minister and respectfully withdrew.

"There is progress in the case?" inquired Ainh.

The minister looked up. "Of a sort. They were able to piece together fragments of the dead man's identity card. It seems he was already well-known to the police."

"Then that explains it!" said Ainh. "Some of these thugs will do anything for a few thousand dong."

"This was no robbery." The minister handed the report to Ainh. "He has connections to the old regime."

Ainh scanned the page. "I see mention only of a woman cousin—a factory worker." He paused, then looked up in surprise. "A mixed blood."

The minister nodded. "She is being questioned now. Shall we look in on her?"

Chantel was slouched on a wooden bench, aiming lethal glares at the policeman in charge of questioning.

"I have done nothing!" she spat out. "Why should I want anyone dead? An American bitch, you say? What, do you think I am crazy? I have been home all night! Talk to the old man who lives above me! Ask him who's been playing my radio all night! Ask him why he's been beating on my ceiling, the old crank! Oh, but I could tell you stories about *him*."

"You accuse an old man?" said the policeman. "*You* are the counterrevolutionary! You and your cousin!"

"I hardly know my cousin."

"You were working together."

Chantal snorted. "I work in a factory. I have nothing to do with him."

The policeman swung a bag onto the table. He took out the items, placed them in front of her. "Caviar. Champagne. Pâté. We found these in your cupboards. How does a factory worker afford these things?"

Chantal's lips tightened, but she said nothing.

The policeman smiled. He gestured to a guard and Chantal, rigidly silent, was led from the room.

The policeman then turned respectfully to the minister,

who, along with Ainh, was watching the proceedings. "As you can see, Minister Tranh, she is uncooperative. But give us time. We will think of a way to—"

"Let her go," said the minister.

The policeman looked startled. "I assure you, she can be made to talk."

Minister Tranh smiled. "There are other ways to get information. Release her. Then wait for the fly to drift back to the honeypot."

The policeman left, shaking his head. But, of course, he would do as ordered. After all, Minister Tranh had far more experience in such matters. Hadn't the old fox honed his skills on years of wartime espionage?

For a long time, the minister sat thinking. Then he picked up the champagne bottle and squinted at the label. "Ah. Taittinger." He sighed. "A favorite from my days in Paris." Gently he set the bottle back down and looked at Ainh. "I sense that Miss Maitland has blundered into something dangerous. Perhaps she is asking too many questions. Stirring up dragons from the past."

"You mean her father?" Ainh shook his head. "That is a very old dragon."

To which the minister said softly, "But perhaps not a vanquished one."

A large black cockroach crawled across the table. One of the guards slapped it with a newspaper, brushed the corpse onto the floor and calmly went on writing. Above him, a ceiling fan whirred in the heat, fluttering papers on the desk.

"Once again, Miss Maitland," said the officer in charge. "Tell me what happened."

"I've told you everything."

"I think you have left something out."

"Nothing. I've left nothing out."

"Yes, you have. There was a gunman."

"I saw no gunman."

"We have witnesses. They heard a shot. Who fired the gun?"

"I told you, I didn't see anyone. The grating was weak—he fell through."

"Why are you lying?"

Her chin shot up. "Why do you insist I'm lying?"

"Because we both know you are."

"Lay off her!" Guy cut in. "She's told you everything she knows."

The officer turned, looked at Guy. "You will kindly remain silent, Mr. Barnard."

"And you'll cut out the Gestapo act! You've been questioning her for two hours now. Can't you see she's exhausted?"

"Perhaps it is time you left."

Guy wasn't about to back down. "She's an American. You can't hold her indefinitely!"

The officer looked at Willy, then at Guy. He gave a nonchalant shrug. "She will be released."

"When?"

"When she tells the truth." Turning, he walked out.

"Hang in," Guy muttered. "We'll get you out of here yet." He followed the officer into the next room, slamming the door behind him.

The arguing went on for ten minutes. She could hear them shouting behind the door. At least Guy still had the strength to shout; she could barely hold her head up.

When Guy returned at last, she could see from his look of disgust that he'd gotten nowhere. He dropped wearily onto the bench beside her and rubbed his eyes.

"What do they want from me?" she asked. "Why can't they just leave me alone?"

"I get the feeling they're waiting for something. Some sort of approval...."

"Whose?"

"Hell if I know."

A rolled up newspaper whacked the table. Willy looked over and saw the guard flick away another dead roach. She shuddered.

It was midnight.

At 1:00 a.m., Mr. Ainh appeared, looking as sallow as an old bed sheet. Willy was too numb to move from the bench. She simply sat there, propped against Guy's shoulder, and let the two men do the talking.

"We are very sorry for the inconvenience," said Ainh, sounding genuinely contrite. "But you must understand—"

"*Inconvenience?*" Guy snapped. "Ms. Maitland was nearly killed earlier tonight, and she's been kept here for three hours now. What the hell's going on?"

"The situation is...unusual. A robbery attempt—on a foreigner, no less—well..." He shrugged helplessly.

Guy was incredulous. "You're calling this an attempted *robbery?*"

"What would you call it?"

"A cover-up."

Ainh shuffled uneasily. Turning, he exchanged a few words in Vietnamese with the guard. Then he gave Willy a polite bow. "The police say you are free to leave, Miss

Maitland. On behalf of the Vietnamese government, I apologize for your most unfortunate experience. What happened does not in any way reflect on our high regard and warm feelings for the American people. We hope this will not spoil the remainder of your visit."

Guy couldn't help a laugh. "Why should it? It was just a little murder attempt."

"In the morning," Ainh went on quickly, "you are free to continue your tour."

"Subject to what restrictions?" Guy asked.

"No restrictions." Ainh cleared his throat and made a feeble attempt to smile. "Contrary to your government propaganda, Mr. Barnard, we are a reasonable people. We have nothing to hide."

To which Guy answered flatly, "Or so it seems."


"I don't get it. First they run you through the wringer. Then they hand you the keys to the country. It doesn't make sense."

Willy stared out the taxi window as the streets of Saigon glided past. Here and there, a lantern flickered in the darkness. A noodle vendor huddled on the sidewalk beside his steaming cart. In an open doorway, a beaded curtain shuddered, and in the dim room beyond, sleeping children could be seen, curled up like kittens on their mats.

"Nothing makes sense," she whispered. "Not this country. Or the people. Or anything that's happened...."

She was trembling. The horror of everything that had happened that night suddenly burst through the numbing dam of exhaustion. Even Guy's arm, which had magically materialized around her shoulders, couldn't keep away the unnamed terrors of the night.

He pulled her against his chest, and only when she inhaled that comfortable smell of fatigue, felt the slow and steady beat of his heart, did her trembling finally stop. He kept whispering, "It's all right, Willy. I won't let anything happen to you." She felt his kiss, gentle as rain, on her forehead.

When the driver stopped in front of the hotel, Guy had to coax her out of the car. He led her through the nightmarish glare of the lobby. He was the pillar that supported her in the elevator. And it was his arm that guided her down the shadowed walkway and past the air-conditioning vent, now ominously silent. He didn't even ask her if she wanted his company for the night; he simply opened the door to his room, led her inside and sat her down on his bed. Then he locked the door and slid a chair in front of it.

In the bathroom, he soaked a washcloth with warm water. Then he came back out, sat down beside her on the bed and gently wiped her smudged face. Her cheeks were pale. He had the insane urge to kiss her, to breathe some semblance of life back into her body. He knew she wouldn't fight him; she didn't have the strength. But it wouldn't be right, and he wasn't the kind of man who'd take advantage of the situation, of her.

"There," he murmured, brushing back her hair. "All better."

She stirred and gazed up at him with wide, stunned eyes. "Thank you," she whispered.

"For what?"

"For..." She paused, searching for the right words. "For being here."

He touched her face. "I'll be here all night. I won't leave you alone. If that's what you want."

She nodded. It hurt him to see her look so tired, so defeated. *She's getting to me,* he thought. *This isn't supposed to happen. This isn't what I expected.*

He could see, from the brightness of her eyes, that she was trying not to cry. He slid his arm around her shoulders.

"You'll be safe, Willy," he whispered into the softness of her hair. "You'll be going home in the morning. Even if I have to strap you into that plane myself, you'll be going home."

She shook her head. "I can't."

"What do you mean, you can't?"

"My father..."

"Forget him. It isn't worth it."

"I made a promise...."

"All you promised your mother was an answer. Not a body. Not some official report, stamped and certified. Just a simple answer. So give her one. Tell her he's dead, tell her he died in the crash. It's probably the truth."

"I can't lie to her."

"You have to." He took her by the shoulders, forcing her to look at him. "Willy, someone's trying to kill you. They've flubbed it twice. But what happens the third time? The fourth?"

She shook her head. "I'm not worth killing. I don't know anything!"

"Maybe it's not what you know. It's what you might find out."

Sniffling, she looked up in bewilderment. "That my father's dead? Or alive? What *difference* does it make to anyone?"

He sighed, a sound of overwhelming weariness. "I don't

know. If we could talk to Oliver, find out who he works for—"

"He's just a kid!"

"Obviously not. He could be sixteen, seventeen. Old enough to be an agent."

"For the Vietnamese?"

"No. If he was one of theirs, why'd he vanish? Why did the police keep hounding you about him?"

She huddled on the bed, her confusion deepening. "He saved my life. And I don't even know why."

There it was again, that raw edge of vulnerability, shimmering in her eyes. She might be Wild Bill Maitland's brat, but she was also a woman, and Guy was having a hard time concentrating on the problem at hand. Why was someone trying to kill her?

He was too tired to think. It was late, she was so near, and there was the bed, just waiting.

He reached up and gently stroked her face. She seemed to sense immediately what was about to happen. Even though her whole body remained stiff, she didn't fight him. The instant their lips met, he felt a shock leap through her, through him, as though they'd both been hit by some glorious bolt of lightning. *My God,* he thought in surprise. *You wanted this as much as I did....*

He heard her murmur, "No," against his mouth, but he knew she didn't mean it, so he went on kissing her until he knew that if he didn't stop right then and there, he'd do something he really didn't want to do.

*Oh, yes I do,* he thought with sudden abandon. *I want her more than I've wanted any other woman.*

She put her hand against his chest and murmured another

"No," this one fainter. He would have ignored it, too, had it not been for the look in her eyes. They were wide and confused, the eyes of a woman pushed to the brink by fear and exhaustion. This wasn't the way he wanted her. Maddening as she could be, he wanted the living, breathing, *real* Willy Maitland in his arms.

He released her. They sat on the bed, not speaking for a while, just looking at each other with a shared sense of quiet astonishment.

"Why—why did you do that?" she asked weakly.

"You looked like you needed a kiss."

"Not from you."

"From someone, then. It's been a while since you've been kissed. Hasn't it?"

She didn't answer, and he knew he'd guessed the truth. *Hell, what a waste,* he thought, his gaze dropping briefly to that perfect little mouth. He managed a disinterested laugh. "That's what I thought."

Willy stared at his grinning face and wondered, *Is it so obvious?* Not only hadn't she been kissed in a long time, she hadn't *ever* been kissed like *that.* He knew exactly how to do it; he'd probably had years of practice with other women. For some insane reason, she found herself wondering how she compared, found herself hating every woman he'd ever kissed before her, hating even more every woman he'd kiss after her.

She flung herself down on the bed and turned her back on him. "Oh, leave me alone!" she cried. "I can't deal with this! I can't deal with you. I'm tired. I just want to sleep."

He didn't say anything. She felt him smooth her hair. It was nothing more than a brush of his fingers, but somehow, that one touch told her that he wouldn't leave, that he'd be there all night, watching over her. He rose from the bed and switched off the lamp. She lay very still in the darkness, listening to him move around the room. She heard him check the windows, then the door, testing how firmly the chair was wedged against it. Then, apparently satisfied, he went into the bathroom, and she heard water running in the sink.

She was still awake when he came back to bed and stretched out beside her. She lay there, worrying that he'd kiss her again and hoping desperately that he would.

"Guy?" she whispered.

"Yes?"

"I'm scared."

He reached for her through the darkness. Willingly, she let him pull her against his bare chest. He smelled of soap and safety. Yes, that's what it was. Safety.

"It's okay to be scared," he whispered. "Even if you are Wild Bill Maitland's kid."

As if she had a choice, she thought as she lay in his arms. The sad part was, she'd never wanted to be the daughter of a legend. What she'd wanted from Wild Bill wasn't valor or daring or the reflected glory of a hero.

What she'd wanted most of all was a father.

Siang crouched motionless in a stinking mud puddle and stared up the road at Chantal's building. Two hours had passed and the man was still there by the curb. Siang could see his vague form huddled in the darkness. A police agent, no doubt, and not a very good one. Was that a snore rumbling in the night? Yes, Siang thought, definitely a snore.

How fortunate that surveillance was always relegated to those least able to withstand its monotony.

Siang decided to make his move.

He withdrew his knife. Noiselessly he edged out of the alley and circled around, slipping from shadow to shadow along the row of hootches. Barely five yards from his goal, he froze as the man's snores shuddered and stopped. The shadow's head lifted, shaking off sleep.

Siang closed in, yanked the man's head up by the hair and slit the throat.

There was no cry, only a gurgle, and then the hiss of a last breath escaping the dead man's lungs. Siang dragged the body around to the back of the building and rolled it into a drainage ditch. Then he slipped through an open window into Chantal's flat.

He found her asleep. She awakened instantly as he clapped his hand over her mouth.

"You!" she ground out through his fingers. "Damn you, you got me in trouble!"

"What did you tell the police?"

"Get away from me!"

"What did you tell them?"

She batted away his hand. "I didn't tell them anything!"

"You're lying."

"You think I'm stupid? You think I'd tell them I have friends in the CIA?"

He released her. As she sat up, the silky heat of her breast brushed against his arm. So the old whore still slept naked, he thought with an automatic stirring of desire.

She rose from the bed and pulled on a robe.

"Don't turn on the lights," he said.

"There was a man outside—a police agent. What did you do with him?"

"I took care of him."

"And the body?"

"In the ditch out back."

"Oh, nice, Siang. Very nice. Now they'll blame me for that, too." She struck a match and lit a cigarette. By the flame's brief glow, he could see her face framed by a tangle of black hair. In the semidarkness she still looked tempting, young and soft and succulent.

The match went out. He asked, "What happened at the police station?"

She let out a slow breath. The smell of exhaled smoke filled the darkness. "They asked about my cousin. They say he's dead. Is that true?"

"What do they know about me?"

"Is Winn really dead?"

Siang paused. "It couldn't be helped."

Chantal laughed. Softly at first, then with wild abandon. "*She* did that, did she? The American bitch? You cannot finish off even a woman? Oh, Siang, you must be slipping!"

He felt like hitting her, but he controlled the urge. Chantal was right. He must be slipping.

She began to pace the room, her movements as sure as a cat's in the darkness. "The police are interested. Very interested. And I saw others there—Party members, I think—watching the interrogation. What have you gotten me into, Siang?"

He shrugged. "Give me a cigarette."

She whirled on him in rage. "Get your own cigarettes! You think I have money to waste on *you*?"

"You'll get the money. All you want."

"You don't know how much I want."

"I still need a gun. You promised me you'd get one. Plus twenty rounds, minimum."

She let out a harsh breath of smoke. "Ammunition is hard to come by."

"I can't wait any longer. This has to be—"

They both froze as the door creaked open. *The police,* thought Siang, automatically reaching for his knife.

"You're so right, Mr. Siang," said a voice in the darkness. Perfect English. "It has to be done. But not quite yet."

The intruder moved lazily into the room, struck a match and calmly lit a kerosene lamp on the table.

Chantal's eyes were wide with astonishment. And fear. "It's you," she whispered. "You've come back…."

The intruder smiled. He laid a pistol and a box of .38-caliber ammunition on the table. Then he looked at Siang. "There's been a slight change of plans."

# Chapter Seven

She was flying. High, high above the clouds, where the sky was so cold and clear, it felt as if her plane were floating in a crystalline sea. She could hear the wings cut the air like knives through silk. Someone said, "Higher, baby. You have to climb higher if you want to reach the stars."

She turned. It was her father sitting in the copilot's seat, quicksilver smoke dancing around him. He looked the way she'd always remembered him, his cap tilted at a jaunty angle, his eyes twinkling. Just the way he used to look when she'd loved him. When he'd been the biggest, boldest Daddy in the world.

She said, "But I don't want to climb higher."

"Yes, you do. You want to reach the stars."

"I'm afraid, Daddy. Don't make me...."

But he took the joystick. He sent the plane upward, upward, into the blue bowl of sky. He kept saying, "This is what it's all about. Yessir, baby, this is what it's all about." Only his voice had changed. She saw that it was no longer her father sitting in the copilot's seat; it was Guy Barnard, pushing them into oblivion. "I'll take us to the stars!"

Then it was her father again, gleefully gripping the

joystick. She tried to wrench the plane out of the climb, but the joystick broke off in her hand.

The sky turned upside down, righted. She looked at the copilot's seat. Guy was sitting there, laughing. They went higher. Her father laughed.

"Who *are* you?" she screamed.

The phantom smiled. "Don't you know me?"

She woke up, still reaching desperately for that stump of a joystick.

"It's me," the voice said.

She stared up wildly. "Daddy!"

The man looking down at her smiled, a kind smile. "Not quite."

She blinked, focused on Guy's face, his rumpled hair, unshaven jaw. Sweat gleamed on his bare shoulders. Through the curtains behind him, daylight shimmered.

"Nightmare?" he asked.

Groaning, she sat up and shoved back a handful of tangled hair. "I don't usually have them. Nightmares."

"After last night, I'd be surprised if you didn't have one."

*Last night.* She looked down and saw she was still wearing the same blood-spattered dress, now damp and clinging to her back.

"Power's out," said Guy, giving the silent air conditioner a slap. He padded over to the window and nudged open the curtain. Sunlight blazed in, so piercing, it hurt Willy's eyes. "Gonna be a hell of a scorcher."

"Already is."

"Are you feeling okay?" He stood silhouetted against the window, his unbelted trousers slung low over his hips. Once again she saw the scar, noticed how it rippled its way down his abdomen before vanishing beneath the waistband.

"I'm hot," she said. "And filthy. And I probably don't smell so good."

"I hadn't noticed." He paused and added ruefully, "Probably because I smell even worse."

They laughed, a short, uneasy laugh that was instantly cut off when someone knocked on the door. Guy called out, "Who's there?"

"Mr. Barnard? It is eight o'clock. The car is ready."

"It's my driver," Guy said, and he unbolted the door.

A smiling Vietnamese man stood outside. "Good morning! Do you still wish to go to Cantho this morning?"

"I don't think so," said Guy, discreetly stepping outside to talk in private. Willy heard him murmur, "I want to get Ms. Maitland to the airport this afternoon. Maybe we can..."

Cantho. Willy sat on the bed, listening to the buzz of conversation, trying to remember why that name was so important. Oh, yes. There was a man there, someone she needed to talk to. A man who might have the answers. She closed her eyes against the window's glare, and the dream came back to her, the grinning face of her father, the sickening climb of a doomed plane. She thought of her mother, lying near death at home. Heard her mother ask, "Are you sure, Willy? Do you know for certain he's dead?" Heard herself tell another lie, all the time hating herself, hating her own cowardice, hating the fact that she could never live up to her father's name. Or his courage.

"So stick around the hotel," Guy said to the driver. "Her plane takes off at four, so we should leave around—"

"I'm going to Cantho," said Willy.

Guy glanced around at her. "What?"

"I said I'm going to Cantho. You said you'd take me."

He shook his head. "Things have changed."

"Nothing's changed."

"The stakes have."

"But not the questions. They haven't gone away. They'll never go away."

Guy turned to the driver. "Excuse me while I talk some sense into the lady...."

But Willy had already risen to her feet. "Don't bother. You can't talk sense into me." She went into the bathroom and shut the door. "I'm Wild Bill Maitland's kid, remember?" she yelled.

The driver looked sympathetically at Guy. "I will get the car."

The road out of Saigon was jammed with trucks, most of them ancient and spewing clouds of black exhaust. Through the open windows of their car came the smells of smoke and sun-baked pavement and rotting fruit. Laborers trudged along the roadside, a bobbing column of conical hats against the bright green of the rice paddies.

Five hours and two ferry crossings later, Guy and Willy stood on a Cantho pier and watched a multitude of boats glide across the muddy Mekong. River women dipped and swayed as they rowed, a strange and graceful dance at the oars. And on the riverbank swirled the noise and confusion of a thriving market town. Schoolgirls, braided hair gleaming in the sunshine, whisked past on bicycles. Stevedores heaved sacks of rice and crates of melons and pineapples onto sampans.

Overwhelmed by the chaos, Willy asked bleakly, "How are we ever going to find him?"

Guy's answer didn't inspire much confidence. He simply shrugged and said, "How hard can it be?"

Very hard, it turned out. All their inquiries brought the same response. "A tall man?" people would say. "And blond?" Invariably their answer would be a shake of the head.

It was Guy's inspired hunch that finally sent them into a series of tailor shops. "Maybe Lassiter's no longer blond," he said. "He could have dyed his hair or gone bald. But there's one feature a man can't disguise—his height. And in this country, a six-foot-four man is going to need specially tailored clothes."

The first three tailors they visited turned up nothing. It was with a growing sense of futility that they entered the fourth shop, wedged in an alley of tin-roofed hootches. In the cavelike gloom within, an elderly seamstress sat hunched over a mound of imitation silk. She didn't seem to understand Guy's questions. In frustration, Guy took out a pen and jotted a few words in Vietnamese on a scrap of newspaper. Then, to illustrate his point, he sketched in the figure of a tall man.

The woman squinted down at the drawing. For a long time, she sat there, her fingers knotted tightly around the shimmering fabric. Then she looked up at Guy. No words were exchanged, just that silent, mournful gaze.

Guy gave a nod that he understood. He reached into his pocket and lay a twenty-dollar bill on the table in front of her. She stared at it in wonder. American dollars. For her, it was a fortune.

At last she took up Guy's pen and, with painful precision, began to write. The instant she'd finished, Guy swept up the scrap of paper and jammed it into his pocket. "Let's go," he whispered to Willy.

"What does it say?" Willy whispered as they headed back along the row of hootches.

Guy didn't answer; he only quickened his pace. In the silence of the alley, Willy suddenly became aware of eyes, everywhere, watching them from the windows and doorways.

Willy tugged on Guy's arm. "Guy..."

"It's an address. Near the marketplace."

"Lassiter's?"

"Don't talk. Just keep moving. We're being followed."

"What?"

He grabbed her arm before she could turn to look. "Come on, keep your head. Pretend he's not there."

She fought to keep her eyes focused straight ahead, but the sense of being stalked made every muscle in her body strain to run. *How does he stay so calm?* she wondered, glancing at Guy. He was actually whistling now, a tuneless song that scraped her nerves raw. They reached the end of the alley, and a maze of streets lay before them. To her surprise, Guy stopped and struck up a cheerful conversation with a boy selling cigarettes at the corner. Their chatter seemed to go on forever.

"What are you doing?" Willy ground out. "Can't we get out of here?"

"Trust me." Guy bought a pack of Winstons, for which he paid two American dollars. The boy beamed and sketched a childish salute.

Guy took Willy's hand. "Get ready."

"Ready for what?"

The words were barely out of her mouth when Guy wrenched her around the corner and up another alley. They made a sharp left, then a right, past a row of tin-roofed shacks, and ducked into an open doorway.

Inside, it was too murky to make sense of their surroundings. For an eternity they huddled together, listening for footsteps. They could hear, in the distance, children laughing and a car horn honking incessantly. But just outside, in the alley, there was silence.

"Looks like the kid did his job," whispered Guy.

"You mean that cigarette boy?"

Guy sidled over to the doorway and peered out. "Looks clear. Come on, let's get out of here."

They slipped into the alley and doubled back. Even before they saw the marketplace, they could hear it: the shouts of merchants, the frantic squeals of pigs. Hurrying along the outskirts, they scanned the street names and finally turned into what was scarcely more than an alley jammed between crumbling apartment buildings. The address numbers were barely decipherable.

At last, at a faded green building, they stopped. Guy squinted at the number over the doorway and nodded. "This is it." He knocked.

The door opened. A single eye, iris so black the pupil was invisible, peered at them through the crack. That was all they saw, that one glimpse of a woman's face, but it was enough to tell them she was afraid. Guy spoke to her in Vietnamese. The woman shook her head and tried to close the door. He put his hand out to stop it and spoke again, this time saying the man's name, "Sam Lassiter."

Panicking, the woman turned and screamed something in Vietnamese.

Somewhere in the house, footsteps thudded away, followed by the shattering of glass.

"Lassiter!" Guy yelled. Shoving past the woman, he raced through the apartment, Willy at his heels. In a back room, they found a broken window. Outside in the alley, a man was sprinting away. Guy scrambled out, dropped down among the glass shards and took off after the fugitive.

Willy was about to follow him out the window when the Vietnamese woman, frantic, grasped her arm.

"Please! No hurt him!" she cried. "Please!"

Willy, trying to pull free, found her fingers linked for an instant with the other woman's. Their eyes met. "We won't hurt him," Willy said, gently disengaging her arm.

Then she pulled herself up onto the windowsill and dropped into the alley.

Guy was pulling closer. He could see his quarry loping toward the marketplace. It had to be Lassiter. Though his hair was a lank, dirty brown, there was no disguising his height; he towered above the crowd. He ducked beneath the marketplace canopy and vanished into shadow.

*Damn,* thought Guy, struggling to move through the crowd. *I'm going to lose him.*

He shoved into the central market tent. The sun's glare abruptly gave way to a close, hot gloom. He stumbled blindly, his eyes adjusting slowly to the change in light. He made out the cramped aisles, the counters overflowing with fruit and vegetables, the gay sparkle of pinwheels spinning on a toy vendor's cart. A tall silhouette suddenly bobbed off to the side. Guy spun around and saw Lassiter duck behind a gleaming stack of cookware.

Guy scrambled after him. The man leapt up and sprinted away. Pots and pans went flying, a dozen cymbals crashing together.

Guy's quarry darted into the produce section. Guy made a sharp left, leapt over a crate of mangoes and dashed up a parallel aisle. "Lassiter!" he yelled. "I want to talk! That's all, just talk!"

The man spun right, shoved over a fruit stand and stumbled away. Watermelons slammed to the ground, exploding in a brilliant rain of flesh. Guy almost slipped in the muck. "Lassiter!" he shouted.

They headed into the meat section. Lassiter, desperate, shoved a crate of ducks into Guy's path, sending up a cloud of feathers as the birds, freed from their prison, flapped loose. Guy dodged the crate, leapt over a fugitive duck and kept running. Ahead lay the butcher counters, stacked high with slabs of meat. A vendor was hosing down the concrete floor, sending a stream of bloody water into the gutter. Lassiter, moving full tilt, suddenly slid and fell to his knees in the offal. At once he tried to scramble back to his feet, but by then Guy had snagged his shirt collar.

"Just—just talk," Guy managed to gasp between breaths. "That's all—talk—"

Lassiter thrashed, struggling to pull free.

"Gimme a chance!" Guy yelled, dragging him back down.

Lassiter rammed his shoulders at Guy's knees, sending Guy sprawling. In an instant, Lassiter had leapt to his feet. But as he turned to flee, Guy grabbed his ankle, and Lassiter toppled forward and splashed, headfirst, into a vat of squirming eels.

The water seemed to boil with slippery bodies, writhing in panic. Guy dragged the man's head out of the vat. They both collapsed, gasping on the slick concrete.

"Don't!" Lassiter sobbed. "Please..."

"I told you, I just—just want to talk—"

"I won't say anything! I swear it. You tell 'em that for me. Tell 'em I forgot everything...."

"Who?" Guy took the other man by the shoulders. "Who are *they*? Who are you afraid of?"

Lassiter took a shaky breath and looked at him, seemed to make a decision. "The Company."

"Why does the CIA want you dead?" Willy asked.

They were sitting at a wooden table on the deck of an old river barge. Neutral territory, Lassiter had said of this floating café. During the war, by some unspoken agreement, V.C. and South Vietnamese soldiers would sit together on this very deck, enjoying a small patch of peace. A few hundred yards away, the war might rage on, but here no guns were drawn, no bullets fired.

Lassiter, gaunt and nervous, took a deep swallow of beer. Behind him, beyond the railing, flowed the Mekong, alive with the sounds of river men, the putter of boats. In the last light of sunset, the water rippled with gold. Lassiter said, "They want me out of the way for the same reason they wanted Luis Valdez out of the way. I know too much."

"About what?"

"Laos. The bombings, the gun drops. The war your average soldier didn't know about." He looked at Guy. "Did you?"

Guy shook his head. "We were so busy staying alive, we didn't care what was going on across the border."

"Valdez knew. Anyone who went down in Laos was in for an education. If they survived. And that was a big *if*. Say you did manage to eject. Say you lived through the G force of shooting out of your cockpit. If the enemy didn't find you, the animals would." He stared down at his beer. "Valdez was lucky to be alive."

"You met him at Tuyen Quan?" asked Guy.

"Yeah. Summer camp." He laughed. "For three years we were stuck in the same cell." His gaze turned to the river. "I was with the 101st when I was captured. Got separated during a firefight. You know how it is in those valleys, the jungle's so thick you can't be sure which way's up. I was going in circles, and all the time I could hear those damn Hueys flying overhead, *right overhead,* picking guys up. Everyone but me. I figured I'd been left to die. Or maybe I was already dead, just some corpse walking around in the trees...." He swallowed; the hand clutching the beer bottle was unsteady. "When they finally boxed me in, I just threw my rifle down and put up my hands. I got force marched north, into NVA territory. That's how I ended up at Tuyen Quan."

"Where you met Valdez," said Willy.

"He was brought in a year later, transferred in from some camp in Laos. By then I was an old-timer. Knew the ropes, worked my own vegetable patch. I was hanging in okay. Valdez, though, was holding on by the skin of his teeth. Yellow from hepatitis, a broken arm that wouldn't heal right. It took him months to get strong enough even to work in the garden. Yeah, it was just him and me in that cell. Three years. We did a lot of talking. I heard all his stories. He said a lot of things I didn't want to believe, things about Laos, about what we were doing there...."

Willy leaned forward and asked softly, "Did he ever talk about my father?"

Lassiter turned to her, his eyes dark against the glow of sunset. "When Valdez last saw him, your father was still alive. Trying to fly the plane."

"And then what happened?"

"Luis bailed out right after she blew up. So he couldn't be sure—"

"Wait," cut in Guy. "What do you mean, 'blew up'?"

"That's what he said. Something went off in the hold."

"But the plane was shot down."

"It wasn't enemy fire that brought her down. Valdez was positive about that. They might have been going through flak at the time, but this was something else, something that blew the fuselage door clean off. He kept going over and over what they had in the cargo, but all he remembered listed on the manifest were aircraft parts."

"And a passenger," said Willy.

Lassiter nodded. "Valdez mentioned him. Said he was a weird little guy, quiet, almost, well, *holy*. They could tell he was a VIP, just by what he was wearing around his neck."

"You mean gold? Chains?" asked Guy.

"Some sort of medallion. Maybe a religious symbol."

"Where was this passenger supposed to be dropped off?"

"Behind lines. VC territory. It was billed as an in-and-out job, strictly under wraps."

"Valdez told *you* about it," said Willy.

"And I wish to hell he never had." Lassiter took another

gulp of beer. His hand was shaking again. Sunset flecked the river with bloodred ripples. "It's funny. At the time we felt almost, well, *protected* in that camp. Maybe it was just a lot of brainwashing, but the guards kept telling Valdez he was lucky to be a prisoner. That he knew things that'd get him into trouble. That the CIA would kill him."

"Sounds like propaganda."

"That's what I figured it was—Commie lies designed to break him down. But they got Valdez scared. He kept waking up at night, screaming about the plane going down...."

Lassiter stared out at the water. "Anyway, after the war, they released us. Valdez and the other guys headed home. He wrote me from Bangkok, sent the letter by way of a Red Cross nurse we'd met in Hanoi right after our release. An English gal, a little anti-American but real nice. When I read that letter, I thought, now the poor bastard's really gone over the edge. He was saying crazy things, said he wasn't allowed to go out, that all his phone calls were monitored. I figured he'd be all right once he got home. Then I got a call from Nora Walker, that Red Cross nurse. She said he was dead. That he'd shot himself in the head."

Willy asked, "Do you think it was suicide?"

"I think he was a liability. And the Company doesn't like liabilities." He turned his troubled gaze to the water. "When we were at Tuyen, all he could talk about was going home, you know? Seeing his old hangouts, his old buddies. Me, I had nothing to go home to, just a sister I never much cared for. Here, at least, I had my girl, someone I loved. That's why I stayed. I'm not the only one. There are other guys like me around, hiding in villages, jungles. Guys who've gone bamboo, gone native." He shook his head. "Too bad Valdez didn't. He'd still be alive."

"But isn't it hard living here?" asked Willy. "Always the outsider, the old enemy? Don't you ever feel threatened by the authorities?"

Lassiter responded with a laugh and cocked his head at a far table where four men were sitting. "Have you said hello to our local police? They've probably been tailing you since you hit town."

"So we noticed," said Guy.

"My guess is they're assigned to protect me, their resident lunatic American. Just the fact that I'm alive and well is proof this isn't the evil empire." He raised his bottle of beer in a toast to the four policemen. They stared back sheepishly.

"So here you are," said Guy, "cut off from the rest of the world. Why would the CIA bother to come after you?"

"It's something Nora told me."

"The nurse?"

Lassiter nodded. "After the war, she stayed on in Hanoi. Still works at the local hospital. About a year ago, some guy—an American—dropped in to see her. Asked if she knew how to get hold of me. He said he had an urgent message from my uncle. But Nora's a sharp gal, thinks fast on her feet. She told him I'd left the country, that I was living in Thailand. A good thing she did."

"Why?"

"Because I don't have an uncle."

There was a silence. Softly Guy said, "You think that was a Company man."

"I keep wondering if he was. Wondering if he'll find me.

I don't want to end up like Luis Valdez. With a bullet in my head."

On the river, boats glided like ghosts through the shadows. A café worker silently circled the deck, lighting a string of paper lanterns.

"I've kept a low profile," said Lassiter. "Never make noise. Never draw attention. See, I changed my hair." He grinned faintly and tugged on his lank brown ponytail. "Got this shade from the local herbalist. Extract of cuttlefish and God knows what else. Smells like hell, but I'm not blond anymore." He let the ponytail flop loose, and his smile faded. "I kept hoping the Company would lose interest in me. Then you showed up at my door, and I—I guess I freaked out."

The bartender put a record on the turntable, and the needle scratched out a Vietnamese love song, a haunting melody that drifted like mist over the river. Wind swayed the paper lanterns, and shadows danced across the deck. Lassiter stared at the five beer bottles lined up in front of him on the table. He ordered a sixth.

"It takes time, but you get used to it here," he said. "The rhythm of life. The people, the way they think. There's not a lot of whining and flailing at misfortune. They accept life as it is. I like that. And after a while, I got to feeling this was the only place I've ever belonged, the only place I ever felt safe." He looked at Willy. "It could be the only place *you're* safe."

"But I'm not like you," said Willy. "I can't stay here the rest of my life."

"I want to put her on the next plane to Bangkok," said Guy.

"Bangkok?" Lassiter snorted. "Easiest place in the world

to get yourself killed. And going home'd be no safer. Look what happened to Valdez."

"But *why?*" Willy said in frustration. "Why would they kill Valdez? Or me? I don't know anything!"

"You're Bill Maitland's daughter. You're a direct link—"

"To *what?* A dead man?"

The love song ended, fading to the *scritch-scritch* of the needle.

Lassiter set his beer down. "I don't know," he said. "I don't know why you're such a threat to them. All I know is, something went wrong on that flight. And the Company's still trying to cover it up...." He stared at the line of empty beer bottles gleaming in the lantern light. "If it takes a bullet to buy silence, then a bullet's what they'll use."

"Do you think he's right?" Willy whispered.

From the backseat of the car, they watched the rice paddies, silvered by moonlight, slip past their windows. For an hour they'd driven without speaking, lulled into silence by the rhythm of the road under their wheels. But now Willy couldn't help voicing the question she was afraid to ask. "Will I be any safer at home?"

Guy looked out at the night. "I wish I knew. I wish I could tell you what to do. Where to go..."

She thought of her mother's house in San Francisco, thought of how warm and safe it had always seemed, that blue Victorian on Third Avenue. Surely no one would touch her there.

Then she thought of Valdez, shot to death in his Houston rooming house. For him, even a POW camp had been safer.

The driver slid a tape into the car's cassette player. A Vietnamese song twanged out, sung by a woman with a sorrowful voice. Outside, the rice paddies swayed like waves on a silver ocean. Nothing about this moment seemed real, not the melody or the moonlit countryside or the danger. Only Guy was real—real enough to touch, to hold.

She let her head rest against his shoulder, and the darkness, the warmth, made sleep impossible to resist. Guy's arm came around her, cradled her against his chest. She felt his breath in her hair, the brush of his lips on her forehead. A kiss, she thought drowsily. It felt so nice to be kissed....

The hum of the wheels over the road seemed to take on a new rhythm, the whisper of the ocean, the soothing hiss of waves. Now he was kissing her all over, and they were no longer in the backseat of the car; they were on a ship, swaying on a black sea. The wind moaned in the rigging, a soulful song in Vietnamese. She was lying on her back, and somehow, all her clothes had vanished. He was on top of her, his hands trapping her arms against the deck, his lips exploring her throat, her breasts, with a conqueror's triumph. How she wanted him to make love to her, wanted it so badly that her body arched up to meet his, straining for some blessed release from this ache within her. But his lips melted away, and then she heard, "Wake up. Willy, wake up...."

She opened her eyes. She was lying in the back seat of the car, her head in Guy's lap. Through the window came the faint glow of city lights.

"We're back in Saigon," he whispered, stroking her face. The touch of his hand, so new yet so familiar, made her tremble in the night heat. "You must have been tired."

Still shaken by the dream, she pulled away and sat up. Outside, the streets were deserted. "What time is it?"

"After midnight. Guess we forgot about supper. Are you hungry?"

"Not really."

"Neither am I. Maybe we should just call it a—" He paused. She felt his arm stiffen against hers. "Now what?" he muttered, staring straight ahead.

Willy followed his gaze to the hotel, which had just swung into view. A surreal scene lay ahead: the midnight glare of streetlights, the army of policemen blocking the lobby doors, the gleam of AK-47s held at the ready.

Their driver muttered in Vietnamese. Willy could see his face in the rearview mirror. He was sweating.

The instant they pulled to a stop at the curb, their car was surrounded. A policeman yanked the passenger door open.

"Stay inside," Guy said. "I'll take care of this."

But as he stepped out of the car, a uniformed arm reached inside and dragged her out as well. Groggy with sleep, bewildered by the confusion, she clung to Guy's arm as voices shouted and men shoved against her.

"Barnard!" It was Dodge Hamilton, struggling down the hotel steps toward them. "What the hell's going on?"

"Don't ask me! We just got back to town!"

"Blast, where's that man Ainh?" said Hamilton, glancing around. "He was here a minute ago...."

"I am here," came the answer in a shaky voice. Ainh, glasses askew and blinking nervously, stood at the top of the lobby steps. He was swiftly escorted by a policeman through the crowd. Gesturing to a limousine, he said to Guy, "Please. You and Miss Maitland will come with me."

"Why are we under arrest?" Guy demanded.

"You are not under arrest."

Guy pulled his arm free of a policeman's grasp. "Could've fooled me."

"They are here only as a precaution," said Ainh, ushering them into the car. "Please get in. Quickly."

It was the ripple of urgency in his voice that told Willy something terrible had happened. "What is it?" she asked Ainh. "What's wrong?"

Ainh nervously adjusted his glasses. "About two hours ago, we received a call from the police in Cantho."

"We were just there."

"So they told us. They also said they'd found a body. Floating in the river…"

Willy stared at him, afraid to ask, yet already knowing. Only when she felt Guy's hand tighten around her arm did she realize she'd sagged against him.

"Sam Lassiter?" Guy asked flatly.

Ainh nodded. "His throat was cut."

# Chapter Eight

The old man who sat in the carved rosewood chair appeared frail enough to be toppled by a stiff wind. His arms were like two twigs crossed on his lap. His white wisp of a beard trembled in the breath of the ceiling fan. But his eyes were as bright as quicksilver. Through the open windows came the whine of the cicadas in the walled garden. Overhead, the fan spun slowly in the midnight heat.

The old man's gaze focused on Willy. "Wherever you walk, Miss Maitland," he said, "it seems you leave a trail of blood."

"We had nothing to do with Lassiter's death," said Guy. "When we left Cantho, he was alive."

"I think you misunderstand, Mr. Barnard." The man turned to Guy. "I do not accuse you of anything."

"Who *are* you accusing?"

"That detail I leave to our people in Cantho."

"You mean those police agents you had following us?"

Minister Tranh smiled. "You made it a difficult assignment. That boy on the corner—an ingenious move. No, we're aware that Mr. Lassiter was alive when you left him."

"And after we left?"

"We know that he sat in the river café for another twenty

minutes. That he drank a total of eight beers. And then he left. Unfortunately, he never arrived home."

"Weren't your people keeping tabs on him?"

"Tabs?"

"Surveillance."

"Mr. Lassiter was a friend. We don't keep…tabs—is that the word?—on our friends."

"But you followed *us*," said Willy.

Minister Tranh's placid gaze shifted to her. "Are you our friend, Miss Maitland?"

"What do you think?"

"I think it is not easy to tell. I think even you cannot tell your friends from your enemies. It is a dangerous state of affairs. Already it has led to three murders."

Willy shook her head, puzzled. "Three? Lassiter's the only one I've heard about."

"Who else has been killed?" Guy asked.

"A Saigon policeman," said the minister. "Murdered last night on routine surveillance duty."

"I don't see the connection."

"Also last night, another man dead. Again, the throat cut."

"You can't blame us for every murder in Saigon!" said Willy. "We don't even know those other victims—"

"But yesterday you paid one of them a visit. Or have you forgotten?"

Guy stared across the table. "Gerard."

In the darkness outside, the cicadas' shrill music rose to a scream. Then, in an instant, the night fell absolutely silent.

Minister Tranh gazed ahead at the far wall, as though divining some message from the mildewed wallpaper. "Are you familiar with the Vietnamese calendar, Miss Maitland?" he asked quietly.

"Your calendar?" She frowned, puzzled by the new twist of conversation. "It—it's the same as the Chinese, isn't it?"

"Last year was the year of the dragon. A lucky year, or so they say. A fine year for babies and marriages. But this year..." He shook his head.

"The snake," said Guy.

Minister Tranh nodded. "The snake. A dangerous symbol. An omen of disaster. Famine and death. A year of misfortune...." He sighed and his head drooped, as though his fragile neck was suddenly too weak to support it. For a long time he sat in silence, his white hair fluttering in the fan's breath. Then, slowly, he raised his head. "Go home, Miss Maitland," he said. "This is not a year for you, a place for you. Go home."

Willy thought about how easy it would be to climb onto that plane to Bangkok, thought longingly of the simple luxuries that were only a flight away. Perfumed soap and clean water and soft pillows. But then another image blotted out everything else: Sam Lassiter's face, tired and haunted, against the sky of sunset. And his Vietnamese woman, pleading for his life. All these years Sam Lassiter had lived safe and hidden in a peaceful river town. Now he was dead. Like Valdez. Like Gerard.

It was true, she thought. Wherever she walked, she left a trail of blood. And she didn't even know why.

"I can't go home," she said.

The minister raised an eyebrow. "Cannot? Or will not?"

"They tried to kill me in Bangkok."

"You're no safer here. Miss Maitland, we have no wish

to forcibly deport you. But you must understand that you put us in a difficult position. You are a guest in our country. We Vietnamese honor our guests. It is a custom we hold sacred. If you, a guest, were to be found murdered, it would seem…" He paused and added with a quietly whimsical lilt, "Inhospitable."

"My visa's still good. I want to stay. I *have* to stay. I was planning to go on to Hanoi."

"We cannot guarantee your safety."

"I don't expect you to." She added wearily, "No one can guarantee my safety. Anywhere."

The minister looked at Guy, saw his troubled look. "Mr. Barnard? Surely you will convince her?"

"But she's right," said Guy.

Willy looked up and saw in Guy's eyes the worry, the uncertainty. It frightened her to realize that even he didn't have the answers.

"If I thought she'd be safer at home, I'd put her on that plane myself," he said. "But I don't think she will be safe. Not until she knows what she's running from."

"Surely she has friends to turn to."

"But you yourself said it, Minister Tranh. She can't tell her friends from her enemies. It's a dangerous state to be in."

The minister looked at Willy. "What is it you seek in the North?"

"It's where my father's plane went down," she said. "He could still be alive, in some village. Maybe he's lost his memory or he's afraid to come out of the jungle or—"

"Or he is dead."

She swallowed. "Then that's where I'll find his body. In the North."

Minister Tranh shook his head. "The jungles are full of skeletons. Americans. Vietnamese. You forget, we have our MIAs too, Miss Maitland. Our widows, our orphans. Among all those bones, to find the remains of one particular man..." He let out a heavy breath.

"But I have to try. I have to go to Hanoi."

Minister Tranh gazed at her, his eyes glowing with a strange black fire. She stared straight back at him. Slowly, a benign smile formed on his lips and she knew that she had won.

"Does nothing frighten you, Miss Maitland?" he asked.

"Many things frighten me."

"And well they should." He was still smiling, but his eyes were unfathomable. "I only hope you have the good sense to be frightened now."

Long after the two Americans had left, Minister Tranh and Mr. Ainh sat smoking cigarettes and listening to the screech of the cicadas in the night.

"You will inform our people in Hanoi," said the minister.

"But wouldn't it be easier to cancel her visa?" said Ainh. "Force her to leave the country?"

"Easier, perhaps, but not wiser." The minister lit another cigarette and inhaled a warm and satisfying breath of smoke. A good American brand. His one weakness. He knew it would only hasten his death, that the cancer now growing in his right lung would feed ravenously on each lethal molecule of smoke. How ironic that the very enemy that had worked so hard to kill him during the war would now claim victory, and all because of his fondness for their cigarettes.

"What if she comes to harm?" Ainh asked. "We would have an international incident."

"That is why she must be protected." The minister rose from his chair. The old body, once so spry, had grown stiff with the years. To think this dried-up carcass had fought two savage jungle wars. Now it could barely shuffle around the house.

"We could scare her into going home—arrange an incident to frighten her," suggested Ainh.

"Like your Die Yankee note?" Minister Tranh laughed as he headed for the door. "No, I do not think she frightens easily, that one. Better to see where she leads us. Perhaps we, too, will learn a few secrets. Or have you lost your curiosity, Comrade?"

Ainh looked miserable. "I think curiosity is a dangerous thing."

"So we let her make the moves, take the risks." The minister glanced back, smiling, from the doorway. "After all," he said. "It is *her* destiny."

"You don't have to go to Hanoi," said Guy, watching Willy pack her suitcase. "You could stay in Saigon. Wait for me."

"While you do what?"

"While I do the legwork up north. See what I can find." He glanced out the window at the two police agents loitering in the walkway. "Ainh's got you covered from all directions. You'll be safe here."

"I'll also go nuts." She snapped the suitcase shut. "Thanks for offering to stick your neck out for me, but I don't need a hero."

"I'm not trying to be a hero."

"Then why're you playing the part?"

He shrugged, unable to produce an answer.

"It's the money, isn't it? The bounty for Friar Tuck."

"It's not the money."

"Then it's that skeleton dancing around in your closet." He didn't answer. "What are you trying to hide? What's the Ariel Group got on you, anyway?" He remained silent. She locked her suitcase. "Never mind. I don't really want to know."

He sat down on the bed. Looking utterly weary, he propped his head in his hands. "I killed a man," he said.

She stared at him. Head in his hands, he looked ragged, spent, a man who'd used up his last reserves of strength. She had the unexpected impulse to sit beside him, to take him in her arms and hold him, but she couldn't seem to move her feet. She was too stunned by his revelation.

"It happened here. In Nam. In 1972." His laugh was muffled against his hands. "The Fourth of July."

"There was a war going on. Lots of people got killed."

"This was different. This wasn't an act of war, where you shoot a few men and get a medal for your trouble." He raised his head and looked at her. "The man I killed was American."

Slowly she went over and sank down beside him on the bed. "Was it...a mistake?"

He shook his head. "No, not a mistake. It was something I did without thinking. Call it reflexes. It just happened."

She said nothing, waiting for him to go on. She knew he *would* go on; there was no turning back now.

"I was in Da Nang for the day, to pick up supplies," he said. "Got a little turned around and wound up on some side street. Just an alley, really, a dirt lane, few old hootches. I got out of the jeep to ask for directions, and I heard this—this screaming...."

He paused, looked down at his hands. "She was just a kid. Fifteen, maybe sixteen. A small girl, not more than ninety pounds. There was no way she could've fought him off. I—I just reacted. I didn't really think about what I was doing, what I was going to do. I dragged him off her, shoved him on the ground. He got up and swung at me. I didn't have a choice but to fight back. By the time I stopped hitting him, he wasn't moving. I turned and saw what he'd done to the girl. All the blood..."

Guy rubbed his forehead, as though trying to erase the image. "By then there were other people there. I looked around, saw all these eyes watching me. Vietnamese. One of the women came up, whispered that I should leave, that they'd get rid of the body for me. That's when I realized the man was dead."

For a long time they sat side by side, not touching, not speaking. He'd just confessed to killing a man. Yet she couldn't condemn him; she felt only a sense of sadness about the girl, about all the silent, nameless casualties of war.

"What happened then?" she asked gently.

He shrugged. "I left. I never said a word to anyone. I guess I was scared to. A few days later I heard they'd found a soldier's body on the other side of town. His death was listed as an assault by unknown locals. And that was the end of it. I thought."

"How did the Ariel Group find out?"

"I don't know." Restless, he rose and went to the window where he looked out at the dimly lit walkway. "There were half a dozen witnesses, all of them Vietnamese. Word must've gotten around. And somehow the Ariel Group got wind of it. What I don't understand is why they waited this long."

"Maybe they only just heard about it."

"Or maybe they were waiting for the right chance to use it." He turned to look at her. "Doesn't it bother you, how we got thrown together? That we *happened* to meet in Kistner's villa? That you *happened* to need a ride into town?"

"And that the man you've been asked to find just happens to be my father."

He nodded.

"They're using us," she said. Then, with rising anger she added, "They're using *me*."

"Welcome to the club."

She looked up. "What do we do about it?"

"In the morning I'll fly to Hanoi, start asking questions."

"What about me?"

"You stay where Ainh can watch you."

"Sounds like a lousy plan."

"Have you got a better one?"

"Yes. I come with you."

"You'll only complicate things. If your father's alive, I'll find him."

"And what happens when you do? Are you going to turn him in? Trade him for silence?"

"I've given up on silence," Guy said quietly. "I'll settle for answers now."

She hauled her packed suitcase off the bed and set it down by the door. "Why am I arguing with you? I don't need your permission. I don't need any man's permission. He's *my* father. I know his face. His voice. After twenty years, *I'm* the one who'll recognize him."

"You're also the one who could get killed. Or is that part of the fun, Junior, going for thrills? Hell." He laughed. "It's probably written in your genes. You're as loony as your old man. He loved getting shot at, didn't he? He was a thrill junkie, and you are, too. Admit it. You're having the time of your life!"

"Look who's talking."

"I'm not in this for thrills. I'm in it because I had to be. Because I didn't have a choice."

"Neither of us has a choice!" She turned away, but he grabbed her arm and pulled her around to face him. He was standing so close it made her neck ache to look up at him.

"Stay in Saigon," he said.

"You must really want me out of the way."

"I want you safe."

"Why?"

"Because I— You—" He stopped. They were staring at each other, both of them breathing so hard neither of them could speak. Without another word he hauled her into his arms.

It was just a kiss, but it hit her with such hurricane force that her legs seemed to wobble away into oblivion. He was all rough edges—stubbled jaw and callused hands and frayed shirt. Automatically, she reached up and her arms closed behind his neck, pulling him hard against her mouth. He needed no encouragement. As his body pressed into hers, those dream images reignited in her head: the swaying deck of a ship, the night sky, Guy's face hovering above hers.

If she let it, it would happen here, now. Already he was nudging her toward the bed, and she knew that if they fell across that mattress, he'd take her and she'd let him, and that was that. Never mind what made sense, what was good for her. She wanted him.

*Even if it's the worst mistake I'll ever make in my life?*

The thump of her legs against the side of the bed jarred her back to reality. She twisted away, pushed him to arm's length.

"That wasn't supposed to happen!" she said.

"I think it was."

"We got our wires crossed and—"

"No," he said softly. "I'd say our wires connected just fine."

She crossed to the door and yanked it open. "I think you should get out."

"I'm not going."

"You're not staying."

But his stance, feet planted like tree roots, told her he most certainly *was* staying. "Have you forgotten? Someone wants you dead."

"But *you're* the one who's threatening me."

"It was just a kiss. Has it been *that* long, Willy? Does it shake you up that much, just being kissed?"

*Yes it does!* she wanted to scream. *It shakes me up because I've never been kissed that way before!*

"I'm staying tonight," he said quietly. "You need me. And, I admit it, I need you. You're my link to Bill Maitland. I won't touch you, if that's what you want. But I won't leave, either."

She had to concede defeat. Nothing she could do or say

would make him budge. She let the door swing shut. Then she went to the bed and sat down. "God, I'm tired," she said. "Too tired to fight you. I'm even too tired to be afraid."

"And that's when things get dangerous. When all the adrenaline's used up. When you're too exhausted to think straight."

"I give up." She collapsed onto the bed, feeling as if every bone in her body had suddenly dissolved. "I don't care what happens anymore. I just want to go to sleep."

He didn't have to say anything; they both knew the debate was over and she'd lost. The truth was, she was glad he was there. It felt so good to close her eyes, to have someone watching over her. She realized how muddled her thinking had become, that she now considered a man like Guy Barnard *safe*.

But safe was what she felt.

Standing by the bed, Guy watched her fall asleep. She looked so fragile, stretched out on the bedcovers like a paper doll.

She hadn't felt like paper in his arms. She'd been real flesh and blood, warm and soft, all the woman he could ever want. He wasn't sure just what he felt toward her. Some of it was good old-fashioned lust. But there was something more, a primitive male instinct that made him want to carry her off to a place where no one could hurt her.

He turned and looked out the window. The two police agents were still loitering near the stairwell; he could see their cigarettes glowing in the darkness. He only hoped they did their job tonight, because he had already crossed his threshold of exhaustion.

He sat down in a chair and tried to sleep.

Twenty minutes later, his whole body crying out for rest, he gave up and went to the bed. Willy didn't stir. What the hell, he thought, She'll never notice. He stretched out beside her. The shifting mattress seemed to rouse her; she moaned and turned toward him, curling up like a kitten against his chest. The sweet scent of her hair made him feel like a drunken man. Dangerous, dangerous.

He'd been better off in the chair.

But he couldn't pull away now. So he lay there holding her, thinking about what came next.

They now had a name, a tentative contact, up north: Nora Walker, the British Red Cross nurse. Lassiter had said she worked in the local hospital. Guy only hoped she'd talk to them, that she wouldn't think this was just another Company trick and clam up. Having Willy along might make all the difference. After all, Bill Maitland's daughter had a right to be asking questions. Nora Walker just might decide to provide the answers.

Willy sighed and nestled closer to his chest. That brought a smile to his face. *You crazy dame,* he thought, and kissed the top of her head. *You crazy, crazy dame.* He buried his face in her hair.

So it was decided. For better or worse, he was stuck with her.

# Chapter Nine

The flight attendant walked up the aisle of the twin-engine Ilyushin and waved halfheartedly at the flies swarming around her head. Puffs of cold mist rose from the air-conditioning vents and swirled in the cabin; the woman seemed to be floating in clouds. Through the fog, Willy could barely read the emergency sign posted over the exit: Escape Rope. Now *there* was a safety feature to write home about. She had visions of the plane soaring through blue sky, trailing passengers on a ten thousand-foot rope.

A bundle of taffy landed in her lap, courtesy of the jaded attendant. "You will fasten your seat belt," came the no-nonsense request.

"I'm already buckled in," said Willy. Then she realized the woman was speaking to Guy. Willy nudged him. "Guy, your seat belt."

"What? Oh, yeah." He buckled the belt and managed a tight smile.

That's when she noticed he was clenching the armrest. She touched his hand. "Are you all right?"

"I'm fine."

"You don't look fine."

"It's an old problem. Nothing, really..." He stared out the window and swallowed hard.

She couldn't help herself; she burst out laughing. "Guy Barnard, don't tell me you're afraid of *flying?*"

The plane lurched forward and began bumping along the tarmac. A stream of Vietnamese crackled over the speaker system, followed by Russian and then very fractured English.

"Look," he protested, "some guys have a thing about heights or closed spaces or snakes. I happen to have a phobia about planes. Ever since the war."

"Did something happen on your tour?"

"End of my tour." He stared at the ceiling and laughed. "There's the irony. I make it through Nam alive. Then I board that big beautiful freedom bird. That's how I met Toby Wolff. He was sitting right next to me. We were both high, cracking jokes as we taxied up the runway. Going home." He shook his head. "We were two of the lucky ones. Sitting in the last row of seats. The tail broke off on impact...."

She took his hand. "You don't have to talk about it, Guy."

He looked at her in obvious admiration. "You're not in the least bit nervous, are you?"

"No. I've been in planes all my life. I've always felt at home."

"Must be something you inherited from your old man. Pilot's genes."

"Not just genes. Statistics."

The Ilyushin's engines screamed to life. The cabin shuddered as they made their take-off roll down the runway. The ground suddenly fell away, and the plane wobbled into the sky.

"I happen to know flying is a perfectly safe way to travel," she added.

"Safe?" Guy yelled over the engines' roar. "Obviously, you've never flown Air Vietnam!"

In Hanoi, they were met by a Vietnamese escort known only as Miss Hu, beautiful, unsmiling and cadre to the core. Her greeting was all business, her handshake strictly government issue. Unlike Mr. Ainh, who'd been a fountain of good-humored chatter, Miss Hu obviously believed in silence. And the Revolution. Only once on the drive into the city did the woman offer a voluntary remark. Directing their attention to the twisted remains of a bridge, she said, "You see the damage? American bombs." That was it for small talk. Willy stared at the woman's rigid shoulders and realized that, for some people on both sides, the war would never be over.

She was so annoyed by Miss Hu's comment that she didn't notice Guy's preoccupied look. Only when she saw him glance for the third time out the back window did she realize what he was focusing on: a Mercedes with darkly tinted windows was trailing right behind them. She and Guy exchanged glances.

The Mercedes followed them all the way into town. Only when they pulled up in front of the hotel did the other car pass them. It headed around the corner, its occupants obscured behind dark glass.

Willy's door was pulled open. Heat poured in, a knock-down, drag-out heat that left her stunned.

Miss Hu stood waiting outside, her face already pearled with sweat. "The hotel is air-conditioned," she said and added, with a note of disdain, "for the comfort of *foreigners*."

As it turned out, the so-called air-conditioning was scarcely functioning. In fact, the hotel itself seemed to be sputtering along on little more than its old French colonial glory. The entry rug was ratty and faded, the lobby furniture a sad mélange of battered rosewood and threadbare cushions. While Guy checked in at the reception desk, Willy stationed herself near their suitcases and kept watch over the lobby entrance.

She wasn't surprised when, seconds later, two Vietnamese men, both wearing dark glasses, strolled through the door. They spotted her immediately and veered off toward an alcove, where they loitered behind a giant potted fern. She could see the smoke from their cigarettes curling toward the ceiling.

"We're all checked in," said Guy. "Room 308. View of the city."

Willy touched his arm. "Two men," she whispered. "Three o'clock..."

"I see them."

"What do we do now?"

"Ignore them."

"But—"

"Mr. Barnard?" called Miss Hu. They both turned. The woman was waving a slip of paper. "The desk clerk says there is a telegram for you."

Guy frowned. "I wasn't expecting any telegram."

"It arrived this morning in Saigon, but you had just left. The hotel called here with the message." She handed Guy the scribbled phone memo and watched with sharp eyes as he read it.

If the message was important, Guy didn't show it. He

casually stuffed it into his pocket and, picking up the suit-
cases, nudged Willy into a waiting elevator.

"Not bad news?" called Miss Hu.

Guy smiled at her. "Just a note from a friend," he said,
and punched the elevator button.

Willy caught a last glimpse of the two Vietnamese men
peering at them from behind the fern, and then the door slid
shut. Instantly, Guy gripped her hand. *Don't say a word,*
she read in his eyes.

It was a silent ride to the third floor.

Up in their room, Willy watched in puzzlement as Guy
circled around, discreetly running his fingers under lamp-
shades and along drawers, opened the closet, searched the
nightstands. Behind the headboard, he finally found what
he was seeking: a wireless microphone, barely the size of a
postage stamp. He left it where it was. Then he went to the
window and stared down at the street.

"How flattering," he murmured. "We rate baby-sitting
service."

She moved beside him and saw what he was looking at:
the black Mercedes, parked on the street below. "What
about that telegram?" she whispered.

In answer, he pulled out the slip of paper and handed it
to her. She read it twice, but it made no sense.

Uncle Sy asking about you. Plans guided tour of Nam.
Happy Trails. Bobbo.

Guy let the curtain flap shut and began to pace furiously
around the room. By the look of him, he was thinking up
a blizzard, planning some scheme.

He suddenly halted. "Do you want something for your stomach?" he asked.

She blinked. "Excuse me?"

"Pepto Bismol might help. And you'd better lie down for a while. That old intestinal bug can get pretty damn miserable."

"Intestinal bug?" She gave him a helpless look.

He stalked to the desk and rummaged in a drawer for a piece of hotel stationery, talking all the while. "I'll bet it's that seafood you ate last night. Are you still feeling really lousy?" He held up a sheet of paper on which he'd scribbled, "Yes!!!"

"Yes," she said. "Definitely lousy. I—I think I should lie down." She paused. "Shouldn't I?"

He was writing again. The sheet of paper now said, "You want to go to the hospital!"

She nodded and went into the bathroom, where she groaned loudly a few times and flushed the toilet. "You know, I feel really rotten. Maybe I should see a doctor...." It struck her then, as she stood by the sink and watched the water hiss out of the faucet, exactly what he was up to. *The man's a genius,* she thought with sudden admiration. Turning to look at him, she said, "Do you think we'll find anyone who speaks English?"

She was rewarded with a thumbs-up sign.

"We could try the hospital," he said. "Maybe it won't be a doctor, but they should have someone who'll understand you."

She went to the bed and sat down, bouncing a few times to make the springs squeak. "God, I feel awful."

He sat beside her and placed his hand on her forehead.

His eyes were twinkling as he said, "Lady, you're really hot."

"I know," she said gravely.

They could barely hold back their laughter.

"She did not seem ill an hour ago," Miss Hu said as she ushered them into the limousine ten minutes later.

"The cramps came on suddenly," said Guy.

"I would say *very* suddenly," Miss Hu noted aridly.

"I think it was the seafood," Willy whimpered from the back seat.

"You Americans," Miss Hu sniffed. "Such delicate stomachs."

The hospital waiting room was hot as an oven and overflowing with patients. As Willy and Guy entered, a hush instantly fell over the crowd. The only sounds were the rhythmic clack of the ceiling fan and a baby crying in its mother's lap. Every eye was watching as the two Americans moved through the room toward the reception desk.

The Vietnamese nurse behind the desk stared in mute astonishment. Only when Miss Hu barked out a question did the nurse respond with a nervous shake of the head and a hurried answer.

"We have only Vietnamese doctors here," translated Miss Hu. "No Europeans."

"You have no one trained in the West?" Guy asked.

"Why, do you feel your Western medicine is superior?"

"Look, I'm not here to argue East versus West. Just find someone who speaks English. A nurse'll do. You have English-speaking nurses, don't you?"

Scowling, Miss Hu turned and muttered to the desk

nurse, who made a few phone calls. At last Willy was led down a corridor to a private examination room. It was stocked with only the basics: an examining table, a sink, an instrument cart. Cotton balls and tongue depressors were displayed in dusty glass jars. A fly buzzed lazily around the one bare lightbulb. The nurse handed Willy a tattered gown and gestured for her to undress.

Willy had no intention of stripping while Miss Hu stood watch in the corner.

"I would appreciate some privacy," Willy said.

The other woman didn't move. "Mr. Barnard is staying," she pointed out.

"No." Willy looked at Guy. "Mr. Barnard is leaving."

"In fact, I was just on my way out," said Guy, turning toward the door. He added, for Miss Hu's benefit, "You know, Comrade, in America it's considered quite rude to watch while someone undresses."

"I was only trying to confirm what I've heard about Western women's undergarments," Miss Hu insisted as she and the nurse followed Guy out the door.

"What, exactly, have you heard?" asked Guy.

"That they are designed with the sole purpose of arousing prurient interest from the male sex."

"Comrade," said Guy with a grin, "I would be delighted to share my knowledge on the topic of ladies' undergarments...."

The door closed, leaving Willy alone in the room. She changed into the gown and sat on the table to wait.

Moments later, a tall, fortyish woman wearing a white lab coat walked in. The name tag on her lapel confirmed that she was Nora Walker. She gave Willy a brisk nod of greeting and paused beside the table to glance through the notes on the hospital clipboard. Strands of gray streaked her mane of brown hair; her eyes were a deep green, as unfathomable as the sea.

"I'm told you're American," the woman said, her accent British. "We don't see many Americans here. What seems to be the problem?"

"My stomach's been hurting. And I've been nauseated."

"How long now?"

"A day."

"Any fever?"

"No fever. But lots of cramping."

The woman nodded. "Not unusual for Western tourists." She looked back down at the clipboard. "It's the water. Different bacterial strains than you're used to. It'll take a few days to get over it. I'll have to examine you. If you'll just lie down, Miss—" She focused on the name written on the clipboard. Instantly she fell silent.

"Maitland," said Willy softly. "My name is Willy Maitland."

Nora cleared her throat. In a flat voice she said, "Please lie down."

Obediently, Willy settled back on the table and allowed the other woman to examine her abdomen. The hands probing her belly were cold as ice.

"Sam Lassiter said you might help us," Willy whispered.

"You've spoken to Sam?"

"In Cantho. I went to see him about my father."

Nora nodded and said, suddenly businesslike, "Does that hurt when I press?"

"No."

"How about here?"

"A little tender."

Now, once again in a whisper, Nora asked, "How is Sam doing these days?"

Willy paused. "He's dead," she murmured.

The hands resting on her stomach froze. "Dear God. How—" Nora caught herself, swallowed. "I mean, how...much does it hurt?"

Willy traced her finger, knifelike, across her throat.

Nora took a breath. "I see." Her hands, still resting on Willy's abdomen, were trembling. For a moment she stood silent, her head bowed. Then she turned and went to a medicine cabinet. "I think you need some antibiotics." She took out a bottle of pills. "Are you allergic to sulfa?"

"I don't think so."

Nora took out a blank medication label and began to fill in the instructions. "May I see proof of identification, Miss Maitland?"

Willy produced a California driver's license and handed it to Nora. "Is that sufficient?"

"It will do." Nora pocketed the license. Then she taped the medication label on the pill bottle. "Take one four times a day. You should notice some results by tomorrow night." She handed the bottle to Willy. Inside were about two dozen white tablets. On the label was listed the drug name and a standard set of directions. No hidden messages, no secret instructions.

Willy looked up expectantly, but Nora had already turned to leave. Halfway to the door, she paused. "There's a man with you, an American. Who is he? A relative?"

"A friend."

"I see." Nora gave her a long and troubled look. "I trust you're absolutely certain about your drug allergies, Miss Maitland. Because if you're wrong, that medication could be very, very dangerous." She opened the door to find Miss Hu standing right outside.

The Vietnamese woman instantly straightened. "Miss Maitland is well?" she inquired.

"She has a mild intestinal infection. I've given her some antibiotics. She should be feeling much better by tomorrow."

"I feel a little better already," said Willy, climbing off the table. "If I could just have some fresh air..."

"An excellent idea," said Nora. "Fresh air. And only light meals. No milk." She headed out the door. "Have a good stay in Hanoi, Miss Maitland."

Miss Hu turned a smug smile on Willy. "You see? Even here in Vietnam, one can find the best in medical care."

Willy nodded and reached for her clothes. "I quite agree."

Fifteen minutes later, Nora Walker left the hospital, climbed onto her bicycle and pedaled to the cloth merchants' road. At a streetside noodle stand she bought a lemonade and a bowl of *pho*, for which she paid the vendor a thousand-dong note, carefully folded at opposite corners. She ate her noodles while squatted on the sidewalk, beside all the other customers. Then, after draining the last of the peppery broth, she strolled into a tailor's shop. It appeared deserted. She slipped through a beaded curtain into a dimly lit back room. There, among the dusty bolts of silks and cottons and brocade, she waited.

The rattle of the curtain beads announced the entrance of her contact. Nora turned to face him.

"I've just seen Bill Maitland's daughter," she said in Vietnamese. She handed over Willy's driver's license.

The man studied the photograph and smiled. "I see there is a family resemblance."

"There's also a problem," said Nora. "She's traveling with a man—"

"You mean Mr. Barnard?" There was another smile. "We're well aware of him."

"Is he CIA?"

"We think not. He is, to all appearances, an independent."

"So you've been tracking them."

The man shrugged. "Hardly difficult. With so many children on the streets, they'd scarcely notice a stray boy here and there."

Nora swallowed, afraid to ask the next question. "She said Sam's dead. Is this true?"

The man's smile vanished. "We are sorry. Time, it seems, has not made things any safer."

Turning away, she tried to clear her throat, but the ache remained. She pressed her forehead against a bolt of comfortless silk. "You're right. Nothing's changed. Damn them. *Damn* them."

"What do you ask of us, Nora?"

"I don't know." She took a ragged breath and turned to face him. "I suppose—I suppose we should send a message."

"I will contact Dr. Andersen."

"I need to have an answer by tomorrow."

The man shook his head. "That leaves us little time for arrangements."

"A whole day. Surely that's enough."

"But there are..." He paused. "Complications."

Nora studied the man's face, a perfect mask of impassivity. "What do you mean?"

"The Party is now interested. And the CIA. Perhaps there are others."

*Others,* thought Nora. Meaning those they knew nothing about. The most dangerous faction of all.

As Nora left the tailor shop and walked into the painful glare of afternoon, she sensed a dozen pairs of eyes watching her, marking her leisurely progress up Gia Ngu Street. The brightly embroidered blouse she'd just purchased in the shop made her feel painfully conspicuous. Not that she wasn't already conspicuous. In Hanoi, all foreigners were watched with suspicion. In every shop she visited, along every street she walked, there were always those eyes.

They would be watching Willy Maitland, as well.

"We've made the first move," Guy said. "The next move is hers."

"And if we don't hear anything?"

"Then I'm afraid we've hit a dead end." Guy thrust his hands into his pockets and turned his gaze across the waters of Returned Sword Lake. Like a dozen other couples strolling the grassy banks, they'd sought this park for its solitude, for the chance to talk without being heard. Flame red blossoms drifted down from the trees. On the footpath ahead, children chattered over a game of ball and jacks.

"You never explained that telegram," she said. "Who's Bobbo?"

He laughed. "Oh, that's a nickname for Toby Wolff. After that plane crash, we wound up side by side in a military hospital. I guess we gave the nurses a lot of grief. You know, a few too many winks, too many sly comments. They got to calling us the evil Bobbsey twins. Pretty soon he was Bobbo One and I was Bobbo Two."

"Then Toby Wolff sent the telegram."

He nodded.

"And what does it mean? Who's Uncle Sy?"

Guy paused and gave their surroundings a thoughtful perusal. She knew it was more than just a casual look; he was searching. And sure enough, there they were: two Vietnamese men, stationed in the shadow of a poinciana tree. Police agents, most likely, assigned to protect them.

Or was it to isolate them?

"Uncle Sy," Guy said, "was our private name for the CIA."

She frowned, recalling the message. *Uncle Sy asking about you. Plans guided tour of Nam. Happy trails. Bobbo.*

"It was a warning," Guy said. "The Company knows about us. And they're in the country. Maybe watching us this very minute."

She glanced apprehensively around the lake. A bicycle glided past, pedaled by a serene girl in a conical hat. On the grass, two lovers huddled together, whispering secrets. It struck Willy as too perfect, this view of silver lake and flowering trees, an artist's fantasy for a picture postcard.

All except for the two police agents watching from the trees.

"If he's right," she said, "if the CIA's after us, how are we going to recognize them?"

"That's the problem." Guy turned to her, and the uneasiness she saw in his eyes frightened her. "We won't."

* * *

So close. Yet so unreachable.

Siang squatted in the shadow of a pedicab and watched the two Americans stroll along the opposite bank of the lake. They took their time, stopping like tourists to admire the flowers, to laugh at a child toddling in the path, both of them oblivious to how easily they could be captured in a rifle's crosshairs, their lives instantly extinguished.

He turned his attention to the two men trailing a short distance behind. Police agents, he assumed, on protective surveillance. They made things more difficult, but Siang could work around them. Sooner or later, an opportunity would arise.

Assassination would be so easy, as simple as a curtain left open to a well-aimed bullet. What a pity that was no longer the plan.

The Americans returned to their car. Siang rose, stamped the blood back into his legs and climbed onto his bicycle. It was a beggarly form of transportation, but it was practical and inconspicuous. Who would notice, among the thousands crowding the streets of Hanoi, one more shabbily dressed cyclist?

Siang followed the car back to the hotel. One block farther, he dismounted and discreetly observed the two Americans enter the lobby. Seconds later, a black Mercedes pulled up. The two agents climbed out and followed the Americans into the hotel.

It was time to set up shop.

Siang took a cloth-wrapped bundle from his bicycle basket, chose a shady spot on the sidewalk and spread out a meager collection of wares: cigarettes, soap and greeting

cards. Then, like all the other itinerant merchants lining the
road, he squatted down on his straw mat and beckoned to
passersby.

Over the next two hours he managed to sell only a single
bar of soap, but it scarcely mattered. He was there simply
to watch. And to wait.

Like any good hunter, Siang knew how to wait.

# Chapter Ten

Guy and Willy slept in separate beds that night. At least, Guy slept. Willy lay awake, tossing on the sheets, thinking about her father, about the last time she had seen him alive.

He had been packing. She'd stood beside the bed, watching him toss clothes into a suitcase. She knew by the items he'd packed that he was returning to the lovely insanity of war. She saw the flak jacket, the Laotian-English dictionary, the heavy gold chains—a handy form of ransom with which a downed pilot could bargain for his life. There was also the Government-issue blood chit, printed on cloth and swiped from a U.S. Air Force pilot.

I am a citizen of the United States of America. I do not speak your language. Misfortune forces me to seek your assistance in obtaining food, shelter and protection. Please take me to someone who will provide for my safety and see that I am returned to my people.

It was written in thirteen languages.

The last item he packed was his .45, the trigger seat filed

to a feather release. Willy had stood by the bed and stared at the gun, struck in that instant by its terrible significance.

"Why are you going back?" she'd asked.

"Because it's my job, baby," he'd said, slipping the pistol in among his clothes. "Because I'm good at it, and because we need the paycheck."

"We don't need the paycheck. We need you."

He closed the suitcase. "Your mom's been talking to you again, has she?"

"No, this is me talking, Daddy. *Me.*"

"Sure, baby." He laughed and mussed her hair, his old way of making her feel like his little girl. He set the suitcase down on the floor and grinned at her, the same grin he always used on her mother, the same grin that always got him what he wanted. "Tell you what. How 'bout I bring back a little surprise? Something nice from Vientiane. Maybe a ruby? Or a sapphire? Bet you'd love a sapphire."

She shrugged. "Why bother?"

"What do you mean, 'why bother'? You're my baby, aren't you?"

"Your baby?" She looked at the ceiling and laughed. "When was I ever *your* baby?"

His grin vanished. "I don't care for your tone of voice, young lady."

"You don't care about anything, do you? Except flying your stupid planes in your stupid war." Before he could answer, she'd pushed past him and left the room.

As she fled down the hall she heard him yell, "You're just a kid. One of these days you'll understand! Grow up a little! Then you'll understand...."

*One of these days. One of these days.*

"I still don't understand," she whispered to the night.

From the street below came the whine of a passing car. She sat up in bed and, running a hand through her damp hair, gazed around the room. The curtains fluttered like gossamer in the moonlit window. In the next bed, Guy lay asleep, the covers kicked aside, his bare back gleaming in the darkness.

She rose and went to the window. On the corner below, three pedicab drivers, dressed in rags, squatted together in the dim glow of a street lamp. They didn't say a word; they simply huddled there in a midnight tableau of weariness. She wondered how many others, just as weary, just as silent, wandered in the night.

*And to think they won the war.*

A groan and the creak of bedsprings made her turn. Guy was lying on his back now, the covers kicked to the floor. By some strange fascination, she was drawn to his side. She stood in the shadows, studying his rumpled hair, the rise and fall of his chest. Even in his sleep he wore a half smile, as though some private joke were echoing in his dreams. She started to smooth back his hair, then thought better of it. Her hand lingered over him as she struggled against the longing to touch him, to be held by him. It had been so long since she'd felt this way about a man, and it frightened her; it was the first sign of surrender, of the offering up of her soul.

She couldn't let it happen. Not with this man.

She turned and went back to her own bed and threw herself onto the sheets. There she lay, thinking of all the ways he was wrong for her, all the ways they were wrong for each other.

The way her mother and father had been wrong for each other.

It was something Ann Maitland had never recognized, that basic incompatibility. It had been painfully obvious to her daughter. Bill Maitland was the wild card, the unpredictable joker in life's game of chance. Ann cheerfully accepted whatever surprises she was dealt because he was her husband, because she loved him.

But Willy didn't need that kind of love. She didn't need a younger version of Wild Bill Maitland.

Though, God knew, she wanted him. And he was right in the next bed.

She closed her eyes. Restless, sweating, she counted the hours until morning.

"A most curious turn of events." Minister Tranh, recently off the plane from Saigon, settled into his hard-backed chair and gazed at the tea leaves drifting in his cup. "You say they are behaving like mere tourists?"

"Typical *capitalist* tourists," said Miss Hu in disgust. She opened her notebook, in which she'd dutifully recorded every detail, and began her report. "This morning at nine-forty-five, they visited the tomb of our beloved leader but offered no comment. At 12:17, they were served lunch at the hotel, a menu which included fried fish, stewed river turtle, steamed vegetables and custard. This afternoon, they were escorted to the Museum of War, then the Museum of Revolution—"

"This is hardly the itinerary of capitalist tourists."

"And then—" she flipped the page "—they went *shopping.*" Triumphantly, she snapped the notebook closed.

"But Comrade Hu, even the most dedicated Party member must, on occasion, shop."

"For antiques?"

"Ah. They value tradition."

Miss Hu bent forward. "Here is the part that raises my suspicions, Minister Tranh. It is the leopard revealing its stripes."

"Spots," corrected the minister with a smile. The fervent Comrade Hu had been studying her American idioms again. What a shame she had absorbed so little of their humor. "What, exactly, did they do?"

"This afternoon, after the antique shop, they spent two hours at the Australian embassy—the cocktail lounge, to be precise—where they conversed in private with various suspect foreigners."

Minister Tranh found it of only passing interest that the Americans would retreat to a Western embassy. Like anyone in a strange country, they probably missed the company of their own type of people. Decades ago in Paris, Tranh had felt just such a longing. Even as he'd sipped coffee in the West Bank cafés, even as he'd reveled in the joys of Bohemian life, at times, he had ached for the sight of jet black hair, for the gentle twang of his own language. Still, how he had loved Paris....

"So you see, the Americans are well monitored," said Miss Hu. "Rest assured, Minister Tranh. Nothing will go wrong."

"Assuming they continue to cooperate with us."

"Cooperate?" Miss Hu's chin came up in a gesture of injured pride. "They are not aware we're following them."

What a shame the politically correct Miss Hu was so

lacking in vision and insight. Minister Tranh hadn't the
energy to contradict her. Long ago, he had learned that
zealots were seldom swayed by reason.

He looked down at his tea leaves and sighed. "But, of
course, you are right, Comrade," he said.

"It's been a day now. Why hasn't anyone contacted us?"
Willy whispered across the oilcloth-covered table.

"Maybe they can't get close enough," Guy said. "Or
maybe they're still looking us over."

The way everyone else was looking them over, Willy
thought as her gaze swept the noisy café. In one glance she
took in the tables cluttered with coffee cups and soup bowls,
the diners veiled in a vapor of cooking grease and cigarette
smoke, the waiters ferrying trays of steaming food. *They're
all watching us,* she thought. In a far corner, the two police
agents sat flicking ashes into a saucer. And through the
dirty street windows, small faces peered in, children straining for a rare glimpse of Americans.

Their waiter, gaunt and silent, set two bowls of noodle
soup on their table and vanished through a pair of swinging
doors. In the kitchen, pots clanged and voices chattered
over a cleaver's staccato. The swinging doors kept slapping
open and shut as waiters pushed through, bent under the
weight of their trays.

The police agents were staring.

Willy, by now brittle with tension, reached for her chopsticks and automatically began to eat. It was modest fare,
noodles and peppery broth and paper-thin slices of what
looked like beef. Water buffalo, Guy told her. Tasty but
tough. Head bent, ignoring the stares, she ate in silence.

Only when she inadvertently bit into a chili pepper and had to make a lunge for her glass of lemonade did she finally put her chopsticks down.

"I don't know if I can take this idle-tourist act much longer." She sighed. "Just how long are we supposed to wait?"

"As long as it takes. That's one thing you learn in this country. Patience. Waiting for the right time. The right situation."

"Twenty years is a long time to wait."

"You know," he said, frowning, "that's the part that bothers me. That it's been twenty years. Why would the Company still be mucking around in what should be a dead issue?"

"Maybe they're not interested. Maybe Toby Wolff's wrong."

"Toby's never wrong." He looked around at the crowded room, his gaze troubled. "And something else still bothers me. Has from the very beginning. Our so-called accidental meeting in Bangkok. Both of us looking for the same answers, the same man." He paused. "In addition to mild paranoia, however, I get also this sense of..."

"Coincidence?"

"Fate."

Willy shook her head. "I don't believe in fate."

"You will." He stared up at the haze of cigarette smoke swirling about the ceiling fan. "It's this country. It changes you, strips away your sense of reality, your sense of control. You begin to think that events are meant to happen, that they *will* happen, no matter how you fight it. As if our lives are all written out for us and it's impossible to revise the book."

Their gazes met across the table. "I don't believe in fate, Guy," she said softly. "I never have."

"I'm not asking you to."

"I don't believe you and I were *meant* to be together. It just happened."

"But something—luck, fate, conspiracy, whatever you want to call it—has thrown us together." He leaned forward, his gaze never leaving her face. "Of all the crazy places in the world, here we are, at the same table, in the same dirty Vietnamese café. And..." He paused, his brown eyes warm, his crooked smile a fleeting glimmer in his seriousness. "I'm beginning to think it's time we gave in and followed this crazy script. Time we followed our instincts."

They stared at each other through the veil of smoke. And she thought, *I'd like nothing better than to follow my instincts, which are to go back to our hotel and make love with you. I know I'll regret it. But that's what I want. Maybe that's what I've wanted since the day I met you.*

He reached across the table; their hands met. And as their fingers linked, it seemed as if some magical circuit had just been completed, as if this had always been meant to be, that this was where fate—good, bad or indifferent—had meant to lead them. Not apart, but together, to the same embrace, the same bed.

"Let's go back to the room," he whispered.

She nodded. A smile slid between them, one of knowing, full of promise. Already the images were drifting through her head: shirts slowly unbuttoned, belts unbuckled. Sweat glistening on backs and shoulders. Slowly she pushed her chair back from the table.

But as they rose to their feet, a voice, shockingly familiar, called to them from across the room.

Dodge Hamilton lumbered toward them through the maze of tables. Pale and sweating, he sank into a chair beside them.

"What the hell are *you* doing here?" Guy asked in astonishment.

"I'm bloody lucky to be here at all," said Hamilton, wiping a handkerchief across his brow. "One of our engines trailed smoke all the way from Da Nang. I tell you, I didn't fancy myself splattered all over some mountaintop."

"But I thought you were staying in Saigon," said Willy.

Hamilton stuffed the handkerchief back in his pocket. "Wish I had. But yesterday I got a telex from the finance minister's office. He's finally agreed to an interview—something I've been working at for months. So I squeezed onto the last flight out of Saigon." He shook his head. "Just about my last flight, period. Lord, I need a drink." He pointed to Willy's glass. "What's that you've got there?"

"Lemonade."

Hamilton turned and called to the waiter. "Hello, there! Could I have one of these—these lemon things?"

Willy took a sip, watching Hamilton thoughtfully over the rim of her glass. "How did you find us?"

"What? Oh, that was no trick. The hotel clerk directed me here."

"How did *he* know?"

Guy sighed. "Obviously we can't take a step without everyone knowing about it."

Hamilton frowned dubiously as the waiter set a napkin and another glass of lemonade on the table. "Probably carries some fatal bacteria." He lifted the glass and sighed. "Might as well live dangerously. Well, here's to the trusty Ilyushins of the sky! May they never crash. Not with me aboard, anyway."

Guy raised his glass in a wholehearted toast. "Amen. From now on, I say we all stick to boats."

"Or pedicabs," said Hamilton. "Just think, Barnard, we could be pedaled across China!"

"I think you'd be safer in a plane," Willy said, and reached for her glass. As she lifted it, she noticed a dark stain bleeding from the wet napkin onto the tablecloth. It took her a few seconds to realize what it was, that tiny trickle of blue. Ink. There was something written on the other side of her napkin....

"It all depends on the plane," said Hamilton. "After today, no more Russian rigs for me. Pardon the pun, but I've been thoroughly dis-Ilyushined."

It was Guy's burst of laughter that pulled Willy out of her feverish speculation. She looked up and found Hamilton frowning at her. Dodge Hamilton, she thought. He was always around. Always watching.

She crumpled the napkin in her fist. "If you don't mind, I think I'll go back to the hotel."

"Is something wrong?" Guy asked.

"I'm tired." She rose, still clutching the napkin. "And a little queasy."

Hamilton at once shoved aside his glass of lemonade. "I *knew* I should have stuck to whiskey. Can I fetch you anything? Bananas, maybe? That's the cure, you know."

"She'll be fine," said Guy, helping Willy to her feet. "I'll look after her."

Outside, the heat and chaos of the street were overwhelming. Willy clung to Guy's arm, afraid to talk, afraid to voice her suspicions. But he'd already sensed her agitation. He pulled her through the crowd toward the hotel.

Back in their room, Guy locked the door and drew the curtains. Willy unfolded the napkin. By the light of a bedside lamp, they struggled to decipher the smudgy message.

"0200. Alley behind hotel. Watch your back."

Willy looked at him. "What do you think?"

He didn't answer. She watched him pace the room, thinking, weighing the risks. Then he took the napkin, tore it to shreds and vanished into the bathroom. She heard the toilet flush and knew the evidence had been disposed of. When he came out of the bathroom, his expression was flat and unreadable.

"Why don't you lie down," he said. "There's nothing like a good night's sleep to settle an upset stomach." He turned off the lamp. By the glow of her watch, she saw it was just after seven-thirty. It would be a long wait.

They scarcely slept that night.

In the darkness of their room, they waited for the hours to pass. Outside, the noises of the street, the voices, the tinkle of pedicab bells faded to silence. They didn't undress; they lay tensed in their beds, not daring to exchange a word.

It must have been after midnight when Willy at last slipped into a dreamless sleep. It seemed only moments had passed when she felt herself being nudged awake. Guy's lips brushed her forehead, then she heard him whisper, "Time to move."

She sat up, instantly alert, her heart off and racing. Carrying her shoes, she tiptoed after him to the door.

The hall was deserted. The scuffed wood floor gleamed dully beneath a bare lightbulb. They slipped out into the corridor and headed for the stairs.

From the second-floor railing, they peered down into the lobby. The hotel desk was unattended. The sound of snoring echoed like a lion's roar up the stairwell. As they moved down the steps, the hotel lounge came into view, and they spotted the lobby attendant sprawled out on a couch, mouth gaping in blissful repose.

Guy flashed Willy a grin and a thumbs-up sign. Then he led the way down the steps and through a service door. Crates lined a dark and dingy hallway; at the far end was another door. They slipped out the exit.

Outside, the darkness was so thick Willy found herself groping for some tangible clue to her surroundings. Then Guy took her hand and his touch was steadying; it was a hand she'd learned she could trust. Together they crept through the shadows, into the narrow alley behind the hotel. There they waited.

It was 2:01.

At 2:07, they sensed, more than heard, a stirring in the darkness. It was as if a breath of wind had congealed into something alive, solid. They didn't see the woman until she was right beside them.

"Come with me," she said. Willy recognized the voice: it was Nora Walker's.

They followed her up a series of streets and alleys, weaving farther and farther into the maze that was Hanoi. Nora said nothing. Every so often they caught a glimpse of her in the glow of a street lamp, her hair concealed beneath a conical hat, her dark blouse anonymously shabby.

At last, in an alley puddled with stagnant water, they came to a halt. Through the darkness, Willy could just make out three bicycles propped against a wall. A bundle was thrust into her hands. It contained a set of pajamalike pants and blouse, a conical hat smelling of fresh straw. Guy, too, was handed a change of clothes.

In silence they dressed.

On bicycles they followed Nora through miles of back streets. In that landscape of shadows, everything took on a life of its own. Tree branches reached out to snag them. The road twisted like a serpent. Willy lost all sense of direction; as far as she knew, they could be turning in circles. She pedaled automatically, following the faint outline of Nora's hat floating ahead in the darkness.

The paved streets gave way to dirt roads, the buildings to huts and vegetable plots. At last, at the outskirts of town, they dismounted. An old truck sat at the side of the road. Through the driver's window, a cigarette could be seen glowing in the darkness. The door squealed open, and a Vietnamese man hopped out of the cab. He and Nora whispered together for a moment. Then the man tossed aside the cigarette and gestured to the back of the truck.

"Get in," said Nora. "He'll take you from here."

"Where are we going?" asked Willy.

Nora flipped aside the truck's tarp and motioned for them to climb in. "No time for questions. Hurry."

"Aren't you coming with us?"

"I can't. They'll notice I'm gone."

"*Who'll* notice?"

Nora's voice, already urgent, took on a note of panic. "Please. Get in *now*."

Guy and Willy scrambled onto the rear bumper and dropped down lightly among a pile of rice sacks.

"Be patient," said Nora. "It's a long ride. There's food and water inside—enough to hold you."

"Who's the driver?" asked Guy.

"No names. It's safer."

"But can we trust him?"

Nora paused. "Can we trust anyone?" she said. Then she yanked on the tarp. The canvas fell, closing them off from the night.

It was a long bicycle ride back to her apartment. Nora pedaled swiftly, her body slicing through the night, her hat shuddering in the wind. She knew the way well; even in the darkness she could sense where the hazards, the unexpected potholes, lay.

Tonight she could also sense something else. A presence, something evil, floating in the night. The feeling was so unshakable she felt compelled to stop and look back at the road. For a full minute she held her breath and waited. Nothing moved, only the shadows of clouds hurtling before the moon. *It's my imagination,* she thought. No one was following her. No one *could* have followed her. She'd been too cautious, taking the Americans up and down so many turns that no one could possibly have kept up unnoticed.

Breathing easier, she pedaled all the way home.

She parked her bicycle in the community shed and climbed the rickety steps to her apartment. The door was unlocked. The significance of that fact didn't strike her until she'd already taken one step over the threshold. By then it was too late.

The door closed behind her. She spun around just as a

light sprang on, shining full in her face. Blinded, she took a panicked step backward. "Who—what—"

From behind, hands wrenched her into a brutal embrace. A knife blade slid lightly across her neck.

"Not a word," whispered a voice in her ear.

The person holding the light came forward. He was a large man, so large, his shadow blotted out the wall. "We've been waiting for you, Miss Walker," he said. "Where did you take them?"

She swallowed. "Who?"

"You went to the hotel to meet them. Where did you go from there?"

"I didn't—" She gasped as the blade suddenly stung her flesh; she felt a drop of blood trickle warmly down her neck.

"Easy, Mr. Siang," said the man. "We have all night."

Nora began to cry. "Please. Please, I don't know anything...."

"But, of course, you do. And you'll tell us, won't you?" The man pulled up a chair and sat down. She could see his teeth gleaming like ivory in the shadows. "It's only a question of when."

From beneath the flapping canvas, Willy caught glimpses of dawn: light filtering through the trees, dust swirling in the road, the green brilliance of rice paddies. They'd been traveling for hours now, and the sacks of rice were beginning to feel like bags of concrete against their backs. At least they'd been provided with food and drink. In an open crate they'd found a bottle of water, a loaf of French bread and four hard-boiled eggs. It seemed sufficient—at first. But as the day wore on and the heat grew suffocating, that single bottle of water became more and more precious. They rationed it, one sip every half hour; it was barely enough to keep their throats moist.

At noon the truck began to climb.

"Where are we going?" she asked.

"Heading west, I think. Into the mountains. Maybe the road to Dien Bien Phu."

"Towards Laos?"

"Where your father's plane went down." In the shadows of the truck, Guy's face, dirty and unshaven, was a tired mask of resolution. She wondered if she looked as grim.

He shrugged off his sweat-soaked shirt and threw it aside, oblivious to the mosquitoes buzzing around them. The scar on his bare abdomen seemed to ripple in the gloom. In silent fascination, Willy started to reach out to him, then thought better of it.

"It's okay," he said softly, guiding her hand to the scar. "It doesn't hurt."

"It must have hurt terribly when you got it."

"I don't remember." At her puzzled look, he added, "I mean, not on any sort of conscious level. It's funny, though, how well I remember what happened just before the plane went down. Toby, sitting next to me, telling jokes. Something about the pilot looking like an old buddy of his from Alcoholics Anonymous. He'd heard in flight school that the best military pilots were always the drunks; a sober man wouldn't dream of flying the sort of junk heap we were in. I remember laughing as we taxied down the runway. Then—" He shook his head. "They say I pulled him out of the wreckage. That I unbuckled him and dragged him out just before the whole thing blew. They even called me a hero." He uncapped the water bottle, took a sip. "What a laugh."

"Sounds like you earned the label," she said.

"Sounds more like I was knocked in the head and didn't know what the hell I was doing."

"The best heroes in the world are the reluctant ones. Courage isn't fearlessness—it's acting in the face of fear."

"Yeah?" He laughed. "Then that makes me the best of the best." He stiffened as the truck suddenly slowed, halted. A voice barked orders in the distance. They stared at each other in alarm.

"What is it?" she whispered. "What're they saying?"

"Something about a roadblock...soldiers are stopping everyone. Some sort of inspection...."

"My God. What do we—"

He put a finger to his lips. "Sounds like a lot of traffic in front. Could take a while before they get to us."

"Can we back up? Turn around?"

He scrambled to the back of the truck and glanced through a slit in the canvas. "No chance. We're socked in tight. Trucks on both sides."

Willy frantically surveyed the gloom, searching for empty burlap bags, a crate, anything large enough in which to hide.

The soldiers' voices moved closer.

*We have to make a run for it,* thought Willy. Guy had already risen to a crouch. But a glance outside told them they were surrounded by shallow rice paddies. Without cover, their flight would be spotted immediately.

*But they won't hurt us,* she thought. *They wouldn't dare. We're Americans.*

As if, in this crazy world, an eagle on one's passport bought any sort of protection.

The soldiers were right outside—two men by the sound of the voices. The truck driver was trying to cajole his way out of the inspection, laughing, offering cigarettes. The man had to have nerves of steel; not a single note of apprehension slipped into his voice.

His attempts at bribery failed. Footsteps continued along the graveled roadside, heading for the back of the truck.

Guy instinctively shoved Willy against the rice sacks, shielding her behind him. He'd be the one they'd see first, the one they'd confront. He turned to face the inevitable.

A hand poked through, gripping the canvas flap....

And paused. In the distance, a car horn was blaring. Tires screeched, followed by the thud of metal, the angry shouts of drivers.

The hand gripping the canvas pulled away. The flap slid shut. There were a few terse words exchanged between the soldiers, then footsteps moved away, crunching up the gravel road.

It took only seconds for their driver to scramble back into the front seat and hit the gas. The truck lurched forward, throwing Guy off his feet. He toppled, landing right next to Willy on the rice sacks. As their truck roared full speed around the traffic and down the road, they sprawled together, too stunned by their narrow escape to say a word. Suddenly they were both laughing, rolling around on the sacks, giddy with relief.

Guy hauled her into his arms and kissed her hard on the mouth.

"What was that for?" she demanded, pulling back in surprise.

"That," he whispered, "was pure instinct."

"Do you always follow your instincts?"

"Whenever I can get away with it."

"And you really think I'll let you get away with it?"

In answer, he gripped her hair, trapping her head against the sacks, and kissed her again, longer, deeper. Pleasure leapt through her, a desire so sudden, so fierce, it left her voiceless.

"I think," he murmured, "you want it as much as I do."

With a gasp of outrage, she shoved him onto his back and climbed on top of him, pinning him beneath her. "Guy Barnard, you miserable jerk, I'm going to give you what you deserve."

He laughed. "Are you now?"

"Yes, I am."

"And what, exactly, do I deserve?"

For a moment she stared at him through the dust and gloom. Then, slowly, she lowered her face to his. "This," she said softly.

The kiss was different this time. Warmer. Hungrier. She was a full and willing partner; he knew it and he responded. She didn't need to be warned that she was playing a dangerous game, that they were both hurtling toward the point of no return. She could already feel him swelling beneath her, could feel her own body aching to accommodate that new hardness. And the whole time she was kissing him, the whole time their bodies were pressed together, she was thinking, *I'm going to regret this. As sure as I breathe, I'm going to pay for this. But it feels so right....*

She pulled away, fighting to catch her breath.

"Well!" said Guy, grinning up at her. "Miss Willy Maitland, I *am* surprised."

She sat up, nervously shoving her hair back into place. "I never meant to do that."

"Yes, you did."

"It was a stupid thing to do."

"Then why did you?"

"It was..." She looked him in the eye. "Pure instinct."

He laughed. In fact, he fell backward laughing, rolling around on the sacks of rice. The truck hit a pothole, bouncing her up and down so hard, she collapsed onto the floor beside him.

And still he was laughing.

"You're a crazy man," she said.

He threw an arm around her neck and pulled her warmly against him. "Only about you."

In a black limousine with tinted windows, Siang sat gripping the steering wheel and cursing the wretched highway—or what this country called a highway. He had never understood why communism and decent roads had to be mutually exclusive. And then there was the traffic, added to the annoyance of that government vehicle inspection. It had given him a moment's apprehension, the sight of the armed soldiers standing at the roadside. But it took only a few smooth words from the man in the back seat, the wave of a Soviet diplomatic passport, and they were allowed to move on without incident.

They continued west; a road sign confirmed it was the highway to Dien Bien Phu. A strange omen, Siang thought, that they should be headed for the town where the French had met defeat, where East had triumphed over West. Centuries before, an Asian scribe had written a prophetic statement.

To the south lie the mountains,
The land of the Viets.
He who marches against them
Is surely doomed to failure.

Siang glanced in the rearview mirror, at the man in the backseat. *He* wouldn't be thinking in terms of East versus West. *He* cared nothing about nations or motherlands or patriotism. Real power, he'd once told Siang, lay in the hands of individuals, special people who knew how to use it, to keep it, and *he* was going to keep it.

Siang had no doubt he would.

He remembered the day they'd first met in Happy Valley, at an American base the GIs had whimsically dubbed "the Golf Course." It was 1967. Siang had a different name then. He was a slender boy of thirteen, barefoot, scratching out a hungry existence among all the other orphans. When he'd first seen the American, his initial impression was of hugeness. An enormous fleshy face, alarmingly red in the heat; boots made for a giant; hands that looked strong enough to snap a child's arm in two. The day was hot, and Siang was selling soft drinks. The man bought a Coca Cola, drank it down in a few gulps and handed the empty bottle back. As Siang took it, he felt the man's gaze studying him, measuring him. Then the man walked away.

The next day, and every day for a week, the American emerged from the GI compound to buy a Coca Cola. Though a dozen other children clamored for his business, each waving soft drinks, the man bought only from Siang.

At the end of the week, the man presented Siang with a brand-new shirt, three tins of corned beef and an astonishing amount of cash. He said he was leaving the valley early the next morning, and he asked the boy to hire the prettiest girl he could find and bring her to him for the night.

It was only a test, as Siang found out later. He passed it. In fact, the American seemed surprised when Siang appeared at the compound gate that evening with an extraordinarily beautiful girl. Obviously, the man had expected Siang to take the money and vanish.

To Siang's astonishment, the man sent the girl away without even touching her. Instead, he asked the boy to stay—not as a lover, as Siang at first feared, but as an assistant. "I need someone I can trust," the man said. "Someone I can train...."

Even now, after all these years, Siang still felt that young boy's sense of awe whenever he looked at the American. He glanced at the rearview mirror, at the face that had changed so little since that day they'd met in Happy Valley. The cheeks might be thicker and ruddier, but the eyes were the same, sharp and all-knowing. Just like the mind. Those eyes almost frightened him.

Siang turned his attention back to the road. The man in the back seat was humming a tune: "Yankee Doodle." A whimsical choice, considering the Soviet passport he was carrying. Siang smiled at the irony of it all.

Nothing about the man was ever quite what it seemed.

# Chapter Eleven

It was late in the day when the truck at last pulled to a halt. Willy, half-asleep among the rice sacks, rolled drowsily onto her back and struggled to clear her head. The signals her body was sending gave new meaning to the word *misery*. Every muscle ached; every bone felt shattered. The truck engine cut off. In the new silence, mosquitoes buzzed in the gloom, a gloom so thick she could scarcely breathe.

"Are you awake?" came a whisper. Guy's face, gleaming with sweat, appeared above her.

"What time is it?"

"Late afternoon. Five or so. My watch stopped."

She sat up and her head swam in the heat. "Where are we?"

"Can't be sure. Near the border, I'd guess..." Guy stiffened as footsteps tramped toward them. Men's voices, speaking Vietnamese, moved closer.

The canvas flap was thrown open. Against the sudden glare of daylight, the faces of the two men staring in were black and featureless.

One of the men gestured for them to climb out. "You follow," he ordered. "Say nothing."

Willy at once scrambled out and dropped onto the spongy jungle floor. Guy followed her. They swayed for a moment, blinking dazedly, gulping in their first fresh air in hours. Chips of afternoon sunlight dappled the ground at their feet. In the branches above, an invisible bird screeched out a warning.

The Vietnamese man motioned to them to move. They had just started into the woods when an engine roared to life. Willy turned in alarm to see the truck rattle away without them. She glanced at Guy and saw in his eyes the same thought that had crossed her mind, *There's no turning back now.*

"No stop. Go, go!" said the Vietnamese.

They moved on into the forest.

The man obviously knew where he was going. Without a trail to guide him, he led them through a tangle of vines and trees to an isolated hut. A tattered U.S. Army blanket hung over the doorway. Inside, straw matting covered the earthen floor and a mosquito net, filmy as lace, draped a sleeping pallet. On a low table was set a modest meal of bananas, cracked coconuts and cold tea.

"You wait here," said the man. "Long time, maybe."

"Who are we waiting for?" asked Guy.

The man didn't answer; perhaps he didn't understand the question. He turned and, like a ghost, slipped into the forest.

For a long time, Willy and Guy lingered in the doorway, waiting, listening to the whispers of the jungle. They heard only the clattering of palms in the wind, the lonely cry of a bird.

How long would they wait? Willy wondered. Hours? Days? She stared up through the dense canopy at the last sunlight sparkling on the wet leaves. It would be dark soon. "I'm hungry," she said, and she turned back into the gloom of the hut.

Together they devoured every banana, gnawed every sliver of coconut from its husk, drank down every drop of tea. In all her life, Willy had never tasted any meal quite so splendid! At last, their stomachs full, their legs trembling with exhaustion, they crawled under the mosquito netting and, side by side, they fell asleep.

At dusk, it began to rain. It was a glorious downpour, monsoonlike in its ferocity, but it brought no relief from the heat. Willy, awake in the darkness, lay with her clothes steeped in sweat. In the shadows above, the mosquito net billowed and fell like a hovering ghost.

She clawed her way free of the netting. If she didn't get some air, she was going to smother.

She left Guy asleep on the pallet and went to the doorway, where she gulped in breaths of rain-drenched air. The swirl of cool mist was irresistible; she stepped out into the downpour.

All around her, the jungle clattered like a thousand cymbals. She shivered in the thunderous darkness as the water streamed down her face.

"What the hell are you doing?" called a sleepy voice. She turned and saw Guy in the doorway.

She laughed. "I'm taking a shower!"

"With your clothes on?"

"It's lovely out here! Come on, before it stops!"

He hesitated, then plunged outside after her.

"Doesn't it feel wonderful?" she cried, throwing her arms out to welcome the raindrops. "I couldn't take the heat any longer. God, I couldn't even stand the smell of my own clothes."

"You think that's bad? Just wait till the mildew sets in." Turning his face to the sky, he let out a satisfied growl. "Now *this* is the way we were meant to take a shower. The way the kids do it. When I was here during the war, I used to get a kick out of seeing 'em run around without their clothes on. Nothing cuter than all those little brown bodies dancing in the rain. No shame, no embarrassment."

"The way it should be."

"That's right," he said. Softly he added, "The way it should be."

All at once, Willy felt him watching her. She turned and stared back. The palms clattered, and the rain beat its tattoo on the leaves. Without a word, he came toward her, stood so close to her, she could feel the heat rippling between them. Yet she didn't move, didn't speak. The rain streaming down her face was as warm as teardrops.

"So what are we doing with our clothes on?" he murmured.

She shook her head. "This isn't supposed to happen."

"Maybe it is."

"A one-night stand—that's all it'd be—"

"Better once than never."

"And then you'll be gone."

"You don't know that. I don't know that."

"I do know it. You'll be gone...."

She started to turn away, but he pulled her back, twisted her around to face him. At the first meeting of their lips, she knew it was over, the battle lost.

*Better once than never,* she thought as her last shred of resistance fell away. *Better to have you once and lose you than to always wonder how it might have been.* Reaching up, she threw her arms around his neck and met his kiss with her own, just as hungry, just as fierce. Their bodies pressed together so tightly, their fever heat mingled through the damp clothes.

He was already fumbling for the buttons of her blouse. She trembled as the fabric slid away and rain trickled down her bare shoulders. Then the warmth of his hand closed around her breast, and she was shivering not with cold but with desire.

Together they stumbled into the darkness of the hut. They were tugging desperately at each other's clothes now, flinging the wet garments into oblivion. When at last they faced each other with no barriers, no defenses, he pulled her face up and gently pressed his lips to hers. No kiss had ever pierced so true to her soul. The darkness swam around her; the earth gave way. She let him lower her to the pallet and felt the mosquito net whisper down around them.

*Making love in the clouds,* she thought as the whiteness billowed above. Then she closed her eyes and lost all sense of where she was. There was only the pounding of the rain and the magical touch of Guy's hands, his mouth. It had been so long since a man had made love to her, so long since she'd bared herself to the pleasure. The pain. And there *would* be pain after it was over, after he was gone from her life. With a man like Guy, the ending was inevitable.

She ignored those whispers of warning, she had drifted beyond all reach of salvation. She pulled him down against her, and whispered, "Now. Please."

He was already struggling against his own needs, his own urgencies. Her quiet plea slashed away his last thread of control.

"I give up," he groaned. Seizing her hands, he pinned her arms above her head, trapping her, his willing captive, beneath him.

His hardness filled her so completely, it made her catch her breath in astonishment. But her surprise quickly melted into pleasure. She was moving against him now, and he against her, both of them driving that blessed ache to new heights of agony.

The world fell away; the night seemed to swirl with mist and magic. They brought each other to the very edge, and there they lingered, between pleasure and torment, unwilling to surrender to the inevitable. Then the jungle sounds of beating rain, of groaning trees were joined by their cries as they plummeted over the brink.

Even when she fell back to earth, she was still floating. In the darkness above, the netting billowed like parachute silk falling through the emptiness of space.

There was no need to speak; it was enough just to lie together, limbs entwined, and listen to the rhythms of the night.

Gently, Guy stroked a tangled lock of hair off her cheek. "Why did you say that?" he asked.

"Say what?"

"That I'd be gone. That I'd leave you."

She pulled away and rolled onto her back. "Because you will."

"Do you want me to?"

She didn't answer. What difference would it make, after all, to bare her soul? And did he really want to hear the truth: that after tonight, she would probably do anything to keep him, to make him love her?

"Willy?"

She turned away. "Why are we talking about this?"

"Because I want to talk about it."

"Well, I don't." She sat up and hugged her knees protectively against her chest. "It doesn't do anyone any good, all this babbling about what comes next, where do we go from here. I've been through it before."

"You really don't trust men, do you?"

She laughed. "Should I?"

"Is it all because your old man walked out on you? Or was it something else? A bad love affair? What?"

"You could say all of the above."

"I see." There was a long silence. She shivered at the touch of his hand stroking her naked back. "Who else has left you? Besides your father?"

"Just a man I loved. Someone who said he loved me."

"And he didn't."

"Oh, I suppose he did, in his way." She shrugged. "Not a very permanent way."

"If it's only temporary, it's not love."

"Now that sounds like the title of a song." She laughed.

"A lousy song."

At once, she fell silent. She pressed her forehead to her knees. "You're right. A lousy song."

"Other people manage to get over rotten love affairs...."

"Oh, I got over it." She raised her head and stared up at the netting. "Took only a month to fall in love with him. And over a year to watch him walk away. One thing I've learned is that it doesn't fall apart in a day. Most lovers don't just get up and walk out the door. They do it by inches, step by step, and every single one hurts. First they start out with,

'Who needs to get married, it's just a piece of paper.' And then, at the end, they tell you, 'I need more space.' Then it's 'How can anyone promise forever?' Maybe it was better the way my dad did it. No excuses. He just walked out the door."

"There's no such thing as a good way to leave someone."

"You're right." She pushed aside the netting and swung her feet out. "That's why I don't let it happen to me anymore."

"How do you avoid it?"

"I don't give any man the chance to leave me."

"Meaning you walk away first?"

"Men do it all the time."

"Some men."

*Including you,* she thought with a distinct twinge of bitterness. "So how did you walk away from your girl-friend, Guy? Did you leave before or after you found out she was pregnant?"

"That was an unusual situation."

"It always is."

"We'd broken up months before. I didn't hear about the kid till after he was born. By then there was nothing I could do, nothing I could change. Ginny was already married to another man."

"Oh." She paused. "That made it simple."

"Simple?" For the first time she heard his anger, and she longed to take back her awful words, longed to cleanse the bitterness from his voice. "You've got some crazy notion that men are all the same," he said. "All of us trying to claw our way free of responsibility, never looking back at the people we've hurt. Let me tell you something, Willy. Having a Y chromosome doesn't make someone a lousy human being."

"I shouldn't have said that," she said, gently touching his hand. "I'm sorry."

He lay quietly in the shadows, staring up at the ceiling. "Sam's three years old now. I've seen him a grand total of twice, once on Ginny's front porch, once on the playground at his preschool. I went over there to get a look at him, to see what kind of kid he was, whether he looked happy. I guess the teachers must've reported it. Not long after, Ginny called me, screaming bloody murder. Said I was messing with her marriage. Even threatened to slap me with a restraining order. I haven't been near him since...." He paused to clear his throat. "I guess I realized I wouldn't be doing him any favors anyways, trying to shove my way into his life. Sam already has a father—a good one, from what I hear. And it would've hurt everyone if I'd tried to fight it out in court. Maybe later, when he's older, I'll find a way to tell him. To let him know how much I wanted to be part of his life."

*And my life?* she thought with sudden sadness. *You won't be part of it, either, will you?*

She rose to her feet and groped around in the darkness for her scattered clothes. "Here's a little advice, Guy," she said over her shoulder. "Don't ever give up on your son. Take it from a kid who's been left behind. Daddies are a precious commodity."

"I know," he said softly. He paused, then said, "You'll never get over it, will you? Your father walking out."

She shook out her wet blouse. "There are some things a kid can't ever forget."

"Or forgive."

Outside, the rain had softened to a whisper. In the thatching above, insects rustled. "Do you think I should forgive him?"

"Yes."

"I suppose I could forgive him for hurting *me*. But not for hurting my mother. Not when I remember what she went through just to—" Her voice died in midsentence.

They both heard it at the same time: the footsteps slapping through the mud outside.

Guy rolled off the pallet and sprang to his feet beside her. Shoes scraped over the threshold, and the shadow of a man filled the doorway.

The intruder held up a lantern. The flood of light caught them in freeze-frame: Willy, clutching the blouse to her naked breasts; Guy, poised in a fighter's crouch. The stranger, his face hidden in the shadow of a drab green poncho, slowly lowered the lantern and set it on the table. "I am sorry for the delay," he said. "The road is very bad tonight." He tossed a cloth-wrapped bundle down beside the lantern. "At ease, Mr. Barnard. If I'd wanted to kill you, you'd be dead now." He paused and added, "Both of you."

"Who the hell are you?" Guy asked.

Water droplets splattered onto the floor as the man shoved back the hood of his poncho. His hair was blond, almost white in the lantern light. He had pale eyes set in a moonlike face. "Dr. Gunnel Andersen," he said, nodding by way of introduction. "Nora sent word you were coming." Raindrops flew as he shook out the poncho and hung it up to dry. Then he sat down at the table. "Please, feel free to put on your clothes."

"How did Nora reach you?" Guy asked, pulling on his trousers.

"We keep a shortwave radio for medical emergencies. Not all frequencies are monitored by the government."

"Are you with the Swedish mission?"

"No, I work for the U.N." Andersen's impassive gaze wandered to Willy, who was self-consciously struggling into her damp clothes. "We provide medical care in the villages. Humanitarian aid. Malaria, typhoid, it's all here. Probably always will be." He began to unwrap the bundle he'd set on the table. "I assume you have not eaten. This isn't much but it's the best I could do. It's been a bad year for crops, and protein is scarce." Inside the bundle was a bamboo box filled with cold rice, pickled vegetables and microscopic flecks of pork congealed in gravy.

Guy at once sat down. "After bananas and coconuts, this looks like a feast to me."

Dr. Andersen glanced at Willy, who was still lingering in the corner, watching suspiciously. "Are you not hungry, Miss Maitland?"

"I'm starved."

"Then why don't you eat?"

"First I want to know who you are."

"I have told you my name."

"Your name doesn't mean a thing to me. What's your connection to Nora? To my father?"

Dr. Andersen's eyes were as transparent as water. "You've waited twenty years for an answer. You can surely wait a few minutes longer."

Guy said, "Willy, you need to eat. Come, sit down."

Hunger finally pulled her to the table. Dr. Andersen had

brought no utensils. Willy and Guy used their fingers to scoop up the rice. All the time she was eating, she felt the Swede's eyes watching her.

"I see you do not trust me," he said.

"I don't trust anyone anymore."

He nodded and smiled. "Then you have learned, in a few shorts days, what took me months to learn."

"Mistrust?"

"Doubt. Fear." He looked around the hut, at the shadows dancing on the walls. "What I call the creeping uneasiness. A sense that things are not right in this place. That, just under the surface, lies some...secret, something...terrible."

The lantern light flickered, almost died. He glanced up as the rain pounded the roof. A puff of wind swept through the doorway, dank with the smells of the jungle.

"You sense it, too," he said.

"All I know is, there've been too many coincidences," said Guy. "Too many tidy little acts of fate. As though paths have been laid out for us and we're just following the trail."

Andersen nodded. "We all have roads laid out for us. We usually choose the path of least resistance. It's when we wander off that path that things become dangerous." He smiled. "You know, at this very minute, I could be sitting in my house in Stockholm, sipping coffee, growing fat on cakes and cookies. But I chose to stay here."

"And has life become dangerous?" asked Willy.

"It's not my life I worry about now. It was a risk bringing you here. But Nora felt the time was right."

"Then it was her decision?"

He nodded. "She thought it might be your last chance for a reunion."

Willy froze, staring at him. "Did you—did you say *reunion?*"

Dr. Andersen met her gaze. Slowly, he nodded.

She tried to speak but found her voice was gone. The significance of that one word reduced her to numb silence.

Her father was alive.

It was Guy who finally spoke. "Where is he?"

"A village northwest of here."

"A prisoner?"

"No, no. A guest. A friend."

"He's not being held against his will?"

"Not since the war." Andersen looked at Willy, who had not yet found her voice. "It may be hard for you to accept, Miss Maitland, but there *are* Americans who find happiness in this country."

She looked at him in bewilderment. "I don't understand. All these years he's been alive...he could have come home...."

"Many men didn't return."

"*He* had the choice!"

"He also had his reasons."

"Reasons? He had every reason to come home!"

Her anguished cry seemed to hang in the room. For a moment neither man spoke. Then Andersen rose to his feet. "Your father must speak for himself..." he said, and he started for the door.

"Then why isn't he here?"

"There are arrangements that have to be made. A time, a place—"

"When will I see him?"

The doctor hesitated. "That depends."

"On what?"

He looked back from the doorway. "On whether your father wants to see *you*."

Long after Andersen had left, Willy stood in the doorway, staring out at the curtain of rain.

"Why *wouldn't* he want to see me?" she cried into the darkness.

Quietly Guy came to stand behind her. His arms came around her shoulders, pulled her into the tight circle of his embrace.

"Why wouldn't he?"

"Willy, stop."

She turned and pressed her face into his chest. "Do you think it was so terrible?" she sobbed. "Being my father?"

"Of course not."

"It must have been. I must have made him miserable."

"You were just a kid, Willy! You can't blame yourself! Sometimes men...change. Sometimes they need—"

"*Why?*" she cried.

"Hey, not all men walk out. Some of us, we hang around, for better or for worse."

Gently, he led her back to the sleeping pallet. Beneath the silvery mosquito net, she let him hold her, an embrace not of passion, but of comfort. The arms of a friend. It felt right, the way their making love earlier that evening had felt right. But she couldn't help wondering, even as she lay in his arms, when this, too, would change, when *he* would change.

It hurt beyond all measure, the thought that he, too, would someday leave her, that this was but a momentary mingling of limbs and warmth and souls. It was hurt she expected, but one she'd never, ever be ready for.

Outside, the leaves clattered in the downpour.

It rained all night.

At dawn the jeep appeared.

"I take only the woman," insisted the Vietnamese driver, planting himself in Guy's path. The man gestured toward the hut. "You stay, GI."

"She's not going without me," said Guy.

"They tell me only the woman."

"Then she's not going."

The two men faced each other, challenge mirrored in their eyes. The driver shrugged and turned for the jeep. "Then I don't take anybody."

"Guy, please," said Willy. "Just wait here for me. I'll be okay."

"I don't like it."

She glanced at the driver, who'd already climbed behind the wheel and started the engine. "I don't have a choice," she said, and she stepped into the jeep.

The driver released the brake and spun the jeep around. As they rolled away, Willy glanced back and saw Guy standing alone among the trees. She thought he called out something—her name, perhaps—but then the jungle swallowed him from view.

She turned her attention to the road—or what served as a road. In truth, it was scarcely more than a muddy track through the forest. Branches slashed the windshield; water flew from the leaves and splattered their faces.

"How far is it?" she asked. The driver didn't answer.

"Where are we going?" she asked. Again, no answer. She sat back and waited to see what would happen next.

A few miles into the forest the mud track petered out, and they halted before a solid wall of jungle. The driver cut the engine. A few rays of sunlight shone dimly through the canopy of leaves. Only the cry of a single bird sliced through the silence.

The driver climbed out and walked around to the rear. Willy watched as he rooted around under a camouflage tarp covering the backseat. Then she saw the blade slide out from beneath the tarp. He was holding a machete.

He turned to face her. For a few heartbeats they stared at each other, gazes meeting over the gleam of razor-sharp steel. Then she saw amusement flash in his eyes.

"We walk now," he said.

A nod was the only reply she could manage. Wordlessly, she climbed out of the jeep and followed him into the jungle.

He moved silently through the trees, the only sound of his passage the whistle and slash of the machete. Vines hung like shrouds from the branches; clouds of mosquitoes swarmed up from stagnant puddles. He moved onward without a second's pause, melting like a phantom through the brush. Willy, stumbling in the tangle of trees, barely managed to keep the back of his tattered shirt in view.

It didn't take long for her to give up slapping mosquitoes. She decided it was a lost cause. Let them suck her dry; her blood was up for grabs. She could only concentrate on moving forward, on putting one foot in front of the other. She was sliding through some timeless vacuum where distance was measured by the gaps between trees, the span between footsteps.

By the time they finally halted, she was staggering from exhaustion. Conquered, she sagged against the nearest tree and waited for his next command.

"Here," he said.

Bewildered, she looked up at him. "But what are you—"

To her astonishment, he turned and trotted off into the jungle.

"Wait!" she cried. "You're not going to leave me here!"

The man kept moving.

"Please, you have to tell me!" she screamed. He paused and glanced back. "Where am I? What is this place?"

"The same place we find *him*," was the reply. Then he slipped away, vanishing into the forest.

She whirled around, scanning the jungle, watching, waiting for some savior to appear. She saw no one. The man's last words echoed in her head.

*What is this place?*

*The same place we find him.*

"Who?" she cried.

In desperation, she stared up at the branches crisscrossing the sky. That's when she saw it, the monstrous silhouette rising like a shark's fin among the trees.

It was the tail of a plane.

# Chapter Twelve

She moved closer. Gradually she discerned, amid the camouflage of trees and undergrowth, the remains of what was once an aircraft. Vines snaked over jagged metal. Fuselage struts reached skyward from the jungle floor, as bare and stark as the bleached ribs of a dead animal. Willy halted, her gaze drawn back to the tail above her in the branches. Years of rust and tropical decay had obscured the markings, but she could still make out the serial number: 5410.

This was Air America flight 5078. Point of origin: Vientiane, Laos. Destination: a shattered treetop in a North Vietnamese jungle.

In the silence of the forest, she bowed her head. A thin shaft of sunlight sliced through the branches and danced at her feet. And all around her the trees soared like the walls of a cathedral. How fitting that this rusted altar to war should come to rest in a place of such untarnished peace.

There were tears in her eyes when she finally forced herself to turn and study the fuselage—what was left of it. Most of the shell had burned or rotted away, leaving only a little flooring and a few crumbling struts. The wings were missing entirely—probably sheared off on impact. She moved forward to the remnants of the cockpit.

Sunlight sparkled through the shattered windshield. The navigational equipment was gutted; charred wires hung from holes in the instrument panel. Her gaze shifted to the bulkhead, riddled with bullet holes. She ran her fingers across the ravaged metal and then pulled away.

As she took a step back, she heard a voice say, "There isn't much left of her. But I guess you could say the same of me."

Willy spun around. And froze.

He came out of the forest, a man in rags, walking toward her. It was the gait she recognized, not the body, which had been worn down to its rawest elements. Nor the face.

Certainly not the face.

He had no ears, no eyebrows. What was left of his hair grew in tortured wisps. He came to within a few yards of her and stopped, as though afraid to move any closer.

They looked at each other, not speaking, perhaps not daring to speak.

"You're all grown up," he finally said.

"Yes." She cleared her throat. "I guess I am."

"You look good, Willy. Real good. Are you married yet?"

"No."

"You should be."

"I'm not."

A pause. They both looked down, looked back up, strangers groping for common ground.

Softly he asked, "How's your mother?"

Willy blinked away a new wave of tears. "She's...dying."

She felt a comfortless sense of retribution at her father's

shocked silence. "It's cancer," she continued. "I wanted her to see a doctor months ago, but you know how she is. Never thinking about herself. Never taking the time to…" Her voice cracked, faded.

"I had no idea," he whispered.

"How could you? You were dead." She looked up at the sky and suddenly laughed, an ugly sound in that quiet circle of trees. "It never occurred to you to write to us? One letter from the grave?"

"It only would have made things harder."

"Harder than *what?* Than it's already been?"

"With me gone, dead, Ann was free to move on," he said, "to…find someone else. Someone better for her."

"But she didn't! She never even tried! All she could think about was *you.*"

"I thought she'd forget. I thought she'd get over me."

"You thought wrong."

He bowed his head. "I'm sorry, Wilone."

After a pause, she said, "I'm sorry, too."

A bird sang in the trees, its sweet notes piercing the silence between them.

She asked, "What happened to you?"

"You mean this?" He gestured vaguely at his face.

"I mean…everything."

"Everything," he repeated. Then, laughing, he looked up at the branches. "Where the hell do I start?" He began to walk in a circle, moving among the trees like a lost man. At last he stopped beside the fuselage. Gazing at the jagged remains, he said, "It's funny. I never lost consciousness. Even when I hit the trees, when everything around me was being ripped apart, I stayed awake all the way down. I remember thinking, 'So when do I get to see heaven?' Or hell, for that matter. Then it all went up in flames. And I thought, 'There's my answer. My eternity...'"

He stopped, let out a deep sigh. "They found me a short way from here, stumbling around under the trees. Most of my face was burned away. But I don't remember feeling much of anything." He looked down at his scarred hands. "The pain came later. When they tried to clean the burns. When the nerves grew back. I'd scream at them to let me die, but they wouldn't. I guess I was too valuable."

"Because you were American?"

"Because I was a pilot. Someone to pump for information, someone to trade. Maybe someone to spread the Party line back home...."

"Did they...hurt you?"

He shook his head. "I guess they figured I'd been hurt enough. It was a quieter sort of persuasion. Endless discussions. Relentless arguments as I recovered. I swore I wasn't going to let the enemy twist my head around. But I was weak. I was far from home. And they said things—so many things—I couldn't argue with. And after a while...after a while it made...well, sense. About this country being their house, about us being the burglars in the house. And wouldn't anyone with burglars in their house fight back?"

He let out a sigh. "I don't know anymore. It sounds so feeble now, but I just got tired. Tired of arguing. Tired of trying to explain what I was doing in their country. Tired of trying to defend God only knew what. It was easier just to agree with them. And after a while, I actually started to believe it. Believe what they were telling me." He looked down. "According to some people, that makes me a traitor."

"To some people. Not to me."

He was silent.

"Why didn't you come home?" she asked.

"Look at me, Willy. Who'd want me back?"

"*We* did."

"No, you didn't. Not the man I'd become." He laughed hollowly. "Everyone would be pointing at me, whispering behind my back, talking about my face. Is that the kind of father you wanted? The kind of husband your mother wanted? Back home, people expect you to have a nose and ears and eyebrows." He shook his head. "Ann...Ann was so beautiful. I—I couldn't go back to that."

"But what do you have here? Look at you, at what you're wearing, at how skinny you are. You're starving, wasting away."

"I eat what the rest of the village eats. It's enough to live on." He picked at the rag that served as his shirt. "Clothes, I never much cared about."

"You gave up a family!"

"I—I found another family, Willy. Here."

She stared at him, stunned.

"I have a wife. Her name's Lan. And we have children. A baby girl and two boys...eight and ten. They can speak English, and a little French...." he said helplessly.

"*We* were at home!"

"But I was here. And Lan was here. She saved my life, Willy. She was the one who kept me alive through the infections, the fevers, the endless pain."

"You said you begged to die."

"Lan was the one who made me want to live again."

Willy stared at that man with half a face, the man she'd

once called her father. The lashless eyes looked back at her, unblinking. Awaiting judgment.

She still had a face, a normal life, she thought. What right did she have to condemn him?

She looked away. "So. What do I tell Mom?"

"I don't know. Maybe nothing."

"She has a right to know."

"Maybe it would be kinder if she didn't."

"Kinder to whom? You or her?"

He looked down at his feet in their dirty slippers. "I suppose I deserve that. Whatever you have to say, I deserve it. But God knows, I wanted to make it up to her. And to you. I sent money—twenty, maybe thirty thousand dollars. You got it, didn't you?"

"We never knew who sent it."

"You weren't supposed to know. Nora Walker arranged it through a bank in Bangkok. It was everything I had. All that was left of the gold."

She gave him a bewildered look and saw that his gaze had shifted toward the plane's fuselage. "You were carrying gold?"

"I didn't know it at the time. It was our little rule at Air America: Never ask about the cargo. Just fly the plane. But after she went down, after I crawled out of the wreckage, I saw it. Gold bars scattered all over the ground. It was crazy. There I was, half my damn face burned off, and I remember thinking, 'I'm rich. If I live through this, son of a bitch, I'm *rich.*'" He laughed, then, at his own lunacy, at the absurdity of a dying man rejoicing among the ashes. "I buried some of the gold, threw some in the bushes. I thought—I guess I thought it would be my ticket out. That if I was captured, I could use it to bargain for my freedom."

"What happened?"

He looked off at the trees. "They found me. NVA soldiers. And they found most of the gold." He shrugged. "They kept us both."

"But not forever. You didn't have to stay—" She stopped. "Didn't you *ever* think of us?"

"I never stopped thinking of you. After the war, after all that—that insanity was over, I came back here, dug up what gold they hadn't found. I asked Nora to get it out to you." He looked at Willy. "Don't you see? I never forgot you. I just..." He stopped, and his voice dropped to a whisper. "I just couldn't go back."

In the trees above, branches rattled in the wind. Leaves drifted down in a soft rain of green.

He turned away. "I suppose you'll want to go back to Hanoi. I'll see that someone drives you...."

"Dad?"

He halted, not daring to look at her.

"Your little boys. You—say they understand English?"

He nodded.

She paused. "Then we ought to understand each other, the boys and I," she said. "I mean, assuming they want to meet me...."

Her father quickly rubbed a hand across his eyes. But when he turned to look at her, she could still see the tears glistening there. He smiled...and held out his hand to her.

She'd been gone too long.

Three hours had passed, and Guy was more than worried. He was scared out of his head. Something wasn't right. It was that old instinct of his, that sense of doom closing in, and he was helpless to do anything about it. A dozen different images kept forming in his mind, each one progressively more terrible. Willy screaming. Dying. Or already dead in the jungle. When at last he heard the rumble of the jeep, he was hovering at the edge of panic.

Dr. Andersen was at the wheel. "Good morning, Mr. Barnard!" he called cheerily as Guy stalked over to him.

"Where is she?"

"She is safe."

"Prove it."

Andersen threw open the door and gestured for him to get in. "I will take you to her."

Guy climbed in and slammed the door. "Where are we going?"

"It is a long drive." Andersen threw the jeep into gear and spun them around onto a dirt track. "Be patient."

The night's rainfall had turned the path to muck, and on either side the jungle pressed in, close and strangling. They might have gone for miles or tens of miles; on a road locked in by jungle, distance was impossible to judge. When Andersen finally pulled off to the side, Guy could see no obvious reason for stopping. Only when he'd climbed out and stood among the trees did he notice the tiny footpath leading into the bush. He couldn't see what lay beyond; the forest hid everything from view.

"From here we walk," said Andersen, foraging around for a few loose branches.

"Why the camouflage?" asked Guy, watching Andersen drape the branches over the jeep.

"Protection for the village."

"What are they afraid of?"

Andersen reached under the tarp on the backseat and pulled out an AK-47. Casually, he slung it over his shoulder. "Everything," he said, and headed off into the jungle.

The footpath led into a shadowy world of hundred-foot trees and tangled vines. Watching Andersen's back, Guy was struck by the irony of a doctor lugging an automatic rifle. He wondered what enemy he planned to use it on.

The smells of rotting vegetation, of mud simmering in the heat were only too familiar. "The whole damn jungle smells of death," the GIs used to say. Guy felt his gait change to a silent glide, felt his reflexes kick into overdrive. His five senses were painfully acute; the snap of a branch under Andersen's boot was as shocking as gunfire.

He heard the sounds of the village before he saw it. Somewhere deep in the forest, children were laughing. And then he heard water rushing and the cry of a baby.

Andersen pushed ahead, and as the last curtain of branches parted, Guy saw, beneath a towering stand of trees, the circle of huts. In the central courtyard, children batted a pebble back and forth with their feet. They froze as Guy and Andersen emerged from the forest. One of the girls called out; instantly, a dozen adults emerged from the huts. In silence they all watched Guy.

Then, in the doorway of one hut, a familiar figure appeared. As Willy came toward Guy, he had the sudden desire to take her in his arms and kiss her right then and there, in view of the whole village, the whole world. But he couldn't seem to move. He could only stare down at her smiling face.

"I found him," Willy said.

He shook his head. "What?"

"My father. He's here."

Guy turned and saw that someone else had emerged from the hut. A man without ears, without eyebrows. The horrifying apparition held out its hand; a fingertip was missing.

William Maitland smiled. "Welcome to Na Co, Mr. Barnard."

Dr. Andersen's jeep was easy to spot, even through the camouflage. How fortunate the rains had been so heavy the night before; without all that mud, Siang would never have been able to track the jeep to this trail head.

He threw aside the branches and quickly surveyed the jeep's interior. On the backseat, beneath a green canvas tarp, was a jug of drinking water, a few old tools and a weathered notebook, obviously a journal, filled with scribbling. The name "Dr. Gunnel Andersen" was written inside the front cover.

Siang left the jeep, tramped a few paces into the jungle and peered through the shadows. It took only a moment to spot the footprints. Two men. Dr. Andersen and who else? Barnard? He followed the tracks a short way and saw that, just beyond the first few trees, the footprints led to a distinct trail, no doubt an old and established path. The village of Na Co must lie farther ahead.

He returned to the limousine where the man was waiting. "They have gone into the forest," Siang said. "There's a village trail."

"Is it the right one?"

Siang shrugged. "There are many villages in these mountains. But the jeep belongs to Dr. Andersen."

"Then it's the right village." The man sat back, satisfied. "I want our people here tonight."

"So soon?"

"It's the way I work. In and out. The men are ready."

In fact the mercenary team had been waiting two days for the signal. They'd been assembled in Thailand, fifteen men equipped with the most sophisticated in small arms. As soon as the order went through, they would be on their way, no questions asked.

"Tell them we need the dogs as well," said the man. "For mopping up. The whole village goes."

Siang paused. "The children?"

"One mustn't leave orphans."

This troubled Siang a little, but he said nothing. He knew better than to argue with the voice of necessity. Or power.

"Is there a radio in the jeep?" asked the man.

"Yes," said Siang.

"Rip it out."

"Andersen will see—"

"Andersen will see nothing."

Siang nodded in instant understanding.

The man drove off in the limousine, headed for a rendezvous spot a mile ahead. Siang waited until the car had disappeared, then he trotted back to the jeep, ripped out the wires connecting the radio and smashed the panel for good measure. He found a cool spot beneath a tree and sat down. Closing his eyes, he summoned forth the strength needed for his task.

Soon he would have assistance. By tonight, the well paid team of mercenaries would stand assembled on this road. He wouldn't allow himself to think of the victims—the women, the children. It was a consequence of war. In every skirmish, there were the innocent casualties. He'd learned to accept it, to shrug it off as inevitable. The act of pulling a trigger required a clear head swept free of emotions. It was, after all, the way of battle.

It was the way of success.

"Does she understand the danger?" asked Maitland.

"I don't know." Guy stood in the doorway and gazed out at the leaf-strewn courtyard where the village kids were mobbing Willy, singing out questions. The wonderful bedlam of children, he thought wistfully. He turned and looked at the mass of scars that was Bill Maitland's face. "I'm not sure *I* understand the danger."

"She said things have been happening."

"Things? More like dead bodies falling left and right of us. We've been followed every—"

"Who's been following you?"

"The local police. Maybe others."

"The Company?"

"I don't know. They didn't come and introduce themselves."

Maitland, suddenly agitated, began to pace the hut. "If they've traced you here…"

"Who're you hiding from? The Company? The local police?"

"To name a few."

"Which is it?"

"Everyone."

"That narrows it down."

Maitland sat down on the sleeping pallet and rested his head in his hands. "I wanted to be left alone. That's all. Just left alone."

Guy gazed at that scarred scalp and wondered why he felt no pity. Surely the man deserved at least a little pity. But at that instant, all Guy felt was irritation that Maitland was thinking only of himself. Willy had a right to a better father, he thought.

"Your daughter's already found you," he said. "You can't change that. You can't shove her back into the past."

"I don't want to. I'm glad she found me!"

"Yet you never bothered to tell her you were alive."

"I couldn't." Maitland looked up, his eyes full of pain. "There were lives at stake, people I had to protect. Lan, the children—"

"Who's going to hurt them?" Guy moved in, confronted him. "It's been twenty years, and you're still scared. Why? What kind of business were you in?"

"I was just a pawn—I flew the planes, that's all. I never gave a damn about the cargo!"

"What *was* the cargo? Drugs? Arms?"

"Sometimes."

"Which?"

"Both."

Guy's voice hardened. "And which side took delivery?"

Maitland sat up sharply. "I never did business with the enemy! I only followed orders!"

"What *were* your orders on that last flight?"

"To deliver a passenger."

"Interesting cargo. Who was he?"

"His name didn't show up on the manifest. I figured he was some Lao VIP. As it turned out, he was marked for death." He swallowed. "It wasn't the enemy fire that brought us down. A bomb went off in our hold. Planted by *our* side. We were meant to die."

"*Why?*"

There was a long silence. At last, Maitland rose and went to the doorway. There he stared out at the circle of huts. "I think it's time we talked to the elders."

"What can they tell me?"

Maitland turned and looked at him. "Everything."

Lan's baby was crying in a corner of the hut. She put it to her breast and rocked back and forth, cooing, yet all the time listening intently to the voices whispering in the shadows.

They were all listening—the children, the families. Willy couldn't understand what was being said, but she could tell the discussion held a frightening significance.

In the center of the hut sat three village elders—two men and a woman—their ancient faces veiled in a swirl of smoke from the joss sticks. The woman puffed on a cigarette as she muttered in Vietnamese. She gestured toward the sky, then to Maitland.

Guy whispered to Willy. "She's saying it wasn't your father's time to die. But the other two men, the American and the Lao, they died because that was the death they were fated all their lives to meet...." He fell silent, mesmerized by the old woman's voice. The sound seemed to drift like incense smoke, curling in the shadows.

One of the old men spoke, his voice so soft, it was almost lost in the shifting and whispers of the audience.

"He disagrees," said Guy. "He says it wasn't fate that killed the Lao."

The old woman vehemently shook her head. Now there was a general debate about why the Lao had really died. The dissenting old man at last rose and shuffled to a far corner of the hut. There he pulled aside the matting that covered the earthen floor, brushed aside a layer of dirt and withdrew a cloth-wrapped bundle. With shaking hands he pulled apart the ragged edges. Reverently, he held out the object within.

Even in the gloom of the hut, the sheen of gold was unmistakable.

"It's the medallion," whispered Willy. "The one Lassiter told us about."

"The Lao was wearing it," said her father.

The old man handed the bundle to Guy. Gingerly, Guy lifted the medallion from its bed of worn cloth. Though the surface was marred by slag from the explosion, the design was still discernable: a three-headed dragon, fangs bared, claws poised for battle.

The old man whispered words of awe and wonder.

"He saw a medallion just like it once before," said Maitland. "Years ago, in Laos. It was hanging around the neck of Prince Souvanna."

Guy took in a sharp breath. "It's the royal crest. That passenger—"

"Was the king's half brother," said Maitland. "Prince Lo Van."

An uneasy murmur rippled through the gathering.

"I don't understand," said Willy. "Why would the Company want him dead?"

"It doesn't make sense," said Guy. "Lo Van was a neutral, shifting to our side. And he was straight-arrow, a clean leader. With our backing, he could've carved us a foothold in Laos. That might have tipped the scales in our favor."

"That's what he was *meant* to do," said Maitland. "That crate of gold was his. To be dropped in Laos."

"To buy an army?" asked Willy.

"Exactly."

"Then why assassinate him? He was on our side, so—"

"But the guys who blew up the plane weren't," said Guy.

"You mean the Communists planted that bomb?"

"No, someone more dangerous. One of ours."

The elders had fallen silent. They were watching their guests, studying them the way a teacher watches a pupil struggle for answers.

Once again the old woman began to speak. Maitland translated.

"'During the war, some of us lived with the Pathet Lao, the Communists in Laos. There were few places to hide, so we slept in caves. But we had gardens and chickens and pigs, everything we needed to survive. Once, when I was new to the cave, I heard a plane. I thought it was the enemy, the Americans, and I took my rifle and went out to shoot it down. But my cell commander stopped me. I could not understand why he let the plane land. It had enemy markings, the American flag. Our cell commander ordered us to unload the plane. We carried off crates of guns and ammunition. Then we loaded the plane with opium, bags and bags of it. An exchange of goods, I thought. This must be a stolen plane. But then the pilot stepped out, and I saw his face. He was neither Lao nor Vietnamese. He was like you. An American.'"

"Friar Tuck," said Guy softly.

The woman looked at them, her eyes dark and unreadable.

"I've seen him, too," said Maitland. "I was being held in a camp just west of here when he landed to make an exchange. I tell you, the whole damn country was an opium factory, money being made left and right on both sides. All under cover of war. I think that's why Lo Van was killed. To keep the place in turmoil. There's nothing like a dirty war to hide your profits."

"Who else has seen the pilot's face?" Guy asked in Vietnamese, looking around the room. "Who else remembers what he looked like?"

A man and a woman, huddled in a corner, slowly raised their hands. Perhaps there were others, too timid to reveal themselves.

"There were four other POWs in that camp with me," said Maitland. "They saw the pilot's face. As far as I know, not a single one made it home alive."

The joss sticks had burned down to ashes, but the smoke still hung in the gloom. No one made a sound, not even the children.

*That's why you're afraid,* thought Willy, gazing at the circle of faces. *Even now, after all these years, the war casts its shadow over your lives.*

*And mine.*

"Come back with us, Maitland," said Guy. "Tell your story. It's the only way to put it behind you. To be free."

Maitland stood in the doorway of his hut, staring out at the children playing in the courtyard.

"Guy's right," said Willy. "You can't spend your life in hiding. It's time to end it."

Her father turned and looked at her. "What about Lan?

The children? If I leave, how do I know the Vietnamese will ever let me back into the country?"

"It's a risk you have to take," said Guy.

"Be a hero—is that what you're telling me?" Maitland shook his head. "Let me tell *you* something, Barnard. The real heroes of this world aren't the guys who go out and take stupid risks. No, they're the ones who hang in where they're needed, where they belong. Maybe life gets a little dull. Maybe the wife and kids drive 'em crazy. But they hang in." He looked meaningfully at Willy, then back at Guy. "Believe me. I've made enough mistakes to know."

Maitland looked back at his daughter. "Tonight, you both go back to Hanoi. You've got to go home, get on with your own life, Willy."

"*If* she gets home," said Guy.

Maitland was silent.

"What do you think her chances are?" Guy pressed him mercilessly. "Think about it. You suppose they'll leave her alone knowing what she knows? You think they'll let her live?"

"So call me a coward!" Maitland blurted out. "Call me any damn name you please. It won't change things. I can't leave this time." He fled the hut.

Through the doorway, they saw him cross the courtyard to where Lan now sat beneath the trees. Lan smiled and handed their baby to her husband. For a long time he sat there, rocking his daughter, holding her tightly to his chest, as though he feared someone might wrench her from his grasp.

*You have the world right there in your arms,* Willy thought, watching him. *You'd be crazy to let it go.*

"We have to change his mind," said Guy. "We have to get him to come back with us."

At that instant Lan looked up, and her gaze met Willy's. "He's not coming back, Guy," Willy said. "He belongs here."

"You're his family, too," Guy protested.

"But not the one who needs him now." She leaned her head in the doorway. A leaf fluttered down from the trees and tumbled across the courtyard. A bare-bottomed baby toddled after it. "For twenty years I've hated that man...." She sighed. And then she smiled. "I guess it's time I finally grew up."

"Something's wrong. Andersen should've been back by now."

Maitland stood at the edge of the jungle and peered up the dirt road. From where the doctor's jeep had been parked, tire tracks led northward. The branches he'd used for camouflage lay scattered at the roadside. But there was no sign of a vehicle.

Willy and Guy wandered onto the road, where they stood puzzling over Andersen's delay.

"He knows you're waiting for him," said Maitland. "He's already an hour late."

Guy kicked a pebble and watched it skitter into the bushes. "Looks like we're not going back to Hanoi tonight. Not without a ride." He glanced up at the darkening sky. "It's almost sunset. I think it's time to head back to the village."

Maitland didn't move. He was still staring up the road.

"He might have a flat tire," said Willy. "Or he ran out of gas. Either way, Dad, it looks like you're stuck with us tonight." She reached out and threaded her arm in his. "Guy's right. It's time to go back."

"Not yet."

Willy smiled. "Are you that anxious to get rid of us?"

"What?" He glanced at his daughter. "No, no, of course not. It's just..." He gazed up the road again. "Something doesn't feel right."

Willy watched him, suddenly sharing his uneasiness. "You think there's trouble."

"And we're not ready for it," he said grimly.

"What do you mean?" said Guy, turning to look at him. "The village must have some sort of defenses."

"We have maybe one working pistol, a few old war relics that haven't been used in decades. Plus Andersen's rifle. He left it today."

"How many rounds?"

"Not enough to—" Maitland's chin suddenly snapped up. He spun around at the sound of an approaching car.

"Hit the deck!" Guy commanded.

Willy was already leaping for the cover of the nearest bush. At the same instant, Guy and Maitland sprang in the other direction, into the foliage across the road from her.

She barely made it to cover in time. Just as she landed in the dirt, a jeep rounded the bend. Through the tangle of underbrush, she saw that it was filled with soldiers. As it roared closer, she tunneled frantically under the branches, mindless of the thorns clawing her face, and curled up among the leaves to wait for the jeep to pass. Something scurried across her hand. Instinctively she flinched and saw a fat black beetle drop off and scuttle into the shadows. Only then, as her gaze followed the insect, did she notice the strange chattering in the branches and she saw that the earth itself seemed to shudder with movement.

Dear God, she was lying in a whole nest of them!

Choking back a scream, she jerked sideways.

And found herself staring at a human hand. It lay not six inches from her nose, the fingers chalk white and frozen into a beckoning claw.

Even if she'd wanted to scream, she couldn't have uttered a sound; her throat had clamped down beyond all hope of any cry. Slowly her gaze traveled along the arm, followed it to the torso, and then, inexorably, to the face.

Gunnel Andersen's lifeless eyes stared back at her.

# Chapter Thirteen

The soldiers' jeep roared past.

Willy muffled her cry with her fist, desperately fighting the shriek of horror that threatened to explode inside her. She fought it so hard her teeth drew blood from her knuckles. The instant the jeep had passed, her control shattered. She stumbled to her feet and staggered backward.

"He's dead!" she cried.

Guy and her father appeared at her side. She felt Guy's arm slip around her waist, anchoring her against him. "What are you talking about?"

"Andersen!" She pointed wildly at the bushes.

Her father dropped to the ground and shoved aside the branches. "Dear God," he whispered, staring at the body.

The trees seemed to wobble around her. Willy slid to her knees. The whole jungle spun in a miserable kaleidoscope of green as she retched into the dirt.

She heard her father say, in a strangely flat voice, "His throat's been cut."

"Clean job. Very professional," Guy muttered. "Looks like he's been here for hours."

Willy managed to raise her head. "Why? Why did they kill him?"

Her father let the bushes slip back over the body. "To keep him from talking. To cut us off from—" He suddenly sprang to his feet. "The village! I've got to get back!"

"Dad! Wait—"

But her father had already dashed into the jungle.

Guy tugged her up by the arm. "We've gotta move. Come on."

She followed him, running and stumbling behind him on the footpath. The sun was already setting; through the branches, the sky glowed a frightening bloodred.

Just ahead, she heard her father shouting, "Lan! Lan!" As they emerged from the jungle, they saw a dozen villagers gathered, watching as Maitland pulled his wife into his arms and held her.

"These people have got to get out of here!" Guy yelled. "Maitland! Tell them, for God's sake! They've got to leave!"

Maitland released his wife and turned to Guy. "Where the hell are we supposed to go? The next village is twenty miles from here! We've got old people, babies." He pointed to a woman with a swollen belly. "Look at her! You think *she* can walk twenty miles?"

"She has to. We all have to."

Maitland turned away, but Guy pulled him around, forcing him to listen. "Think about it! They've killed Andersen. You're next. So's everyone here, everyone who knows you're alive. There's got to be somewhere we can hide!"

Maitland turned to one of the village elders and rattled out a question in Vietnamese.

The old man frowned. Then he pointed northeast, toward the mountains.

"What did he say?" asked Willy.

"He says there's a place about five kilometers from here. An old cave in the hills. They've used it before, other times, other wars...." He glanced up at the sky. "Almost sunset. We have to leave now while there's still enough light to cross the river."

Already, the villagers had scattered to gather their belongings. Centuries of war had taught them survival meant haste.

Five minutes was all the time Maitland's family took to pack. Lan presided over the dismantling of her household, the gathering of essentials—blankets, food, the precious family cooking pot. She spared no time for words or tears. Only outside, when she allowed herself a last backward glance at the hut, did her eyes brim. She swiftly, matter-of-factly, wiped away the tears.

The last light of day glimmered through the branches as the ragged gathering headed into the jungle. Twenty-four adults, eleven children and three infants, Willy counted. *And all of us scared out of our wits.*

They moved noiselessly, even the children; it was unearthly how silent they were, like ghosts flitting among the trees. At the edge of a fast-flowing river, they halted. A waterwheel spun in the current, an elegant sculpture of bamboo tubes shuttling water into irrigation sluices. The river was too deep for the little ones to ford, so the children were carried to the other bank. Soaked and muddy, they all slogged up the opposite bank and moved on toward the mountains.

Night fell. By the light of a full moon, they journeyed through a spectral land of wind and shadow where the very darkness seemed to tremble with companion spirits. By now the children were exhausted and stumbling. Still, no one had to coax them forward; the fear of pursuit was enough to keep them moving.

At last, at the base of the cliff, they halted. A giant wall of rock glowed silvery in the moonlight. The village elders conferred softly, debating which way to proceed next. It was the old woman who finally led the way. Moving unerringly through the darkness, she guided them to a set of stone steps carved into the mountain and led them up, along the cliff face to what appeared to be nothing more than a thicket of bushes.

There was a general murmur of dismay. Then one of the village men shoved aside the branches and held up a lit candle. Emptiness lay beyond. He thrust his arm into the void, into a darkness so vast, it seemed to swallow up the feeble light of the flame. They were at the mouth of a giant cavern.

The man crawled inside, only to scramble out as a flurry of wings whooshed past him. Nervous laughter rippled through the gathering.

Bats, Willy thought with a shudder.

The man took a deep breath and entered the cave. A moment later, he called for the others to follow.

Guy gave Willy a nudge. "Go on. Inside."

She swallowed, balking. "Do I have a choice?"

His answer was immediate. "None whatsoever."

The village was deserted.

Siang searched the huts one by one. He overturned pallets and flung aside mats, searching for the underground tunnels that were common to every village. In times of peace, those tunnels were used for storage; in times of war, they served as hiding places or escape routes. They were all empty.

In frustration, he grabbed an earthenware pot and smashed it on the ground. Then he stalked out to the court-yard where the men stood waiting in the moonlight, their faces blackened with camouflage paint.

There were fifteen of them, all crack professionals, rough-hewn Americans who towered above him. They had been flown in straight from Thailand at only an hour's notice. As expected, Laotian air defense had been a large-meshed sieve, unable to detect, much less shoot down, a lone plane flying in low through their airspace. It had taken a mere four hours to march here from their drop point just inside the Vietnamese border. The entire operation had been flawless.

Until now.

"It seems we've arrived too late," a voice said.

Siang turned to see his client emerge from the shadows, one more among this gathering of giants.

"They have had only a few hours' head start," said Siang. "Their evening meals were left uneaten."

"Then they haven't gone far. Not with women and children." The man turned to one of the soldiers. "What about the prisoner? Has he talked?"

"Not a word." The soldiers shoved a village man to the ground. They had captured the man ten miles up the road, running toward Ban Dan. Or, rather, the dogs had caught him. Useful animals those hounds, and absolutely essential in an operation where a single surviving eyewitness could prove disastrous. Against such animals, the villager hadn't stood a chance of escape. Now he knelt on the ground, his black hair silvered with moonlight.

"Make him talk."

"A waste of time," grunted Siang. "These northerners are stubborn. He will tell you nothing."

One of the soldiers gave the villager a kick. Even as the man lay writhing on the ground, he managed to gasp out a string of epithets.

"What? What did he say?" demanded the soldier.

Siang shifted uneasily. "He says that we are cursed. That we are dead men."

The soldier laughed. "Superstitious crap!"

Siang looked around at the darkness. "I'm sure they sent other messengers for help. By morning—"

"By morning we'll have the job done. We'll be out of here," said his client.

"If we can find them," Siang said.

"Find a whole village? No problem." The man turned and snapped out an order to one of the soldiers. "That's what the dogs are for."

A dozen candles flickered in the cavern. Outside, the wind was blowing hard; puffs of it shuddered the blanket hanging over the cave mouth. Through the dancing shadows floated murmuring voices, the frantic whispers of a village under siege. Children gathered stones or twisted vines into rope. Women whittled stalks of bamboo, sharpening them into punji stakes. Only the babies slept. In the darkness outside, men dug the same lethal traps that had defended their homeland through the centuries. It was an axiom of jungle warfare that battles were won not by strength or weaponry but by speed and cunning and desperation.

Most of all, desperation.

"The cylinder's frozen," muttered Guy, sighting down the

barrel of an ancient pistol. "You could squeeze off a single shot, that's all."

"Only two bullets left anyway," said Maitland.

"Which makes it next to worthless." Guy handed the gun back to Maitland. "Except for suicide."

For a moment Maitland weighed the pistol in his hand, thinking. He turned to his wife and spoke to her gently in Vietnamese.

Lan stared at the gun, as though afraid to touch it. Then, reluctantly, she took it and slipped away into the shadows of the cave.

Guy reached for Andersen's assault rifle and gave it a quick inspection. "At least this baby's in working order."

"Yeah. Nothing like a good old AK-47," said Maitland. "I've seen one fished out of the mud and still go right on firing."

Guy laughed. "The other side really knew how to make 'em, didn't they?" He glanced around as Willy approached. "How're you holding up?"

She sank down wearily beside him in the dirt. "We've carved enough stakes to skewer a whole army."

"We'll need more," said her father. He glanced toward the cave entrance. "My turn to do some digging...."

"I was just out there," said Guy. "Pits are all dug."

"Then they'll need help with the other traps—"

"They know what they're doing. We just get in the way."

"It's hard to belive," said Willy.

"What is?"

"That we can hold off an army with vines and bamboo."

"It's been done before," said Maitland. "Against bigger

armies. And we're not out to win a war. We just have to hold out until our runners get through."

"How long will that take?"

"It's twenty miles to the next village. If they have a radio, we might get help by midmorning."

Willy gazed around at the sleeping children who, one by one, had collapsed in exhaustion. Guy touched her arm. "You need some rest, too."

"I can't sleep."

"Then just lie down. Go on."

"What about you two?"

Guy snapped an ammunition clip into place. "We'll keep watch."

She frowned at him. "You don't really think they'd find us tonight?"

"We left an easy trail all the way."

"But they'll need daylight—"

"Not if they have a local informant," said her father. "Someone who knows these caves. We found our way in the dark. So could they." He grabbed the rifle and slung it over his shoulder. "Minh and I'll take the first watch, Guy. Get some sleep."

Guy nodded. "I'll relieve you in a few hours."

After her father left, Willy's gaze shifted back to the sleeping children, to her little half brothers, now curled up in a tangle of blankets. *What will happen to them?* she wondered. *To all of us?* In a far corner, two old women whittled bamboo stalks; the scrape of their blades against the wood made Willy shiver.

"I'm scared," she whispered.

Guy nodded. The candlelight threw harsh shadows on his face. "We're all scared. Every last one of us."

"It's my fault. I can't stop thinking that if I'd just left well enough alone..."

He touched her face. "I'm the one who should feel responsible."

"Why?"

"Because I used you. For all my denials, I planned to use you. And if something were to happen to you now..."

"Or to you," she said, her hand closing over his. "Don't you ever make me weep over your body, Guy Barnard. Because I couldn't stand it. So promise me."

He pressed her hand to his mouth. "I promise. And I want you to know that, after we get out of here, I..." He smiled. "I plan to see a lot more of you. If you'll let me."

She returned the smile. "I'll insist on it."

*What stupid lies we're telling each other,* she thought. *Our way of pretending we have a future.* In the face of death, promises mean everything.

"What if they find us?" she whispered.

"We do what we can to stay alive."

"Sticks and stones against automatics? It should be a very quick fight."

"We have a defensible position. Traps waiting in the path. And we have some of the smartest fighters in the world on our side. Men who've held off armies with not much more than their wits." He gazed up at the darkness hovering above the feeble glow of candlelight. "This cave is said to be blessed. It's an ancient sanctuary, older than anyone can remember. Follow that tunnel back there, and you'll come out at the east base of the cliff. They're clever, these people. They never back themselves into a corner. They always leave an escape route." He looked at the families dozing in the shadows. "They've been fighting wars since the Stone Age. And they can do it in their bare feet, with only a handful of rice. When it comes to survival, *we're* the novices."

Outside, the wind howled; they could hear the trees groan, the bushes scrabbling against the cliff. One of the children cried out in his sleep, a sob of fear that was instantly stilled by his mother's embrace.

The little ones didn't understand, thought Willy. But they knew enough to be afraid.

Guy took her in his arms. Together, they sank to the ground, clinging to each other. There was no need for words; it was enough just to have him there, to feel their hearts beating together.

And in the shadows, the two old women went on whittling their stalks of bamboo.

Willy was asleep when Guy rose to stand his watch. It wasn't easy leaving her. In the few short hours they'd clung together on the hard ground, their bodies had somehow melted together in a way that could never be reversed. Even if he never saw her again, even if she was suddenly swept out of his life, she would always be part of him.

He covered her with a blanket and slipped out into the night.

The sky was a dazzling sea of stars. He found Maitland huddled on a ledge a short way up the cliff face. Guy settled down beside him on the rock shelf.

"Dead quiet," said Maitland. "So far."

They sat together beneath the stars, listening to the wind, to the bushes thrashing against the cliff. A rock clattered down the mountain. Guy glanced up and saw, on a higher ledge, one of the village men silhouetted against the night sky.

"Did you get some sleep?" asked Maitland.

Guy shook his head. "You know, I used to be able to sleep through anything. Chopper landings. Sniper fire. But not now. Not here. I tell you, this isn't my kind of fight."

Maitland handed the rifle to Guy. "Yeah. It's a whole different war when people you love are at stake, isn't it?" He rose to his feet and walked off into the darkness.

*People you love?* It filled Guy with a sense of wonder, the thought that he *was* in love. Though it shouldn't surprise him. On some level, he'd known it all along: he had fallen hard for Bill Maitland's daughter.

It was something he'd never planned on, something he'd certainly never wanted. He wasn't even sure *love* was the right word for what he felt. They'd just spent a week together in hell. *And in heaven,* he thought, remembering that night in the hut, under the mosquito net. He knew he couldn't stand the thought of her being hurt, that he'd do anything to keep her safe. Was *love* the name for that feeling?

Somewhere in the night, an animal screamed.

He tightened his grip on the rifle.

Four more hours until dawn.


At first light the attack came.

Guy had already handed the rifle to the next man on watch and was starting down the cliff face when a shot rang out. Sheer reflexes sent him diving for cover. As he scrambled behind a clump of bushes, he heard more automatic gunfire and a scream from the ledge above, and he knew his relief man had been hit. He peered up to see how badly the man was hurt. Through fingers of morning mist, he could make out the man's bloodied arm dangling lifelessly over the ledge. More gunfire erupted, spattering the cliff face. There was no return fire; the village's only rifle now lay in the hands of a dead man.

Guy glanced down and saw the other villagers scrambling for cover among the rocks. Unarmed, how long could they defend the cave? It was the booby traps they were counting on now, the trip wires and the pits and the stakes that would hold off the attackers.

Guy looked up at the ledge where the rifle lay. That precious AK-47 could make all the difference in the world between survival and slaughter.

He spotted a boulder a few yards up, with a few scraggly bushes as cover along the way. There was no other route, no other choice. He crouched, tensing for the dash to first base.

Willy was stirring a simmering pot of rice and broth when she heard the gunshots. Her first thought as she leapt to her feet was, *Guy. Dear God, has he been hurt?*

But before she could take two steps, her father grabbed her arm. "No, Willy!"

"He may need help—"

"You can't go out there!" He called for his wife. Somehow, Lan heard him through the bedlam and, taking her arm, pulled Willy toward the back of the cave. Already the other women were herding the children into the escape tunnel. Willy could only watch helplessly as the men grabbed what primitive weapons they had and scrambled outside.

More gunfire thundered in the distance, and rocks clattered down the mountainside.

*Where's our return fire?* she thought. *Why isn't anyone firing back?*

Outside, something skittered across the ground and popped. A finger of smoke wafted into the cave, its vapor so sickening it made Willy reel backward, gasping for air.

"Get back, get back!" her father yelled. "Into the tunnel, all of you!"

"What about Guy?"

"He can take care of himself! Go and get the kids out of here!" He gave her a brutal shove into the tunnel. *"Move!"*

There was no other choice. But as she turned to flee and heard the rattle of new gunfire, she felt she was abandoning a part of herself on the embattled cliff.

The children had already slipped into the tunnel. Just ahead, Willy could hear a baby crying. Following the sound, she plunged into pitch blackness.

A light suddenly flickered in the passage. It was a candle. By the flame's glow, she saw the leathery face of the old woman who'd guided them to the cave. She was now leading the frightened procession of women and children.

Willy, bringing up the rear, could barely keep track of the candle's glow. The old woman moved swiftly; obviously, she knew where she was going. Perhaps she'd fled this way before, in another battle, another war. It offered some small comfort to know they were following in the footsteps of a survivor.

The first step down was a surprise. For an instant, Willy's

heel met nothingness, then it landed on slippery stone. How much farther? she wondered as she reached out to steady herself against the tunnel wall. Her fingers met clumps of dried wax, the drippings of ancient candles. How many others before her had felt their way down these steps, had stumbled in terror through these passages? The fear of all those countless other refugees seemed to permeate the darkness.

The tunnel took a sharp left and moved ever downward. She wondered how far they'd come; it began to seem like miles. The sound of gunfire had faded to a distant *tap-tap-tap*. She wouldn't let herself think about what was happening outside; she could only concentrate on that tiny pinpoint of light flickering far ahead.

Suddenly the light seemed to flare brighter, exploding into a dazzling luminescence. No, she realized with sudden wonder as she rounded the curve. It wasn't the candle. It was daylight!

Murmurs of joy echoed through the passageway. All at once, they were all scrambling forward, dashing toward the exit and into the blinding sunshine.

Outside, Willy stood blinking painfully at trees and sky and mountainside. They were on the other side of the cliff. Safe. For now.

Gunfire rattled in the distance.

The old woman ordered them forward, into the jungle. At first Willy didn't understand the urgency. Was there some new danger she hadn't recognized? Then she heard what was frightening the old woman: dogs.

Now the others heard the barking, too. Panic sent them all dashing into the forest. Lan alone didn't move. Willy spotted her standing perfectly still. Lan appeared to be listening to the dogs, gauging their direction, their distance. Her two boys, alarmed by their mother's refusal to run, stood watching her in confusion.

Lan shoved her sons forward, commanding them to flee. The boys shook their heads; they wouldn't leave without their mother. Lan gave the baby to her eldest son, then gave both boys another push. The younger boy was crying now, shaking his head, clinging to her sleeve. But his mother's command could not be disobeyed. Sobbing, he was led away by his older brother to join the other children in flight.

"What are you doing?" Willy cried. Had the woman gone mad?

Calmly, Lan turned to face the sound of the dogs.

Willy glanced ahead at the forest, saw the children fleeing through the trees. They were so small, so helpless. How far would they get?

She looked back at Lan, who was now purposefully shuffling through the dirt, circling back toward the dogs. Suddenly Willy understood what Lan was doing. She was leaving her scent for the dogs. Trying to make them follow her, to draw them away from the children. By this action, this choice, the woman was offering herself as a sacrifice.

The barking grew louder. Every instinct Willy possessed told her to run. But she thought of Guy and her father, of how willingly, how automatically they had assumed the role of protectors, had offered themselves to the enemy. She saw the last of the children vanish into the jungle. They needed time, time no one else could give them.

She, too, began to stamp around in the dirt.

Lan glanced back in surprise and saw what Willy was

doing. They didn't exchange a word; just that look, that sad and knowing smile between women, was enough.

Willy ripped a sleeve off her blouse and trampled the torn cloth into the dirt. The dogs would surely pick up the scent. Then she turned and headed south, back along the cliff base. Away from the children. Lan, too, headed away from the villagers' escape route.

Willy didn't hurry. After all, she was no longer running for *her* life. She wondered how long it would take for the dogs to catch up. And when they did, how long she could hold them off. A weapon was what she needed. A club, a stick. She snatched up a fallen branch, tore off the twigs and swung it a few times. It was good and heavy; it would make the dogs think twice. Prey she might be, but she'd damn well fight back.

The barking grew steadily closer, a demon sound, relentless and terrifying. But now it mingled with something else, a rhythmic, monotonous thumping that, as it grew louder, seemed to make the ground itself shudder. Not gunfire...

A helicopter!

Wild with hope, she glanced up at the sky and saw, in the distance, a pair of black specks against the vista of morning blue. Was it the rescue party they'd been waiting for?

She scrambled up on a mound of rocks and began waving her arms. It was their only chance—Guy's only chance—for survival.

All her attention focused on those two black pinpricks hovering in the morning sky, she didn't see the dogs moving in until it was too late.

A flash of brown shot across her peripheral vision. She jerked around as a pair of jaws lunged straight for her throat. Her response was purely reflex. She twisted away and a hundred pounds of fur and teeth slammed into her shoulder. Thrown to the ground, she could only cry out as powerful jaws clamped onto her arm.

Footsteps thudded close. A voice shouted, "Back off! I said back *off!*"

The dog released her and stood back, growling.

Slowly Willy raised her head and saw two men in camouflage garb towering above her. *Americans,* she thought in confusion. What were they doing here?

Rough hands hauled her to her feet. "Where are the others?" one of the men demanded.

"You're hurting me—"

"Where are the others?"

"There are no others!" she screamed.

His savage blow knocked her back to the ground. Too dazed to move, she sprawled helplessly at their feet and fought to clear her head.

"Finish her off."

*No,* she thought. *Please, no...*

But she knew that no amount of begging would change their minds. She lay there, hugging herself, waiting for the end.

Then the other soldier said, "Not yet. She might come in handy."

She was dragged back to her feet to stand, sick and swaying, before them.

An expressionless face, blackened with camouflage grease, stared down at her. "Let's see what the good Friar thinks."

# Chapter Fourteen

Made it to third base. Time to go for that home run.

Guy, sprawled behind a boulder, scouted out the next twenty yards to the gun. His only cover would be a few bushes and, midway, a pathetic excuse for a tree. He could see the AK-47's barrel extending over the rock ledge, so close, he could practically spit at it, but still beyond reach.

Slowly, he rose to a crouch and got ready for the final dash.

Gunfire splattered the cliff. Instantly, he flopped back to the dirt. *This is a crazy-ass idea, Barnard. The dumbest idea you've ever had.*

He glanced below and saw Maitland trying to signal him. What the hell was he trying to say? Guy couldn't be sure, but Maitland seemed to be telling him to wait, to hold on. But there was so little time left. Already, Guy spotted men in camouflage fatigues moving through the brush toward the cliff base. Toward the first booby trap. *God, slow 'em down. Give us time.*

He heard, rather than saw, the first victim drop into the trap. A shriek echoed off the cliff face, the cry of a man who had just slid into a bed of stakes. Now there were other shouts, curses, the sounds of confusion as soldiers dragged their injured comrade to safety.

*Just a taste, fellas,* Guy thought with a grim sense of satisfaction. *Wait till you see what comes next.*

The attackers didn't delay long. A shouted order sent a half-dozen soldiers scrambling up the cliff path, closer and closer to the second trap: a trip wire poised to unleash a falling tree trunk. But now the attackers were warned; they knew that every step was a gamble, and they were searching for hazards, considering every rock, every bush with the practiced eyes of men well versed in jungle combat.

*We're almost down to our last resort,* thought Guy. *Prayer.*

Then he heard it. They all heard it. A familiar rumble that made them turn their gazes to the sky. Choppers.

That was the instant Guy ran, when everyone's eyes were focused on the heavens. His sudden dash took the soldiers by surprise, left them only a split second to respond. Then the maelstrom broke loose as bullets chewed the ground, throwing up a storm cloud of dust. By then he was halfway to his goal, scrambling through the last thicket. Time seemed to slow down. Each step took an eternity. He saw puffs of dirt explode near his feet, heard a far-off shriek and the thud of the poised tree trunk, the second trap, slamming onto the soldiers in the path.

He launched himself through the air and tumbled onto the ledge. Time leapt to fast forward. He yanked the AK-47 out of the dead man's grasp, took aim and began firing.

One soldier, standing exposed below, went down at once. The others beat a fast retreat into the jungle. Two lay dead on the path, victims of the latest booby trap.

*Welcome to the Stone Age, Rambo.*

Guy held his fire as the attackers slipped out of view and into the cover of trees. He watched, waiting for any flash of movement, any sign of a renewed attack. A standoff?

He turned his gaze to the sky and searched for the choppers. To his dismay, they were moving away; already they had faded to mere specks. In despair he watched them slip away into a field of relentless blue.

Then, from below, he heard shouts in Vietnamese and saw smoke spiral up the cliff face, the blackest, most glorious smoke he'd seen in his whole damn life. The villagers had set the mountainside on fire!

Quickly he scanned the heavens again, hoping, praying. Within seconds he spotted them, like two flies hovering just above the horizon. Was it only wishful thinking, or were they actually moving closer?

A new hint of movement at the bottom of the cliff drew his attention. He looked down to see two figures emerge from the forest and approach the cliff base. Automatically, he swung his gun barrel to the target and was about to squeeze off a round when he saw who it was standing below. His finger froze on the trigger.

A man stood clutching a human shield in front of him. Even from that distance, Guy recognized the prisoner's face, could see her blanched and helpless expression.

"Drop it, Barnard!" The command of an unseen man, hidden among the trees, echoed off the mountainside. The voice was disturbingly familiar.

Guy remained frozen in the pose of a marksman, his finger on the trigger, his cheek pressed against the rifle. Frantically he wracked his brain for a plan, for some way to pull Willy out of this alive. A trade? It was the only possibility: her life for his. Would they go for it?

"I said *drop it!*" the disembodied voice shouted.

Willy's captor raised a pistol barrel to her head.

"Or would you like to see what a bullet will do to that pretty face?"

"Wait!" Guy screamed. "We can trade—"

"No deals."

The barrel was pressed to Willy's temple.

"No!" Guy's voice, harsh with panic, reverberated off the cliff.

"Then drop the gun. *Now.*"

Guy let the AK-47 fall to the ground.

"Kick it away. Go on!"

Guy gave the gun a kick. It tumbled off the ledge and clattered to the rocks below.

"Out where I can see you. Come on, come on!"

Slowly, Guy rose to his full height, expecting an instantaneous hail of bullets.

"Now come down. Off the cliff. You, too, Maitland! I haven't got all day, so *move.*"

Guy made his way down the cliff path. By the time he reached bottom, Maitland was already waiting there, his arms hooked behind his head in surrender. Guy's first concern was Willy. He could see she'd been hurt; her shirt was torn and bloodied, her face alarmingly white. But the look she gave him was one of heartwrenching courage, a look that said, *Don't worry about me. I'm okay. And I love you.*

Her captor smiled and let the pistol barrel drop from her head. Guy instantly recognized his face: it was the same man he'd tackled on the terrace of the hotel in Bangkok. The Thai assassin—or was he Vietnamese?

"Hello, Guy," said a shockingly familiar voice.

A man strolled into the sunshine, a man whose powerful shoulders seemed to strain against the fabric of his camouflage fatigues.

Maitland took in a startled breath. "It's him," he murmured. "Friar Tuck."

*"Toby?"* said Guy.

"Both," said Tobias Wolff, smiling. He stood before them, his expression hovering somewhere between triumph and regret. "I didn't want to kill you, Guy. In fact, I've done everything I could to avoid it."

Guy let out a bitter laugh. "Why?"

"I owed you. Remember?"

Guy frowned at Toby's legs, noticing there were no braces, no crutches. "You can walk."

Toby shrugged. "You know how it is in army hospitals. The surgeons gave me the bad news, said there was nothing they could do and then they walked away. Shoved me into a corner and forgot about me. But I wasn't a lost cause, after all. First I got the feeling back in my toes. Then I could move them. Oh, I never bothered to tell Uncle Sam. It gave me the freedom to carry on with my business. That's the nice thing about being a paraplegic. No one suspects you of a damn thing." He grinned. "Plus, I get that monthly disability check."

"A real fortune."

"It's the principle of things. Uncle Sam owes me for all those years of loyal service." He glanced at Maitland. "He was the only detail that worried me. The last witness from Flight 5078. I'd heard he was alive. I just didn't know how to find him."

He squinted up at the sky as the rumble of the choppers drew closer. They were moving in, attracted by the smoke from the cliff fire. "Time's up," said Toby. Turning, he yelled to his men, "Move out!"

At once, the soldiers started into the woods in a calm but hasty retreat. Toby looked at the hit man and nodded. "Mr. Siang, you know what to do."

Siang shoved Willy forward. Guy caught her in his arms; together, they dropped to their knees. There was no time left for last words, for farewells. Guy wrapped himself around her in a futile attempt to shield her from the bullets.

"Finish it," said Toby.

Guy looked up at him. "I'll see you in hell."

Siang raised the pistol. The barrel was aimed squarely at Guy's head. Still cradling Willy, Guy waited for the explosion. The darkness.

The blast of the pistol made them both flinch.

In wonderment, Guy realized he was still kneeling, still breathing. *What the hell? Am I still alive? Are we both still alive?*

He looked up in time to see Siang, shirt bloodied, crumple to the ground.

"There! She's there!" Toby shouted, pointing at the trees.

In the shadow of the forest they saw her, clutching the ancient pistol in both hands. Lan stood very still, as though shocked by what she'd just done.

One of the soldiers took aim at her.

"No!" screamed Maitland, flinging himself at the gunman.

The shot went wild; Maitland and the soldier thudded to the ground, locked in combat.

From the cliff above came shouts; Guy and Willy hit the dirt as arrows rained down. Toby cried out and fell. What remained of his army scattered in confusion.

In the melee, Guy and Willy managed to crawl to cover. But as they rolled behind a boulder, Willy suddenly realized her father hadn't followed them.

"Dad!" she screamed.

A dozen yards away, Maitland lay bloodied. Willy turned to go to him, but Guy dragged her back down.

"Are you nuts?" he yelled.

"I can't leave him there!"

"Wait till we're clear!"

"He's hurt!"

"There's nothing you can do!"

She was sobbing now, trying to wrench free, but her protests were drowned out by the *whomp-whomp* of the helicopters moving in. An army chopper hovered just above them. The pilot lowered the craft through a slot in the trees. Gently, the skids settled to the ground.

The instant it touched down, a half-dozen Vietnamese soldiers jumped out, followed by their commanding officer. He pointed at Maitland and barked out orders. Two soldiers hurried to the wounded man.

"Let me go," Willy said and she broke free of Guy's grasp.

He watched her run to her father's side. The soldiers had already opened their medical field kit, and a stretcher was on the way. Guy's gaze shifted back to the chopper as one last passenger stepped slowly to the ground. Head bowed beneath the spinning blades, the old man made his way toward Guy.

For a long time, they stood together, both of them silent as they regarded the rising cloud of smoke. The flames seemed to engulf the mountain itself as the last of the village men scrambled down the cliff path to safety.

"A most impressive signal fire," said Minister Tranh. He looked at Guy. "You are unhurt?"

Guy nodded. "We lost some people...up on the mountain. And the children—I don't know if they're all right. But I guess...I think..."

He turned and watched as Willy followed her father's stretcher toward the chopper. At the doorway, she stopped and looked back at Guy.

He started toward her, his arms aching to embrace her. He wanted to tell her all the things he'd been afraid to say, the things he'd never said to any woman. He had to tell her now, while he still had the chance, while she was still there for him to touch, to hold.

A soldier suddenly blocked Guy's way and commanded, "Stay back!"

Dust stung Guy's eyes as the chopper's rotor began to spin. Through the tornado-like wash of whirling leaves and branches, Guy saw a soldier in the chopper shout at Willy to climb aboard. With one last backward glance, she obeyed. Time had run out.

Through the open doorway, Guy could still see her face gazing out at him. With a sense of desolation, he watched the helicopter rise into the sky, taking with it the woman he loved. Long after the roar of the blades had faded to silence, he was staring up at that cloudless field of blue.

Sighing, he turned back to Minister Tranh. That's when he noticed that someone else, just as desolate, had watched the chopper's departure. At the forest edge stood Lan, her gaze turned to the sky. At least she, too, had survived.

"We are glad to find you alive," Minister Tranh said.

"How *did* you find us?" Guy asked.

"One of the men from the village reached Na Khoang early this morning. We'd been concerned about you. And when you vanished…" Minister Tranh shook his head. "You have a talent for making things difficult, Mr. Barnard. For us, at least."

"I had to. I didn't know who to trust." Guy looked at the other man. "I still don't know who to trust."

Minister Tranh considered this statement for a moment. Then he said quietly, "Do we ever really know?"

"A toast," said Dodge Hamilton, leaning against the hotel bar. "To the good fight!"

Guy stared down moodily at his whiskey glass and said, "There's no such thing as a good fight, Hamilton. There are only fights you can't avoid."

"Well—" grinning, Hamilton raised his drink "—then let's drink to the unavoidable."

That made Guy laugh, though it was the last thing he felt like doing. He supposed he *ought* to be celebrating. The ordeal was over, and for the first time in days, he felt human again. After a good night's sleep, a shower and a shave, he could once again stand the sight of his own face in the mirror. *For all the difference it makes,* he thought bleakly. *She's not here to notice.*

He was having a hell of a time adjusting to Willy's absence. Over and over he replayed that last image of her sad backward glance as she'd climbed into the chopper. No last words, no goodbyes, just that look. He wished he could erase the image from his memory.

No, no, that wasn't what he wanted.

What he wanted was another chance.

He set the whiskey glass down and forced a smile to his lips. "Anyway, Hamilton," he said, "looks like you got your story, after all."

"Not quite the one I expected."

"Think it's front-page material?"

"Indeed! It has everything. Old war ghosts come to life. Ex-enemies joining sides. *And* a happy ending! A story that ought to be heard. But…" He sighed. "It'll probably get shoved to the back page to make room for some juicy royal scandal. As if the fate of the world depends on who does what to whom in Buckingham."

Guy shook his head and chuckled. Some things, it seemed, never changed.

"He'll be all right, won't he? Maitland?"

Guy looked up. "I think so. Willy called me from Bangkok a few hours ago. Maitland's stable enough to be transferred."

"They're flying him to the States?"

"Tonight."

Hamilton cocked his head. "Aren't you joining them?"

"I don't know. I've got a job to wrap up, a few last minute details. And she'll be busy with other things…."

He looked down at his whiskey and thought of that last phone conversation. They'd had a lousy connection, lots of static on the line, and they'd both been forced to shout. She'd been standing at a hospital telephone; he'd been on his way out to meet Vietnamese officials. It had hardly been the time for romantic conversation. Yet he'd been ready to say anything, if only she'd given him some hint that she wanted to hear it. But there'd been only awkward how arc-yous and is-your-arm-all-right and yes-it's-fine-I'm-all-patched-up-now and then, in the end, a hasty goodbye.

When he'd hung up the receiver, he'd known she was gone. *Maybe it's for the best,* he thought. Every idiot knew wartime romances never lasted. When you were huddled together in the trenches and the bullets were whizzing overhead, it was easy to fall in love.

But now they were back in the real world. She didn't need him any longer, and he liked to think he didn't need *her* either. After all, he'd never needed anyone before.

He drained his whiskey glass. "Anyway, Hamilton," he said, "I guess I'll have a hell of a story to tell the guys back home. How I fought in Nam all over again—this time with the other side."

"No one'll believe you."

"Probably not." Guy looked off at a painting on the wall—Ho Chi Minh smiling like someone's merry uncle. "You know, I have a confession to make." He looked back at his drinking partner. "At one point, I was so paranoid that I thought *you* were the CIA."

Hamilton burst out laughing.

"Can you believe it?" Guy said, laughing as well. "You of all people!"

Hamilton, still grinning, set his glass down on the counter. "Actually," he said after a pause, "I am."

There was a long silence. "What?" said Guy.

Hamilton gazed back, his expression blandly pleasant and utterly unrevealing. "General Kistner sends his regards. He's happy to hear you're alive and well."

"Kistner sent you?"

"No, he sent *you.*"

Guy stiffened. "You got it wrong. I don't work for those people. I was on my own the whole—"

"Were you, now?" Hamilton's smile was maddening. "Quite a stroke of luck, wouldn't you say, that meeting between you and Miss Maitland at Kistner's villa? Damned odd about her driver vanishing like that, just as you were heading back to town."

Guy looked down at his glass, swirled the whiskey. "I *was* set up," he muttered. "That mysterious appointment with Kistner—"

"Was to get you and Miss Maitland together. She was in dangerous waters, already floundering. We knew she'd need help. But it had to be someone completely unconnected with the Company, someone the Vietnamese wouldn't suspect. As it turned out, *you* were it."

Guy's fists tightened on the countertop. "I did your dirty work—"

"You did Uncle Sam a favor. We knew you were slated to go to Saigon. That you knew the country. A bit of the language. We also knew you had a...shall we say, *vulnerable* aspect to your past." He gave Guy a significant look.

*They know,* Guy thought. *They've probably always known.* Slowly, he said, "That visit from the Ariel Group..."

"Ah, yes. Ariel. Lovely ring to it, don't you think? It happens to be the name of General Kistner's youngest granddaughter." Hamilton smiled. "You needn't worry, Guy. We can be discreet. Especially when we feel we've been well served."

"What if you'd been wrong about me? What if I was working for Toby Wolff? I could have killed her."

"You wouldn't."

"I had a 'vulnerable' aspect to my past, remember?"

"You're clean, Guy. Even with your past, you're cleaner than any flag-waving patriot in Washington."

"How would you know?"

Hamilton shrugged. "You'd be amazed at the things we know about you. About everyone."

"But you couldn't predict what I'd do! What Willy would do. What if she'd told me to go to hell?"

"It was a gamble. But she's an attractive woman. And you're a resourceful man. We took a chance on chemistry."

*And it worked,* thought Guy. *Damn you, Hamilton, the chemistry worked just fine.*

"At any rate," said Hamilton, sliding a few bills onto the bar, "you'll be rewarded with the silence you crave. I'm afraid the bounty's out of the question, though—budget deficit and all. But you'll have the distinct pleasure of knowing you served your country well."

That's when Guy burst into unstoppable laughter. He laughed so hard, tears came to his eyes; so loud, a dozen heads turned to look at him.

"Have I missed the joke?" Hamilton inquired politely.

"The joke," said Guy, "is on me."

He laughed all the way out the door.

# Chapter Fifteen

Her father, once again, was leaving.

Early on a rainy morning, Willy stood in the bedroom doorway and watched him pack his suitcase, the way she'd watched him pack it long ago. She'd had him home such a short time, only a few days since his release from the hospital. And he'd spent every moment pining for his family—his other family. Oh, he hadn't complained or been unkind, but she'd seen the sadness in his gaze, heard his sighs as he'd wandered about the house. She'd known it was inevitable: that he'd be walking out of her life again.

He took one last look in the closet, then turned to the dresser.

She glanced down at a pair of brand-new loafers that he'd set aside in the closet. "Dad, aren't you taking your shoes?" she asked.

"At home, I don't wear shoes."

"Oh." *This used to be your home,* she thought.

She wandered into the living room, sat down by the window and stared out at the rain. It seemed as if a lifetime of sorrow had been crammed into these past two weeks she'd been home. While her father had recuperated in a military hospital, in a civilian hospital a few miles away, her mother had lain dying. It had been wrenching to drive back and forth between them, to shift from seeing her father regain his strength to seeing her mother fade. Ann's death had come more quickly than the doctors had predicted; it was almost as if she'd held on just long enough to see her husband one last time, then had allowed herself to quietly slip away.

She'd forgiven him, of course.

Just as Willy had forgiven him.

Why was it always women who had to do the forgiving? she'd wondered.

"I'm all packed," her father said, carrying his suitcase into the living room. "I've called a cab."

"Are you sure you've got everything? The kids' toys? The books?"

"It's all in here. What a delivery! They're going to think I'm Santa Claus." He set the suitcase down and sat on the couch. They didn't speak for a moment.

"You won't be coming back, will you?" she said at last.

"It may not be easy."

"May I come see you?"

"Willy, you know you can! Both you and Guy. And next time, we'll make it a decent visit." He laughed. "Nice and quiet and dull. Guy'll appreciate that."

There was a long silence. Her father asked, "Have you spoken to him lately?"

She looked away. "It's been two weeks."

"That long?"

"He hasn't called."

"Why haven't you called him?"

"I've been busy. A lot of things to take care of. But you know that."

"He doesn't."

"Well, he *ought* to know." Suddenly agitated, she rose and paced the room, finally returning to the window. "I'm not really surprised he hasn't called. After all, we had our little adventure, and now it's back to life as usual." She glanced at her father. "Men hate that, don't they? Life as usual."

"Some men do. On the other hand, some of us change."

"Oh, Dad, I've been around the block. I can tell when things are over."

"Did Guy say that?"

She turned and gazed back out the window. "He didn't have to."

Her father didn't comment. After a while, she heard him go back into the bedroom, but she didn't move. She just kept staring out at the rain, thinking about Guy. Wondering for the first time if maybe *she* had done the running away.

No, it wasn't running. It was facing reality. Together they'd had the time of their lives, a crazy week of emotions gone wild, of terror and exhilaration, when every breath, every heartbeat had seemed like a gift from God.

Of course, it hadn't lasted.

But whose fault was that?

She felt herself drawn almost against her will to the telephone. Even as she dialed his number, she wondered what she'd say to him *Hello, Guy. I know you don't want to hear this, but I love you.* Then she'd hang up and spare him the ordeal of admitting the feeling wasn't mutual. She let it ring twelve times, knowing it was 4:00 a.m. in Honolulu, knowing he *should* be home.

There were tears in her eyes when she finally hung up. She stood staring down at the phone, wondering how that inanimate collection of wires and plastic could leave her feeling so betrayed. *Damn you,* she thought. *You never even gave me the chance to make a fool of myself.*

The sound of tires splashing across wet streets made her look out the window. Through pouring rain she saw a cab pull up at the curb.

"Dad?" she called. She went to her father's bedroom. "Your taxi's here."

"Already?" He glanced around to see if he'd forgotten anything. "Okay. I guess this is it, then."

The doorbell rang. He threw on his raincoat and strode across the living room. Willy wasn't watching as he opened the door, but she heard him say, "I don't believe it." She turned.

"Hello, Maitland," said Guy.

The two men, both wearing raincoats, both holding suit-cases, grinned at each other across the threshold.

Guy shook the raindrops from his hair. "Mind if I come in?"

"Gee, I don't know. I'd better ask the boss." Maitland turned to his daughter. "What do you think? Can the man come in?"

Willy was too stunned to say a word.

"I guess that's a yes," her father said, and he motioned for Guy to enter.

Guy stepped over the threshold and set his suitcase down. Then he just stood there, looking at her. Rain had plastered his hair to his forehead, lines of exhaustion mapped his face, but no man had ever looked so wonderful. She tried to remind herself of all the reasons she didn't want to see him, all the reasons she should throw him out into the rain. But she couldn't seem to find her voice. She could only stare at him in wonder and remember how it had felt to be in his arms.

Maitland shuffled uneasily. "I...uh...I think I forgot to pack something," he muttered, and he discreetly vanished into the bedroom.

For a moment, the only sound was the water dripping from Guy's raincoat onto the wood floor.

"How's your mother?" Guy asked.

"She died, five days ago."

He shook his head. "Willy, I'm sorry."

"I'm sorry, too."

"How are you? Are you okay?"

"I'm...fine." She looked away. *I love you,* she thought. *And yet here we are, two strangers engaging in small talk.* "Yeah, I'm fine," she repeated, as though to convince him—to convince herself—that the anguish of these past two weeks had been a minor ache not worth mentioning.

"You look pretty good, considering."

She shrugged. "You look terrible."

"Not too surprising. Didn't get any sleep on the plane. And there was this baby screaming in the next seat, all the way from Bangkok."

"Bangkok?" She frowned. "You were in Bangkok?"

He nodded and laughed. "It's this crazy business I'm in. Got home from Nam, and a week later, they asked me to fly back...for Sam Lassiter." He paused. "I admit I wasn't thrilled about getting on another plane, but I figured it was something I had to do." He paused and added quietly, "No soldier should have to come home alone."

She thought about Lassiter, about that evening in the river café, the love song scratching from the record player, the paper lanterns fluttering in the wind. She thought about his body drifting in the waters of the Mekong. And she thought about the dark-eyed woman who'd loved him. "You're right," she said. "No soldier should have to come home alone."

There was another pause. She felt him watching her, waiting.

"You could have called me," she said.

"I wanted to."

"But you never got the chance, right?"

"I had plenty of chances."

"But you didn't bother?" She looked up. All the hurt, all the rage suddenly rose to the surface. "Two weeks with no word from you! And here you have the gall to show up unannounced, walk in my door and drop your damn suitcase in my living—"

The last word never made it to her lips. But he did. She was dragged into a rain-drenched embrace, and everything she'd planned to say, all the hurt and angry words, were swept away by that one kiss. The only sound she could manage was a small murmur of astonishment, and then she was whirled up in a wild maelstrom of desire. She lost all sense of where she ended and he began. She only knew, in that instant, that he had never really left her, that as long as she lived, he'd be part of her. Even as he pulled back to look at her, she was still drunk with the taste of him.

"I *did* want to call you. But I didn't know what to say…"

"I kept waiting for you to call. All these days…"

"Maybe I was...I don't know. Scared."

"Of what?"

"Of hearing it was over. That you'd come to your senses and decided I wasn't worth the risk. But then, when I got to Bangkok, I stopped at the Oriental Hotel. Had a drink on the terrace for old time's sake. Saw the same sunset, the same boats on the river. But it just didn't feel the same without you." He sighed. "Hell, nothing feels the same without you."

"You never told me. You just dropped out of my life."

"It never seemed like...the right time."

"The right time for what?"

"You know."

"No, I don't."

He shook his head in irritation. "You never make it easy, do you?"

She stepped back and gave him a long, critical look. Then she smiled. "I never intended to."

"Oh, Willy." He threw his arms around her and pulled her tightly against his chest. "I can see you and I are going to have a lot of things to settle."

"Such as?"

"Such as..." He lowered his mouth to hers and whispered, "Such as who gets to sleep on the right side of the bed...."

"Oh," she murmured as their lips brushed. "You will."

"And who gets to name our firstborn...."

She settled warmly into his arms and sighed. "I will."

"And who'll be first to say 'I love you.'"

There was a pause. "That one," she said with a smile, "is open to negotiation."

"No, it's not," he said, tugging her face up to his.

They stared at each other, both longing to hear the words but stubbornly waiting for the other to give in first.

It was a simultaneous surrender.

"I love you," Willy heard him say, just as the same three words tumbled from her lips.

Their laughter was simultaneous, too, bright and joyous and ringing with hope.

The kiss that followed was warm, seeking, but all too brief; it left her aching for more.

"It gets even better with practice," he whispered.

"Saying 'I love you?'"

"No. Kissing."

"Oh," she murmured. She added in a small voice, "Then can we try it again?"

Outside, a horn honked, dragging them both back to reality. Through the window they saw another taxi waiting at the curb.

Reluctantly Willy pulled out of Guy's arms. "Dad?" she called.

"I'm coming, I'm coming." Her father emerged from the bedroom, pulling on his raincoat again. He paused and looked at her.

"Uh, why don't you two say goodbye," said Guy, diplomatically turning for the front door. "I'll take your suitcase out to the car."

Willy and her father were left standing alone in the room. They looked at each other, both knowing that this, like every goodbye, could be the last.

"Are things okay between you and Guy?" Maitland asked.

Willy nodded.

There was another silence. Then her father asked softly, "And between you and me?"

She smiled. "Things are okay there, too." She went to him then, and they held each other. "Yes," she murmured against his chest, "between you and me, things are definitely okay."

A little reluctantly, he turned to leave. In the doorway, he and Guy shook hands.

"Have a good trip back, Maitland."

"I will. Take care of things, will you? And, Guy— thanks a lot."

"For what?"

Maitland glanced back at Willy. It was a look of regret. And redemption. "For giving me back my daughter," he said.

As Wild Bill Maitland walked out the door, Guy walked in. He didn't say a thing. He just took Willy in his arms and hugged her.

As the taxi drove away, she thought, *My father has left me. Again.*

She looked up at Guy. *And what about you?*

He answered her unspoken question by taking her face in his hands and kissing her. Then he gave the door a little kick; with a thud of finality, it swung shut.

And she knew that this time, the man would be staying.